ALWAYS BRAVE,

SOMETIMES KIND

All rights reserved. No part of this publication may be reproduced, stored in a retrieval system, or transmitted in any form or by any means, electronic, mechanical, photocopying, recording, or otherwise, without the prior written permission of the publisher. For more information, contact the publisher at:

Brindle & Glass
An imprint of TouchWood Editions
touchwoodeditions.com

Edited by Claire Philipson
Interior design by Sydney Barnes

The newspaper article referenced on p. 51 is drawn from the CBC News story of March 20, 2018, "Creator of Sixties Scoop adoption program says it wasn't meant to place kids with white families" (https://www.cbc.ca/news/indigenous/creator-of-sixties-scoop-adoption-program-says-it-wasn-t-meant-to-place-kids-with-white-families-1.4584342)

CATALOGUING INFORMATION AVAILABLE FROM LIBRARY AND ARCHIVES CANADA

ISBN 9781927366912 (softcover)
ISBN 9781927366929 (electronic)

TouchWood Editions gratefully acknowledges that the land on which we live and work is within the traditional territories of the Lkwungen (Esquimalt and Songhees), Malahat, Pacheedaht, Scia'new, T'Sou-ke and WSÁNEĆ (Pauquachin, Tsartlip, Tsawout, Tseycum) peoples.

We acknowledge the financial support of the Government of Canada through the Canada Book Fund and the Canada Council for the Arts, and of the Province of British Columbia through the British Columbia Arts Council and the Book Publishing Tax Credit.

Printed in Canada at Friesens

This book was produced using FSC®-certified, acid-free papers, processed chlorine free, and printed with soya-based inks.

24 23 22 21 20   1 2 3 4 5

ALWAYS BRAVE, SOMETIMES KIND

A Novel

Katie Bickell

BRINDLE
AND GLASS

For Amy and Miranda and Jordan,
and Jenna Jewel and Jarrett Jude,
and all the children we do not know.

PROLOGUE
ALL THE CHILDREN WE DO NOT KNOW

1995

AN AURA BRIGHTENS the dark staff room and wakes Rhanji. The doctor gasps upon his rush to consciousness. He had dreamt of skin—skin as blue and translucent as water in Nanni's dyeing vat: cadaverous, pallid, with indigo residue. In the last moments of the dream, the flesh had melted into a liquid in which Rhanji began to drown. In that blurred place between slumber and reality, he'd thought the fluorescent light was the sun as seen from under the sea; the girl in the centre of the glow, an angel. High notes had sounded her arrival, like the bracelets that used to chime on his late wife's arm.

Sunita?

No.

Only young Carrie Quentin, a first-year nursing student, peppering him with nervous apologies in singsong pitch. "Sorry, doctor! I'm so sorry!"

Her regret only confuses Rhanji more. Sympathy? Why?

"The child's body has been found?"

"No!" Carrie gasps. "I just didn't mean to wake you!"

Rhanji massages the deep lines of his forehead. *Canadians.*

He pulls himself from the couch and stumbles into the hall, squinting under the hallway lights. The night's charge nurse leans out from room 112. Sandra resembles a Q-tip wand dressed up in white scrubs, that tight mass of bleached spirals on her head. The thought is unkind; Sandra is a dear friend and a skilled nurse. Likely, Rhanji would not have had such a dislike for the hairstyle had it not made her resemble the silly woman on the *Lamb Chop's Play-Along* program. The show had polluted Rhanji's formerly quiet home for nearly a year, his daughter arguing the correlation between pre-school rhymes and early developmental growth.

The nurse scans left to right before spotting the doctor and summoning him to the room. Inside, a little girl moans a singular phrase at sharp volume, a phrase from a language Rhanji does not know. She cries the unknown word without hope, her small head lolling from one side to another, heavy eyes blinking wide when fear presents itself more acutely than her pain. She is feverish, dehydrated, and, if further tests confirm Rhanji's suspicions, suffering appendicitis. Worst of all, the child is alone.

"Her name's Miranda," her foster mother spat before abandoning her to the emergency room earlier that day. "She's from up north, and boy, she's got some pipes."

Beside the child, a man stoops under wild hair and a well-worn toque, swatting away the red-scrubbed hands that pull on the sleeves of his too-large jacket. Wilf. A bunker bag hangs from Wilf's shoulder, the kind firefighters use to carry gear. Likely, the bag is a thrift shop find.

"Nikâwiy wants you too, little one! She wants you to be brave. Hush, niece. Stop crying."

The man sways as he speaks. Is Wilf really the child's uncle? The girl cowers, brown eyes bottomless with fear. Doubtful, Rhanji thinks. Still, it would be better if Wilf were actually a relative. Rhanji's heart aches at the sight of the lonely little girl. His own daughter was the same age when Sunita died.

Wilf has no right to trespass, Sandra scolds. She's right, of course; the man is merely a patient himself, though perhaps a favourite of the doctor and becoming something of a fixture, as days grow colder. Rhanji guides Wilf from the bed to the hall.

"You know our patients require privacy, Wilf. If this happens again, I will ask you to vacate the hospital."

Wilf nods repeatedly, listening as intently as a parent in consultation until he grasps the meaning of the doctor's words. His face falls, eyes lowering to the toes of his worn boots. He'll go back to the waiting room.

"I'm sorry, doctor. I heard her crying, all alone. I just wanted to help."

Rhanji nods. Of course Wilf would want to help. When Rhanji began practising in Canada in the early seventies, he was appalled by the number of Indigenous children removed from their homes, and entirely bewildered to find the majority of his young patients in fine health and without any obvious signs of neglect or disclosed history of abuse. He scanned intake forms for details explaining their removal and found reasons so petty they'd make more sense justifying a school detention: truancy, poor grades, pilfering candy bars. The younger ones were often taken upon birth for such common things as a family's poor economic standing, or the marital status of the mother, or even whether delivery staff deemed a labouring woman uncooperative during her child's birth.

However, Rhanji soon discovered that even if the children had left their mother's arms or wombs strong, rarely did they stay that way. Most moved from foster home to foster home so frequently that Rhanji was unable to track their medical needs; some were transferred as far away from home as the southern states. The ones he was able to track seemed to shrink in size and, seemingly, in spirit; their bodies growing gaunt, skin yellowing with mysterious bruises, shoulders pulling inward in near-constant stances of cowering. These were the ones he may have assessed as needing intervention, these children showing the signs of abuse, neglect, failure to thrive. How could this outcome have been preferable to the lives they had previously led?

There was no sense to it.

Once, Rhanji had performed a wellness check on a sunny, beautiful boy slated for adoption by a local Mormon couple. The boy and his siblings had been taken from their mother because her husband was recently deceased.

"There'd be no way she could afford them on her own, y'know?" the boy's social worker said during Rhanji's examination, as though the three-year-old weren't in the room. Upon the loss of her husband, the child's mother had applied for financial aid. Family services waited until the family had buried their breadwinner and removed the children the very next day.

The social worker snapped chewing gum in his mouth as he spoke. Rhanji was taken aback. Silently, he stopped his work and sat in his office chair, hiding his eyes by massaging his temples, pretending to make notes in the boy's file. He thought of his elderly Nanni bent over the dyeing vat in the years that followed his own parents' deaths as he, then a small child, played nearby. He thought of tiny, beloved Yasmin and the life Rhanji carved out for her in a new country after they lost Sunita. If misfortune were reason enough to steal children, both Rhanji and his daughter might have been prime candidates. As soon the terms of his immigration allowed, Rhanji transferred out of childhood health. Until then, he did his best to get through, developing the mantra that made his medical performance possible for more than two decades:

I do not know this child. This child is not mine.

"Just don't kick me out," Wilf says, clutching his stomach. "Appendicitis must be going round, eh? Ten outta ten for pain."

Rhanji watches the man limp toward the waiting room.

"Wait," he calls. "Wilf!"

Wilf turns and Rhanji moves closer to him, lowering his voice as he speaks. Rhanji tries to match a tone of casual friendship; he attempts to fix his face into an understanding smile. Male camaraderie never had come easy for him, but he knows the numbers: those suffering addiction rarely recover without social support.

"My friend, have you been attending the meetings I found you?" he asks. "You look strong."

Wilf laughs. His steady hand moves as though batting the doctor's words from the air. "Oh yeah, yeah," he jokes. "I'm a He-Man now, doctor."

"If the meetings aren't the right fit, we can find another group—"

Wilf shakes his head. "No, no. One Fourteenth Street, nine-thirty, every morning."

Rhanji nods. "Okay. Okay, that's good, Wilf. We don't want you in withdrawal again, do we?"

Wilf's smile doesn't falter but instead becomes static, only a mask of mirth. He looks away, his shoulders slumped. Rhanji cringes. Why would he say such a thing? Shame, he knows, is more poison than the drug itself. He searches for words to heal the connection.

"Wilf," Rhanji tries again, "We need you to be well. The whole world does, but especially little ones like her." He nods to Miranda's room. "Your life . . . well, you can draw a roadmap home for her, for children like her. Do you understand? You can heal them in a way that I can't."

Wilf swallows hard. He turns from the doctor and shakes his head, a small, sad smile forming, and waves with one big swoop of his arm as he retreats to the waiting room. Rhanji watches the man for a moment before re-entering room 112. He is just about to step inside when the lonesome wail of a harmonica cries out.

"Not indoors," Rhanji calls without turning. He has already requested that Wilf refrain from panhandling. Wilf's noise ceases at high pitch.

"Sorry, doctor!"

Rhanji purses his lips, hiding the first smile he has felt in weeks.

Carrie calls to Rhanji from triage. She leans into the hall, covering a phone's receiver with her palm, tethered to an office desk by its black cord. She is the picture of inexperience: young and nervous in teddy-bear print scrubs. But Rhanji is biased; he remembers a time when professionals wore only white. The hospital is lucky for the free labour of university students. The rest of the Sandras, those steady nurses—militant in their confidence, expertise, and technique—have gone to the picket line or elsewhere, their positions more than halved by government cuts made by a premier who refuses to blink.

"Um . . . Dr. Rhanji? Trauma incoming via Northern Air. They say five minutes."

Rhanji shakes his head. "We're at capacity." Ambulances have been refused all day, sent to taxi patients throughout the city and beyond in search of beds.

Carrie lifts the phone and relays the message before dropping it to her palm again.

"Everywhere else is full too. There's a collision north of Fort Mac. Two intensive-care patients but one's going to the Royal Alex. They say that's the last bed in the city."

"The trauma room's free," Sandra shouts from 112.

"We don't have a bed in it!"

"We'll have to treat him on the stretcher, then. Figure the rest out later."

Rhanji and the nurses meet the aircrew at the elevator's steel doors. The stretcher carries in November's bitter chill and a pungency of urine, oil, alcohol. Medics share details as quickly as the team moves the patient through the hall: a thirty-year-old male in a half-ton truck, broken right humerus, broken right femur, fractured sternum. Signs of significant spinal injury.

"Let me guess," Sandra asks, rechecking vitals en route. "Shoulda seen the other guy?"

"Something like that," the lead responds. "Girl in a Toyota four door, seven months pregnant. Hit just a few kilometres from home. Her dad was first on scene."

In an instant Rhanji imagines the father's discovery as if it were his own: his own heavy footsteps breaking a highway snowbank, a steering wheel pressed into the rounded womb of his daughter, her thighs coated with sticky black ice. Rhanji's throat tightens.

Sweetu!

No.

I do not know that child. That child is not mine.

Rhanji refocuses to the patient at hand. The man roars. He can't breathe, can't feel his legs. The doctor palpates the abdomen as they rush the stretcher into the trauma room. Over the heart: a deep internal sore. No, not a bruise, no bleeding. A tattoo, dark red. A maple leaf, bolded black lettering above and below: *Fuck Off, We're Full.*

Something thick and warm and wet hits Rhanji's eyes.

"Get a spit guard on him!" Sandra shouts.

Stop, turn, hands up. Rhanji feels a friend's hand on his shoulder and a rush of saline pours over his lids.

"Don't talk," Sandra says. "Keep your mouth and eyes shut."

A new voice joins the chaos. Dr. Anderson has arrived to relieve Rhanji's fourteen-hour shift, his voice clear and calm, steady with the optimism of his youth.

Rhanji dries his face with a towel and opens his eyes, trying to ignore the thought of sinister microbes seeping into his ocular membrane, en route to poison his blood or seize his immune system. Sandra, pushing morphine into the drip, jokes above the noise of their frantic patient.

"Savour the terry cloth, Rhanji."

It's black humour, funny because it's true. The laundry workers went on strike that morning. A year ago, all non-essential hospital staff had accepted pay cuts with the promise of continued job security, but now the Alberta government had announced plans to annihilate laundry-worker positions in favour of hiring a private contracting facility. Scoffing at the idea of helping those who betrayed them make a clean transition, the workers walked off the job and were soon joined by cafeteria workers, janitors, and administrative staff. Clean linens were quickly becoming as rare and valuable as available hospital beds.

"I don't know where we'll put him," Rhanji tells the younger physician. Rhanji's hands are shaking. Is his anger as obvious as it feels?

"No worries, mate." Anderson's thick Australian accent is unable to sound anything but unworried. He ushers Rhanji away from the trauma room.

"There's an old cot in basement storage," Sandra calls behind the men. Carrie's already left to retrieve it. They'll get the little girl into a wheelchair and the new patient off the stretcher, put him in her place in 112. Miranda can stay on the army duck canvas in the hall until something better opens up.

"Time to go home now, eh? You 'right?"

Rhanji nods. He will go home but not before completing a final task. The doctor takes the medic's clipboard to his office and transfers the Northern Air patient's information to official intake papers: name, injuries, healthcare card.

Patient's birth date: the day and month are the very same as Yasmin's.

Rhanji hears the man shout again in a weaker voice now: cracking, begging, pleading for his mother.

"Nikâwiy," the little girl matches in desperation. "Nikâwiy! Nikâwiy!"

I do not know this child, Rhanji repeats and repeats. *This child is not mine.*

※

Rhanji parks on the street in front of his house. He kills the vehicle's ignition and silences the radio's rabid arguments for and against the hospital worker's strike and its majority of protesting widows, mothers, and immigrants.

Outside, skin freezes within thirty seconds of exposure. The sky is as though Nanni pours her shade over the whole world, all homes awash in Rhanji's drowning dream. In Alberta, in November, four o'clock is a desolate time of day.

The doctor thinks of the old joke, a child's double entendre: *Your hands are blue, Nanni.*

Her palms were always stained indigo.

Yearn. Your hands yearn.

It is the truest thing in all the world.

Three houses over, a man is doubled in size by Gore-Tex, gloves, and balaclava. Clumsily, he drags a string of holiday lights up a ladder. Twelve weeks ago, this street was bright with porch lights, a gesture of hope for Yasmin's missing child. The community herded around Rhanji's daughter: private groups organized citywide searches and volunteer transit check-stops. Dr. Anderson's young girlfriend, Kelly, filled Rhanji's freezer with so many casseroles and bags of soup that Rhanji had to ask his colleague to tell her to stop. Sandra spent countless hours at Yasmin's side. The nurse had been at the boy's birth, picking up extra evening hours at the Grey Nuns, the former hospital recently downgraded to a perpetually short-staffed clinic. Sandra's hands had been the first to hold the boy, and she had been the one to discover the abandoned child in the room his birth mother had laboured in. She'd been the one to name him, in fact, after a favourite song.

But now Jude is just one more gone in a system so many vanish from. Houses are no longer lit. Inside the front window of Rhanji's home, his daughter's silhouette holds the last glowing tribute in the form of a cigarette raised and lowered from her lips. It is a terrible scene and one Rhanji is powerless to heal.

Rhanji had not approved of the child's impending adoption and had made his feelings clear even up to the very night before Jude was taken. Yasmin was too young, Rhanji insisted, only twenty-two, still unmarried. She'd just started her career the year prior, and the hours of a social worker were so long and so difficult for such little pay. Had she not already given enough without assuming the responsibility of a child?

But Yasmin argued she owed the boy. Sometime before his birth, she had placed a teenager and her two-year-old sister—two of the first case files Yasmin had inherited when a senior co-worker walked off the job—in a less than ideal home. The night after the older girl had run away from the foster mother's care, Yasmin had confessed to Rhanji that she'd never trusted the woman. Too often Mariam had passed judgment on biological families, and, at times, she seemed almost fanatical. Yasmin described how once, when she had outlined the important role a foster family could play in preserving a child's culture, the woman had laughed in a blurting, chilling, singular spurt, exposing her most defining feature: a discoloured front tooth, dark and dead as dirt on snow. "That laugh, the tooth—it made me want to run, too, you know?" Yasmin said.

Weeks later, Yasmin showed Rhanji a notebook filled with carefully jotted information. Yasmin had travelled far north to interview the girl's grandmother, a woman in her late fifties. Until Yasmin reached out, the woman hadn't known her eldest granddaughter was

pregnant, never mind lost. Her own daughter—the girls' mother—
had also gone missing before the children had gone into care.

"She had this huge binder," Yasmin said, flipping through the
pages she'd copied off the woman, so Rhanji could see. "It was filled
with newspaper clippings, details about each time she'd asked about
her daughter's case, a timeline of the disappearance itself. Organized,
like she's the lead investigator." Yasmin shook her head. "Honestly,
at this point, she probably is. She said she reads papers and calls
hospitals and shelters and watches the news for 'clues' every day,
but that no one will return her calls anymore, or, if they do, they
say she's too rural when she asks to meet with them. She's even travelled to offices only to have appointments cancelled minutes before
they're supposed to begin.

"But you know what's really terrible?" Yasmin continued.
"Apparently, she had applied for kinship care as soon as they were
placed in care. All this time she's been trying to get custody of
her own grandchildren, and I didn't even know. She's even begun
working with a child's advocate. I just sat there like a dummy when
she told me. Like, I know the system's a mess. We're totally under-
funded, and it feels like every time we get things organized there's
another staffing change-up. Still, those girls could have been with
their grandmother this whole time, and now one's missing."

Rhanji placed his hand on the back of Yasmin's head as tears
dropped from her eyes to the front of her sweater. She wiped her
face with the back of her wrist and took a breath.

"She told me to write everything down, and asked if I'd draft a
statement of support, which, yeah, of course. But Dad, the paper-
work hadn't been processed. There was no application to attach my
statement to when I looked through files, so I mailed her another

but, of course, that hasn't made it in yet, either. And then all this information still has to go to a committee that'll consider it anywhere up to a year from after it's submitted. It's this system—I can barely navigate it, and I'm in it! This family has so much stacked against them. She made me promise I'd do the best I could, and I will. I'll do everything to help her get custody of her youngest. But, honestly . . . there's no quick or easy route to take here."

A couple of months later, after the boy was born and assigned to Yasmin's roster of young clients, Yasmin chose not to place the newborn in a temporary home and instead applied for emergency guardianship herself. Sandra had reported to her a physical description of the boy's mother that matched Yasmin's runaway, and while there was no way to know for sure if they were one and the same, Yasmin was convinced.

"Then you already know this child's family," Rhanji said the night Yasmin brought the child home. He had been chopping carrots but stopped when she arrived, balancing the handle of a bulky carseat on her arm. "Why did you bring him here?"

Yasmin shook her head. Privacy laws were clear: Yasmin had no right to tell the woman the details of a newborn who may or may not be related to her.

"Besides," she said, resting the carseat on the floor to unbuckle the infant from his harness, "even if we could confirm the relationship, there isn't a caseworker employed who'd place a newborn and a two-year-old in solo kinship care at the same time. It would be asking her to choose between the granddaughter she's been fighting for, and an infant that might not even be her great-grandson." She ran a finger down the side of the baby's cheek. "It's too cruel. I'll take care of him."

Rhanji didn't understand. He lay the knife on the chopping block and crossed his arms. "How is it fair that you should end up with an unwanted child?"

"He's not unwanted," Yasmin scolded, lifting the child to rest against her chest.

"This is not your problem!"

"This is my obligation!" Yasmin deepened her voice in response to the rise in Rhanji's. She held the infant tight against her body, cradling his head in her palm. "I promised to do my best, Dad. This is what that looks like right now."

"These people are strangers, Yasmin."

"No. Jude is my son. Your grandson."

Rhanji shook his head. "He is only a stranger to me."

And then he left the room.

In the months that followed, Rhanji's heart had not softened. To him, the child seemed parasitic, growing larger and louder as circles darkened around Yasmin's eyes, as though he siphoned youth as hungrily as he took formula from the bottle. When Rhanji looked at the baby all he saw was a wide-open mouth, insatiable hunger, and manipulating tears. Small limbs that kicked and struck, fists that fought for more comfort and attention than a young single woman could ever possibly give. His wails were those of an emergency siren, a warning of how badly things had gone wrong. In his presence, nothing was right.

I do not know this child. He is not mine.

And Yasmin, Rhanji's own child, his *sweetu*, had not forgotten or forgiven his resentment. She had not spoken to him in kindness since the child was taken.

Cold claims the vehicle and Rhanji opens the car door, its hinges whining. The air is biting but the muffled noise of the suburban street is preferable to the silence of Rhanji and Yasmin's house. Rhanji shuffles along the icy driveway to the garage for a shovel and ice chipper. Once his home had enjoyed unending conversation, music, and easy laughter. Father and daughter had tested one another's English at breakfast, compared Canadian customs at lunch, shared fading remembrances of Sunita in the quiet evenings that followed soccer practices, drama club, piano lessons. When Yasmin reached adulthood, they had renovated the basement and she moved into the underground suite. They spent evenings together, taking in the daily news as they had in her childhood.

But these days all Rhanji hears of Yasmin's voice are the awkward attempts at Hindi that drift up through the floorboards as she seeks solace in a grandmother a whole world away instead of her own father waiting only a floor above. Why didn't Yasmin simply go to her, Rhanji wondered. He had asked her as much.

"The boy is gone. Go now and discover your roots. Have adventures and find love. I will buy you the ticket, and no one will judge, sweetu. You are so young. You have surely done more for the child than most would."

But Yasmin only shook her head. "I'm not going to give up on my son."

She left the room and Rhanji paced it as though the empty steps could cover the distance between his heart and hers. Perhaps Yasmin believes she knows a loss that he does not, he thought, but it is she who does not understand.

All grieve children. No one is immune.

Yearn, your hands yearn.

Now the doctor steadies himself over the ice of his driveway and grips the chipper's handle. He lifts the pole above his shoulders and brings the blade down hard, thinking of the boy, not killed or beaten or abandoned like so many other children in this world but simply taken. Witnesses who had been in the parking lot that day described the woman who had slipped into Yasmin's running truck as young, calm, careful. The act happened so quickly that she must have watched as the child and groceries were loaded into the vehicle, she must have waited for Yasmin to return the cart to the corral. Police didn't say so outright, but after no immediate leads, Rhanji sensed that they had given up.

"Women just aren't prone to violence," an officer said only days after the disappearance stopped making headlines. There was every reason to consider that the child belonged to the woman who had taken him. She could be the birth mother, regretful of a decision made in great pain and fear. "Even women who chose their kid's adoptive parents change their minds. It happens all the time."

Please let that be the truth, Rhanji asks of the sky, of Nanni's gods, of no one at all. *Let the boy be with his and me with mine and all will be as it should be again.*

The ice does not chip. Rhanji juts the blade and tries to recall the heft of the child in his arms. Had he ever held the boy? He thinks of Yasmin, in high school. She had been tasked with protecting a raw egg for two weeks, the project a metaphor for the necessary vigilance of parenthood. Careless, she had left it on the couch where Rhanji sat and crushed it. He imagines the boy like this now: alone, helpless, fragile. The child had not yet taken his first steps. Would a teenager know how to care for someone so young? How long will a baby call if no one picks him up? Rhanji doesn't know. He never let Yasmin cry.

Over and over, the blade bounces, leaving only superficial lines. A Chevy roars into the cul-de-sac, spitting out clouds of black smoke before fishtailing back onto the street from which it came. Rhanji flinches and slips, falling hard on his back, winded on the ice.

Dusk has given way to night, but Rhanji imagines a frozen field at high sun, its purity marred only by the smouldering of a truck, plastic bags melted to singed upholstery. He imagines the eager yelps of thick-haired dogs and sees them, leashes taut.

A child's car seat, overturned in the snow.

Skin as blue as a garment dyer's vat.

"Dad?"

A door creaks and booted feet shuffle toward him as quickly as the ice underfoot will allow. Yasmin's voice is a weak thread to a bitter reality. Rhanji imagines what it would be like to go this way, exposed. Hypothermia causes the release of an excess of endorphins, the body mercifully softening an otherwise painful death. It would be quick, euphoric even, in the end.

Above, Nanni's gods spy through pinholes in the sky, laughing or crying or disinterested in the lives of those living on a frozen prairie so far from home.

✳

The day is frigid and bright, the entrance to the hospital a hive of activity. Rhanji is greeted at the main doors by protestors arriving with food-bank donations and placards:

Jobs with Justice!
Tell Us Where It Hurts!

Food-service workers and housekeeping staff from other facilities have joined the laundry workers' ranks, as well as work-to-rule nurses, out-of-work social workers, overworked teachers. Senior citizens and a variety of union reps add to their masses. In another life, these women could have been Nanni and her contemporaries, the female labour force used and abused, underpaid and unseen. Rhanji is surprised by the support from those who drive by, but mostly he just wants to go inside. Crystallized piss coats the wall by the entrance doors.

Rhanji stops at the triage desk to overlook the waiting room. Wilf sleeps with his legs spread over three plastic chairs, his red bunker bag occupying another two. In fits, the man startles and flinches before pulling his large jacket tighter around his shoulders, resuming loud snores. The noise of his harmonica would almost be preferable, Rhanji thinks. He checks his watch: 9:28 AM. Wilf will miss his daily meeting.

The doctor considers waking the sleeping man, but it's too late now. Besides, the waiting room is surprisingly quiet and sleep is one of the most important parts of recovery. Still, there is an uncomfortable worry in the forefront of Rhanji's mind: Is this sleep natural, or has Wilf been drinking again?

Rhanji feels the disappointment well but dismisses the thought. Yes, it is possible, but with so much wrong in this world he needs something, someone, to hold out hope for. He retrieves a folded blanket from behind the triage desk and walks into the room, unfolding the material and draping it over the snoring man.

"Oh, doctor," Wilf says, suddenly wide eyed before recognizing Rhanji. "I'm sorry, doctor. I'm just tired. I promise. Just very, very tired." He closes his eyes again and immediately his breathing sinks into the sounds of sleep.

"It's alright, Wilf," Rhanji tells him. "Rest, my friend."

"All electives and non-emergency care have been cancelled," Carrie reports from behind the desk as Rhanji returns, her hand over the telephone receiver. Hold music hums from the earpiece, a top-forty song, Alanis Morissette. Rhanji raises his brows. So the minister of health has acknowledged frontline's problems. Will he fix them?

He flips through patient folders, scanning the file notes Anderson made the night before.

"Did you see on the news about that girl our drunk driver hit?" Carrie asks.

Rhanji shakes his head and frowns as he reads. Appendicitis confirmed for the pediatric patient; an aggressive course of antibiotics is prescribed. In the next folder, injury to the lumbar vertebrae and fifth sacral vertebrae confirmed for the drunk driver, definitive evidence of cellular damage.

"Well," Carrie continues, "you know she lost her baby, right? And only nineteen years old! Anyway, she was heading home from the Alberta Vocational College up in Slave Lake, studying to be a social worker. Just like your daughter. The news said she was studying for a job in child services because her dream was to help prevent kids in her own community from being, like, you know, automatically taken. And only a month from graduating . . . isn't that sad?"

Rhanji ignores her. "Someone has urinated on the entrance walls."

"Oh." She blushes. "But janitorial's on strike, remember?"

Rhanji looks at her until she blinks and smiles, finally taken off hold with whoever is on the end of her line. Are new staff members unversed in the rules of seniority? Then again, he remembers, Carrie is a volunteer.

Down the hall, the pediatric patient howls like a crisis siren. Rhanji checks the little girl's saline and vitals: her temperature is high but her urine bag is clear. Mucus crusts Miranda's mouth and nose and she screams when Rhanji tries to wipe it away. A nurse skirts around them, en route to the front desk.

"Has anyone heard from this child's guardian?"

The nurse barely slows her steps. "Her caseworker was recently let go and her foster mom is adamant the child is going into kinship care and is no longer in her custody. But as far as I know, Kohkum is still only petitioning for it. So, beats me. Miranda won't be assigned to another worker until Monday, at least, so I guess . . . she's ours until then?"

Rhanji shakes his head. "Can we at least get her passages cleared?"

"Not if she won't let us, we can't."

Rhanji attempts to comfort the girl with a friendly nod. The child hides under her sheets as RCMP officers exit 112. Inside, the spinal patient stares at the ceiling, the fragility of his paper gown in stark contrast to the large biceps underneath. The space is dark but for a lamp on the far side of the room.

Rhanji ignores the patient's wince as the doctor lights the lamp above his bed. "How are we this morning?"

"Best kind," the man whispers. "Yourself?"

"Relieved to discover a lack of communicable diseases in your system. Any complaints?"

The patient attempts to shield his face from the bulb but stops short, his right hand brought to the fault in his chest. "Jesus Mary," he whimpers. "This. And some bad head."

"Fractured sternum," Rhanji explains. "And a hangover, I suspect. Probably competing with the concussion."

The man points his jaw to the hall where Miranda has increased in pitch, screaming as if in competition with their conversation. "Or that."

"Anything else?"

"The other fella, the Aussie? He says I won't be wanting no surgery."

The injury is severe, Rhanji explains, surgery is not viable. "With or without treatment, it is unlikely you will ever regain the use of your legs."

Rhanji waits. He expects the man will weep, or beg, or pray. A better person might accept the paralysis as comeuppance for the woman he injured, for the death of her unborn child. But this man is silent until he screams at the small child in the hall.

"Shut up! Shut up yer prate!"

Rhanji replaces his pen cap. Silence.

"Well, they can't bloody well put no cripple in no prison now, can they?" the man whispers. "They'll have to fly me home." He chokes at the end of his words and begins to sob.

Rhanji turns to leave. "All government buildings are wheelchair accessible."

✳

Rhanji returns home to find Yasmin looking like a corpse before the pyre, skin ashen in the television's glow. "Alberta's hospital crisis reaches critical condition with 2,700 workers on the picket line and another 3,000 poised to walk," Peter Mansbridge reports on CBC. "Alarming new details emerge on André Dallaire's attempt on the prime minister's life. The Princess of Wales admits to adultery. A woman with the tattoo of a bird vanishes from the streets of Edmonton."

"What kind of world is this?" Yasmin asks. A cardboard box is set on the floor beside her, overpacked with coffee mugs, books, a half-dead plant.

"What's this?" Rhanji asks, nudging the container with his foot.

"Stuff from my office," she says. She does not look up, the tone of her voice flat, deadpan. "I don't work there anymore."

Rhanji's heart sinks. "Since?"

"A few days ago. Government cuts."

Rhanji reaches for the remote and the screen flickers to dark. "Let's talk."

His daughter moves from couch to kitchen still clutching the blanket around her shoulders. Red and gold bangles sound upon her wrist, the treasured jewellery that once upon a time belonged to her mother.

"You can't live like this anymore, Yasmin."

She pulls open a drawer and lights a cigarette. "No?"

"I know it feels like everything has ended, but there will be other jobs, sweetu. And you can still be a mother, but do it right next time! Fall in love, get married, have a baby all your own."

She takes a drag, eyes hard and dark.

"You don't have to squeeze out a kid for him to be your own, Dad."

The hard woman before Rhanji is a stranger in their home, completely unknown to him. But then her chin trembles under a stream of smoke as she exhales and, as if by magic, Yasmin is once again the baby girl he loves, the one for whom he can make everything right. He lifts his arms and steps forward, but she stops him, the cigarette end burning the space between.

"And he was your own, too." Her voice breaks and she wipes a tear from her face with the heel of her hand balancing the cigarette. "Emphasis on 'was,' I guess."

She does not look back when retreating downstairs.

He rests his head on the back of the couch and waits to hear the language of women he has lost. He lifts the remote. Men combing white fields replace the image of the Grey Nuns' hospital and then: a smouldering truck, a police officer in front of a microphone.

The news is bad, and good, and meaningless.

The pregnant girl is dead.

Yasmin's stolen truck is found.

The missing child is still gone. No leads.

On the coffee table, he is shocked to find a plane ticket in his daughter's name.

His daughter has broken, Rhanji thinks. Yasmin has given up.

What kind of world is this? Yasmin had asked.

One Rhanji can barely stand anymore.

꙳

By morning, protestors have multiplied. Rhanji is in no mood to deal with the mounting drama. Local 18 machinists have joined the noisy ranks, as well as top union dogs. Children have been dragged from school and into their parents' public tantrums. A woman flanked by two boys in ratty snowsuits smiles through her tears.

"They see us now," she sobs to a news camera as Rhanji walks past. "They finally see us!"

Who sees you? Alberta doesn't give a shit and neither do I, Rhanji thinks. Let the goddamn hospitals crumble for all he cares. Give the voters what they asked for. He just wants to do his goddamn job.

There's another night's worth of frozen piss sticking to the entrance wall. Behind the glass doors, Rhanji can see Wilf sitting on the floor, red bunker bag behind him like a pillow propped against the wall. Why has he set up camp in there?

The sliding doors part and Rhanji is hit with the too-loud wails of Wilf's harmonica and the campfire stink of the corridor. Something's not right.

"Wilf?"

"There's the good doctor!" Wilf slurs as Rhanji kneels down. He wears the straps of his red bag on his shoulders. As he lifts his arms in greeting, the bag shifts and spills empty liquor bottles to the floor. Both men watch the bottles roll, and Wilf begins to laugh.

"This is what you want?" Rhanji asks. "After all I've done . . . you do this here, in my hospital?"

Wilf snorts. "Oh, come on, doctor! Lighten up, *my friend*," he says, mocking Rhanji's accent. "It's cold. How else are we supposed to keep warm? It's a party in here!"

Wilf raises his hands and pretends to dance, wiggling the upper half of his body. Rhanji lifts the man by the straps of his bunker bag and his too-large jacket and pushes him into the protestors outside. The bag swings and throws Wilf off balance. He hits the ground, shaking hands still stretched out to Rhanji.

"Go to a meeting!" Rhanji shouts.

"Ease up!" scolds a voice from the sea of placards.

Rhanji does not look at the woman's face.

In triage, he slaps his palm against the desk. Carrie, on the phone, flinches.

"What the hell was that bum doing in here?"

"Excuse me?" She blinks.

"Do your goddamn job, Carrie."

Down the hall Miranda switches from singing to screaming as Rhanji nears. Toys litter the bed, small gifts dropped off by nurses to appease her temper. The antibiotics have run their course; her eyes are clear, her fever subsided.

Sandra walks past with a pasted smile, hair done up like mutton.

"Why is she still here?" Rhanji snaps.

"I'm sorry?"

"The child. Figure it out. We need these beds."

He turns and enters room 112. One nurse lifts the drunk-driving rigger so another can sponge his back.

"Not bad if you can get it, eh, b'y?" The man winks.

"The girl's dead," Rhanji says. "The girl you crushed? You killed her. She's dead."

✳

Rhanji is relieved for the rest of the day. Dr. Anderson will cover his shift.

Sandra told Rhanji to go home, but instead he took to his office and watched the day turn to dusk outside his window. Now he lays his head on his desk, humiliated. To whom does he not owe an apology? He picks up the phone and dials his own number, connecting with the machine. He imagines Yasmin listening from the couch, a cigarette's glow illuminating her face. He leaves a message. "I'm so sorry, sweetu. He was mine because he was yours, and I wasted it." He feels the truth of these words as he speaks them and lets the tears wash over his face. "I wasted it."

Sandra knocks at the door, a mug in either hand. Rhanji hangs up the phone and wipes his eyes as the nurse sits opposite and sips.

"Sandra," he starts, but the woman lifts her hand to stop him. She shakes her head and smiles.

"So quiet tonight," she says. "Thank god."

Rhanji nods.

They stare into their mugs, resting in the silence, until they realize. *No.*

Where is the singing? Where is the screaming? Where is Nikâwiy?

Where is Miranda?

They drop their coffee cups, rising and running as a unit to the child's bed in the hall.

Empty.

Sandra turns, shouting to triage, "Lock down, Carrie! Lock down! No one leaves this building!"

Fluorescent lights hum and blur as Rhanji stares at Miranda's mussed sheets, her scattered toys. Not another child gone. Not another child. Panicked, Rhanji shouts to no one and to everyone.

"Where is the girl? Where is the girl! Who has this girl?"

"B'y."

Rhanji turns. The spinal patient holds a finger to his lips. Miranda is asleep under his arm, her small head resting over the buried crack in his chest, her pink lips parted but hushed, only gently snoring.

"Couldn't let her suffer alone no more, could I?" Tears run down his face, over dark bruises as he looks down at the face of the child. "God knows I've caused enough suffering."

Rhanji's heart slows but his knees are weak. He pulls a chair bedside and sits by the man, and together they listen to the girl's quiet breathing. He senses Sandra at the door, hears her voice catch in surprise and relief before she calls off the search. The young man stifles a sob, striving for stillness to let the girl sleep despite the pain of the fracture in his chest.

"I'm scared," he tells Rhanji. "I'm so scared. I want my mom. Isn't that sad?" He shakes his head. "The size of me, and I just want my mom."

Rhanji offers the patient his hand. They sit like this, child and patient and doctor, until man and girl sleep.

Later, Sandra tiptoes into the room and places a hand on Rhanji's tired shoulder. "It's a good news day," she whispers. The workers' strike is over. Better yet: Miranda's Kohkum has finally won custody.

She reaches over and brushes hair from the child's face. "This little one's going home."

Rhanji blinks back tears. He tilts his head so it rests on Sandra's steady arm and together they look out into the blackness of the night through the caged hospital window.

And Rhanji thinks about all the children he does not know.

＊

Rhanji stops at triage before leaving. It's a slow night and Carrie has already left. He asks Sandra to pass along his apologies if she sees the student nurse first. Rhanji will call in the morning and ask her forgiveness himself.

The doctor turns to leave but finds the waiting room wanting, silent.

"Where's Wilf?"

Sandra presses her lips together. She shakes her head and shrugs. "I don't know. But it's a cold one tonight. I'm worried about him."

"Call me if he comes in?"

Outside, snow falls slow in soft, thick flakes. Streetlamps make cones of light in the parking lot. Rhanji sits for a moment, warming the interior of his car. They'll find the child together, he thinks; he'll promise Yasmin they won't give up. Together they will find this child and they'll love him and they'll love his desperate mother, too. Rhanji will do the best he can.

The silent vow is interrupted by a scream. Rhanji cranes his neck to look out the passenger window and is startled by a pounding on the driver's-side door.

Wilf.

Rhanji opens the door and Wilf falls into his arms. Something feels warm and wet and when Rhanji pulls his hand away he sees dark droplets staining the icy snow outside the vehicle. Blood. He stands and steadily lowers the man to the frozen asphalt, propping Wilf's back against the vehicle's tire. Then Rhanji lays on the horn until he sees Sandra rush into the light of the entrance.

"He's all alone!" Wilf cries. "No one could see him! He was left! All alone!"

Rhanji tries to peel back Wilf's layers, but the man resists. He'll freeze, Wilf cries and cries. "He'll freeze and he's all alone!"

"Who's alone, Wilf? You're not alone. I'm here. Where does it hurt?"

Wilf's hands are stained red. His knuckles are swollen and displaced. Rhanji tries to lift the sleeves of the man's oversized parka to inspect further but Wilf turns from him, holding tight to his jacket, arms locked across his body. Finally, Rhanji breaks the lock and pulls the injured arm to him. The flesh is torn, shards of glass sparkling in the moonlight.

"Wilf, did you punch a window?"

Rhanji loosens his own scarf from around his neck, wrapping it above the wound to slow blood loss. A team arrives with a stretcher but Wilf leans harder into Rhanji, snowflakes catching on his unkempt beard, littering his long black hair.

"It hurts. He can't be alone. It hurts!"

"Who, Wilf?"

Wilf lifts his face and wails. He finally lets slack the arm still clutching his coat, opening his large jacket to expose what was hidden, cradled within. Young eyes stare out, big and brown and unafraid, a little face framed by soft curly hair. The tiny child clings to Wilf's thin torso underneath the enormous parka, small but strong limbs wrapped around his hero.

"He was left alone. Left alone, crying! In a car! No one could see him. It hurts!"

Rhanji takes the child. The boy protests and kicks, but Rhanji holds him close in one hand and clutches the tourniquet in the other as the howls of boy and man combine.

"I've got him, Wilf. I've got him. He's all right. You're a hero, Wilf. He's not alone. I've got you too. I see you."

Sandra covers her mouth with her hands as her eyes fill and glisten. "Jude," she whispers. She kneels in the snow by Wilf and takes hold of Rhanji's blood-soaked scarf.

"Rhanji, that's Jude. Wilf! Wilf, you found him!"

"I gotta go home," Wilf sobs. "I just want to go home."

"We'll help you, Wilf," Sandra promises. "We'll help you get home."

Rhanji tries to place the child in the warmth of his running vehicle but the boy clings to his neck so Rhanji tightens the embrace, first to warm him, and then to feel the stillness. The weight in his arms is so familiar, so right, so much like home.

BUT FOR THE STREETLAMPS AND THE MOON
AND ALL THE STARS

1991

"BITCH."

The word hisses out of Patty's mouth like air escaping from the pop bottle Lacey opened to use as mix. Not that Patty really thinks Mrs. Simperson is a bitch. Really, Mrs. Simperson is smart and passionate and kind. But she's also a love bead–wearing weirdo who talks about things like *the patriarchy* and always has crusty eye boogers and once said she wished she were a tree so she could pray all day. That kind of weird is fair game. Besides, everyone knows better than to take on Shannon.

Shannon passes Patty the cigarette held between her thumb and index finger. Lacey kneels nearby in the playground sand, pouring blue Sour Puss and Orange Crush into the thin necks of empty water bottles. She exhales with a huff and blows barrel-curled bangs out of her eyes as she buries the base of each plastic bottle so they won't fall over. Patty was filling the bottles first but Lacey pushed her out of the way. She loves taking care of little details like mixing drinks and decorating teacher's classrooms. She even packs the snacks for her brother's hockey team. "Can you guys even imagine how nice my house is going be someday?" Lacey always brags. "I'm going to be, like, the best mom ever."

"Seriously!" Shannon says, coughing smoke, " 'I can't stand the sound of your laughter?' I mean, oh my god!"

Lacey snorts. "Yeah, Simperson lost it on you, man. I didn't think teachers were allowed to talk like that."

"They're not." Shannon grabs a bottle from the sand and climbs onto the balance beam. She flexes and points her feet like a ballerina as she walks. The Celtic cross ring she wears on a long chain around her neck catches the sun's last rays as though it were Shannon's own heart sparkling in the dying light. "She's having, like, a midlife crisis or something. You know she's paying some chick to get pregnant with her dead son's baby? She, like, saved his sperm, or something. Gross."

Lacey's mouth falls wide open. "Oh. My. God."

Patty feels the other girls waiting for her to agree but Patty pretends she didn't hear. She knows Shannon is lying but doesn't want to be a know-it-all. Patty isn't a total spaz. Still . . .

"How'd she get her son's sperm?"

Shannon raises her eyebrows at Lacey. They erupt in high-pitched laughter. "Wouldn't you like to know, Pervy Pat!"

Patty tries to laugh like she's in on the joke. "No, I mean, like . . ."

"Oh, no!" Lacey clasps her hands over her chest, her feathered hair shaking in its heavily sprayed shape. She pretends to cradle a head on her lap. "My son! Let me give you a quick hand job before your balls rot, my boy." Her fist moves up and down furiously over the invisible man's crotch.

Patty looks away and takes a swig of her drink. Shannon rolls her eyes.

"Ugh, I'm bored. Let's go somewhere."

"Mikey's friends are over and me and Mom turned the basement into a games den so there's, like, more privacy. He'd probably let us hang out."

"Yeah," Shannon says, "but Patty's not allowed to be around boys, remember?"

"So? She's not allowed to drink or smoke, either."

"Yeah," Shannon says slowly, with *enunciation*, "but if we go to your house, your mom will see her, and then she'll mention it to Patty's mom at the arena next week."

"Oh. Yeah." Lacey stifles a laugh. Patty cringes, imagining what Lacey's thinking: Mom barefaced and in a hairnet, scowling so her brown tooth shows like an old popcorn kernel stuck at the front of her mouth. "I forgot Mariam's the canteen lady now." Lacey crosses her arms, eyes narrowed at Patty. "Don't you think it's kind of mean that you're not allowed to come to my house? Like, my brother's some kind of danger or something, just because he's a boy?"

Shannon shakes her head. "Not very Christian," she says. "I mean, what about 'no one should judge,' right?"

"Thou shalt not judge." Patty shifts from one foot to the other, envying the invisible man, dead in the sand.

Her mom got really religious after Patty's dad left: daily Bible study groups and abortion clinic protests and all. Now it seems like she gets a little crazier every day, and Patricia's not allowed to watch TV or listen to music and she's certainly not allowed to date. Dating is "worldly." Apparently good Christian girls are supposed to *court*, but only if they're ready to get married, and only if the boy gets approval from the girl's family first. Patricia doesn't even have words for how dumb the whole thing is. If she ever has a daughter, she's going to teach her to be free and to chase her dreams above anything else. Who cares if she wants to date boys? The only thing that matters is that you don't lose yourself in someone else.

But Mariam kind of counts on girls losing themselves. Last week she was even talking about taking in teenage foster kids because apparently the church says girls who become Christian before they're old enough to know better are most likely to stay that way. Not that Mariam's had any luck converting Patty.

"We are the daughters of the king," she tells Patty every day before school, palm pressed against her daughter's forehead, the other lifted in prayer.

But just this morning Patty ducked away from her mother's hand.

"I'm dust, Mom, and so are you. We're all just dust—stardust! There is no king. No tooth fairy, either."

Mariam swallowed hard as her arms dropped to her sides. She looked away with wet eyes and Patty almost felt bad, but then she moved quick as Patty blinked and smacked her right across the face. The sting surprised Patty, but she looked Mariam in the eyes anyway, even if it was through tears she couldn't help but let fill up.

"You can be mad about it all you want," Patty whispered. "But it's true." The day before their science teacher had lectured about how almost everything is created from the burning of interstellar gases. Everything: stardust. Besides, the whole Bible freak routine . . . it was crazy, silly, *ludicrous*. Science, fact, logic, and proof—that's where it's at, not that she'd ever say anything so uncool to Shannon and Lacey.

Besides, knowing everyone's just made of dust—of dirt, basically—well, it makes everything a little easier to deal with. Like, everyone's a little special, but mostly everyone's all the same, and we're
all just made of space junk, so it doesn't really matter what happens.
Like, Patty knows life is awful. Terrible things happen all the time:
parents are dying, kids are left alone and afraid, whole groups of
people are wiped out for no good reason. Sometimes World Vision
commercials come on and Patricia feels sick for the rest of the day,
thinking about those little kids. But when she reminds herself that
everyone's made of dust, things are put in perspective, like those
shitty things might as well happen to a rock or a pebble or *anything* because even though people have feelings right now, we're
just nothing when all's said and done. Or maybe we're everything.
Or, whatever—we're the same as everything else. We're just history.
Stardust: sparkly, but in the end, just dirt.

As in, nothing really matters, so Patty shouldn't worry about everyone so much.

"I know," Patty says to her friends. "It sucks. She's so
overprotective."

"Whatever," Lacey mouths, making an L on her forehead with
her fingers. The girls leave the playground, hands stuffed into the
pockets of their hoodies, capped bottles hiding up their sleeves.

They walk nowhere but forward, hoping their aimless steps take
them someplace good. Patty and Lacey's houses aren't an option,
but Shannon doesn't suggest her own and neither of the other girls
will either—they know they can't go there until everyone's asleep.
Last time they went too early and Shannon's mom's live-in boyfriend
came into the bedroom and tried to hang out, holding Shannon's

hand. It was weird but Patty and Lacey didn't say anything. No one with any smarts wants to make Shannon mad.

The April night air is crisp but the Sour Puss makes Patty feel warm, alive, *euphoric*. Stars shine in the cloudless sky and she imagines them shining brighter just for her, recognizing her as one of their own. Patty stretches her arms and pictures starlight pouring in through her eyes, setting off billions of particles so she radiates with the same glittery brilliance. She wishes she could feel like this always.

"Check out PP." Lacey giggles.

"Huh?"

Behind her Shannon and Lacey walk arm in arm, identical smirks between curtains of blond hair.

"PP," Lacey shrieks, "Pervy Pat!"

Shannon laughs until she squirms, clasping her crotch. "I'm gonna pee!" She totters behind a thin tree and drops her jeans.

A screen door squeaks and they hear a man, "Hey! What are you doing?"

"Oh my god!" Lacey squeals. "Run!"

When they feel they've gone far enough, the girls collapse on the grass of a corner lot, laughing without noise, without air, ribs burning with the pleasure of it. Lacey lies on her back and pulls her knees to her chest, ripping a loud fart.

"Oh, no!" Shannon says, pulling denim from her leg. "I peed on myself!"

More laughter.

"Here." Patty takes off her sweater and hands it to her, generously, *benevolently*. "Tie this around so you don't get cold."

The sweater is almost too big for Shannon to tie the arms around her nonexistent hips. "Are you sure?" The way she coos reminds Patty of how Dave carried Shannon's desk to the gym during midterms (which made Lacey cry. Dave is supposed to be *her* crush).

"I'm fine," Patty says. She's better than fine. She takes a sip from her bottle and realizes she's swallowed her last mouthful. Patty takes aim and pitches the bottle down the street, smiling as it pings off a yield sign.

"Whoa!" Lacey shouts, swaying. "Good one, PP!" She puts her arm around Patty's shoulder.

A few feet ahead, Shannon stands fixed at a Dodge Spirit in front of a yellow-sided house.

"Do you know whose car this is?" The black liner smudging Shannon's eyes makes her seem older, more sure. Dangerous.

"No."

"This is Simperson's car."

"How can you tell?"

Shannon rolls her eyes. "Come on, Patty. Look!"

Patty peers into the windows and sees red velvet seats. *Wild Geese* sits on the backbench, the same novel the girls are supposed to be reading in class. Photocopy paper pokes from between its pages: *Grade 9 Vocab Words, April 15–19.*

"You see that, there?" Shannon points at a brown pouch dangling from the rear-view mirror. "You know what that is?"

"Air freshener?"

"That's her kid's fucking ashes," Shannon whispers. "She says he keeps her safe. Like he's her guardian angel, or something." She pulls at the passenger side's door handle. "Holy shit. It's open!"

The street is empty and dark but for the streetlamps and the moon and all the stars.

Lacey and Shannon ransack the car while Patty paces the sidewalk, chewing on her thumbnail. They put Simperson's books in a pile on the lawn, laying a wool cardigan beside them, a pair of Sorel boots on top, balancing three empty coffee cups on union papers. It's done quietly, carefully, *ceremoniously*. Finished, Shannon walks to Patty and presses something soft into the palm of her hand. A beaded pink flower reflects moonlight at the centre of the leather bag.

"Come on, Patty. You're the creative one."

"Yeah, right!" Lacey snorts. "PP's Simperson's pet. They're best buds with their lesbo poems and nerd books." She stumbles and falls onto the pile of books, her wrist catching the corner of the top hardcover. "Shit!" She presses the scratch with her thumb.

Patty's cheeks burn. It is super lame, staying after school to write, but Mrs. Simperson says she has talent, *a voice*. She even assigns Patty extra vocabulary words the other kids don't get. Patty sticks them in her head and pulls them to the front of her mind whenever she can: *ethereal, evanescent, eviscerate*. It is weird getting special attention like that, though. Good weird, but like she doesn't know how to act or what to say. It makes her think of Mom and the awkwardness of before-school prayers.

"Well?"

Patty shrugs. She slides the pouch out of Shannon's hand the way potheads pass baggies in the cafeteria: quick, cool, *nonchalant*. She walks to a plastic birdbath in the middle of the Simperson's lawn. Slowly, Patty unties the pouch's drawstring, smoothing the ruched material. Pinching the bag by its corners, she flips it, dumping its contents into the dry birdbath.

She expected a cloud of white soot to pillow her face, but the ashes fall in a clump, like dirt, kicking up only a little dust. She doesn't feel awful or evil, either, like she thought she would. She feels big, brave, *victorious*. The girls clap from the sidewalk. It'll probably end up being good for Mrs. Simperson, Patty tells herself; maybe now she can move on, let go. Driving around with your kid's dead body, that can't be easy. He must have died years ago.

Patty turns with her fist in the air like the braless protestors in the photos that hang in Simperson's classroom. While she keeps lookout, Shannon kicks the books across the lawn, picking up the heavier ones, ripping out their pages. Lacey pulls down her leggings and tries to squat over the birdbath but falls and takes the lawn ornament down with her. She sits in the bowl, bum right on the ashes, and pees.

"Run!"

A light shines through the Simpersons' front window. Patty stuffs the empty pouch into the waistband of her jeans. No one squeals, this time. No one escapes, either.

The girls huddle behind three garbage cans across the street, flinching when they hear a man shout. A door slams and Mrs. Simperson's faraway voice breaks with sleep.

A man: "You'd better come out here, love."

"Darling, what's wrong?"

And then Patty hears her moan.

Patty hears the clap-clap-clap of slipper-clad feet, running so close to where they hide. She hears Mrs. Simperson cry out again and again and again. Jamie, Jamie, her voice keens.

"Jamie, Jamie, Jamie!"

There is a quiet ache, a pause. Mrs. Simperson's cries are muffled. The man is holding her, Patty realizes. It's strange to think of Mrs. Simperson in someone's arms, of her being loved like that. The girls squat until their knees shake, pressing their mouths to their shoulders to keep from making noise when their thighs begin to burn. Then, at the sound of a shutting screen, they run.

They stick to suburban tree lines, creeping between houses when possible, staying off main roads. They travel north until they're back in Rundle Park, headed toward the low-income complex where Patty and Shannon live. Shannon walks ahead as if she's trying to lose the others. By the time they reach the trails that lead to Shannon's house Patty has one arm propped under Lacey's shoulder, helping her walk.

"Can I still sleep over, Shannon?" Lacey asks, slurring her words.

"Are you for real?" Shannon snaps. She quickens her pace but walks backward, facing the other girls. "As if! You're disgusting, Lacey, just gross. You fucking pissed on someone's ashes. Like, you actually peed on a dead body. Ew!"

Lacey starts to cry. "I can't go home this drunk!" Her voice is the same low moan as Simperson's. Spit drools down her chin. "My dad will freak out! Your mom doesn't even care!"

Shannon stops walking and shakes her head slowly, *incredulously*. She tucks her diamond ring necklace under the collar of her sweater and unties Patty's sweater from around her waist, letting it fall to the ground before stepping over it with dirty sneakers.

"Whatever," Shannon says. She smirks at first, but her chin starts to quiver. "I can't even believe you!" she shouts. Then she turns and quickens her pace, disappearing around the bend of the trail.

Lacey starts to heave. She lets go of Patty's shoulder and drops to the ground. She turns to her right and throws up, catching vomit in her hair. Patty sits beside her, rubbing her shoulders.

"I'm sorry I'm so mean to you, Patty," Lacey whimpers. She wipes her mouth with the sleeve of her sweatshirt. "I'm just so tired of everything." She starts to sob.

"Today Mom told me Dad spent my college money on Mikey's hockey camps. She didn't even care, just mentioned like it was nothing, like we both knew I wouldn't need it."

She hiccups and curls into herself, presses her forehead into Patty's leg. Patty moves fallen bangs out of Lacey's sad blue eyes.

"A woman's place is with her family, Mom always says. She thinks I'm too stupid. Useless," Lacey whispers. "Why does everyone think I'm so dumb?"

Patty lies down and stares up at the sky. The stars are dim, cold, just balls of gas burning a hundred trillion miles away. Something pinches at her hip and she pulls Simperson's soft pouch from her waistband, feeling grains and powder under her fingertips, watching the bag's embroidered beads twinkle in what little light there is.

None of this matters, she thinks. It's just a pocket of stardust.

No.

Jamie.

Jamie.

ANGELS IN THE SNOW

1998 / 1978

EARL CLOSES THE door and the cold rushes in, prickling Dolly's arms before warming to match the temperature of the house. Not that Dolly would describe the house as warm. It's too large. Sterile. The baseboards are still scuffed, blackened by little shoes, and the window trim is still chipped where the baby gnawed, but the marks are just memories now, only ghosts. The space is painful in its emptiness.

"Cold one today," Earl says, breathing into his hands. "Minus thirty. Should've plugged the truck in."

Dolly's heart beats in her ears. The skin around her mouth hardens and puckers, falling into deep vertical lines.

"Don't leave us. You can't leave."

Earl's eyebrows knot as he reaches for her but she pulls away. "Doll, I'm not leaving. I'm never leaving. I'll be home tonight."

She almost believes him, but that girl comes in. She steps into their home without so much as a knock, a man's flannel coat pulled around her, shapeless as a sack of potatoes, Sorels thumped on Dolly's welcome mat. Dolly wore bright colours when she was young: florals and geometric prints, skirts and kitten heels. She would have taken the time to button up, at the very least.

What's her name? Colleen? No, Car-something. Carlene? Carly? That must be it. There was a Kar-en once, in the old days, when the kids were little. She was young, too. There's always a girl like that, waiting in the wings, ready to take a woman's man. Earl says the new girl's here to help, but it's all a ruse, plain as day. Weren't they just in the hall together yesterday? Oh, they didn't think Dolly was watching, but she was.

"I don't think I can do this much longer," the girl whispered. "It doesn't feel right." At least she had the decency to blush, the coy thing.

Earl wrapped his arms around her, hugging her against his chest, resting his chin on her head. "Angel, I don't know what else to do."

It wasn't the embrace that stung. It was the tenderness. Angel? In thirty-six years of marriage, he'd never once given Dolly a pet name, nothing more than "doll," anyway.

"Oh, it's slippy out there!" Carly says, shrugging off her coat.

Slippy. Like a child. Pretty idiot.

Slippery, Dolly tries to correct, but the word doesn't come out right. "Ery," her voice sounds. "Slippy-ery. Her means."

The girl frowns and nods and Dolly cringes inside, so horribly embarrassed. *Agrammatic*, Dr. Anderson had called her at last week's appointment. He was a nice young man, Australian by birth and new at the university hospital after spending a few years at the Grey Nuns. Words and syllables are getting mixed up alongside dates and times and names, he explained; Dolly is losing track of how to place everything in its proper order. She was non-fluent.

But did he know she had all the children reading by the time they were only three years old? She wanted Earl to tell him, but she just couldn't find the words.

"Let's get you someplace warmer, shall we?"

Carly takes Dolly's arm and she's put on the sofa like some fussy old cat, pillows propped and fluffed and the blinds of a nearby window opened. But listen! Look! There they are, whispering in the hall again.

"I'm not sure I should leave," Earl says. "It's a difficult day, for everyone."

The girl shakes her head. "I don't think she knows. She doesn't even . . . she calls me Carly."

Earl pushes his fist to his lips. Tears? Why? The girl places a hand on his arm and leans in and—oh! She's kissed him! Right on the cheek, look, lipstick marks, right there!

"Just make sure she takes her medicine, eh?" Earl whispers. "There's a good girl."

There's screaming inside of Dolly. She breathes deep through her nose, out through her mouth. Her heart will stop, smothered by this anger.

She remembers this from long ago, this raging panic, heavy in her belly like the worry stones she'd find in little Jack's pockets. She'd visit and revisit it all day, caressing its sides, forcing herself to believe it. She can't say now what it was that upset her so, but recalls crying into scrambled eggs before serving them with a smile. That's motherhood, isn't it? Hum through the pain. *Little pitchers have big ears.* Sob into a pillow later. Claim a headache—God bless sleeping pills—take to bed and let your busy little world move all around you. Back when life was wild, all Dolly wanted was stillness.

Now life is still and all Dolly wants is wild. She would scratch faces, upset tables, pull hair, tear clothes—if only this clumsy body would cooperate.

That's the only real reason she needs a nurse; it's the aging, the shutting down. Dr. Anderson can *early onset* this and *Broca's aphasia* that until the cows come home, but the problem's in stiff joints, shaky fingers, and atrophied muscles; there's not a bit wrong with her mind. *Given to flights*, she's been that way since she was a girl, like that time she got caught in a daydream and dropped the church's new china pitcher.

"I saw something, in my head," Dolly explained after the fellowship picnic. She sat in the back of her father's Chrysler, hands unthreading a skirt hem, picking at her cuticles. "There were white walls on either side of me and only blue in front. I was very tired and then realized I was lying down and the walls were running up beside me. I was dying, I think, or dead."

Her mother blinked and blushed deep scarlet, staring straight ahead, mouth locked in her lopsided frown. She reached for the dash and turned the radio dial high to drown out Dolly's voice. Dolly never mentioned pitcher-white walls again.

Oh look, it's happened just now. She's gotten lost in her head and that damned nurse is giving her a strange look.

"Did you hear me, Mom?"

Well, isn't she bold? It's Dorothy—no, Mrs. Quentin, to her!

"What?"

The nurse is unfolding something—oh, it's Dolly's shawl. She wraps it around Dolly's shoulders, smoothing the material with warm hands. Well, that's thoughtful. There's a tightness in Dolly's throat. She must have it wrong. The girl isn't frumpy or stupid.

Carly is kind, really, so kind, and so fresh and so sweet and so young. Earl is an old man, what would Carly want with him? Oh, it's lovely to feel another's hands. It used to annoy her, the children always pawing, pulling at her clothes, messing her hair. Now Dolly is desperate for touch.

"I was just saying if you wanted to go to church today, maybe light a candle or leave some flowers, I could skip my afternoon classes."

Oh.

Oh, no. Dolly's not much for religion. She left the church as a newlywed, she and Earl both, when they moved up to Alberta. Those were the days. How exciting it was: the freedom of adulthood, the weightlessness of leaving, the beauty of letting go what no longer served. And the sex! She and Earl couldn't get enough of one another then. Dolly presses her fist into her lap.

Oh dear, Carly is upset. Her dark-pencilled lips make an uneven arch, reminding Dolly of her mother.

"It's just, you usually want to do *something*. You know?"

What? Nonsense. Is young Carly trying to convert her? Dolly ought to have Earl put a notice on the door: *No Solicitors, Not Even Jesus.* Anyway, she must be firm. The children are expecting her. They might want to dye eggs. Easter is only a week away—early this year, being in March. Dolly shakes her head.

"Want me to turn on the TV? Or we could play cards."

Dolly shakes her head again.

What Dolly really wants to do is go upstairs and see what the little ones are up to. But she won't let Carly in on that secret; it's too wonderful. She's going to show Earl this weekend. How happy he'll be! They'll make an occasion of it, take them to Rundle Park and toboggan, just like they used to. Why, she'll even have a go, old bones be damned! No doubt Jack will want some hot chocolate and Carrie some cake. Susan will ask for sips of her father's coffee and she'll cross her legs, ever the lady, when he gives her a cup of her own. Then they'll hold the children until they sleep, and Earl will look at Dolly, touch her hair and kiss below her ear, and it will all be as it used to be.

Dolly wakes from her daydream with a dry mouth, her eyes slow to focus.

"Twelve o'clock," Carly says, helping her up. "Time to rest."

Dolly opens and closes her mouth. They haven't even had lunch yet! She's sure the nurse moves the clock ahead when she's not paying attention. Suddenly Dolly is repulsed by the thought of herself, lips smacking like an old pervert with knuckles pressed between her legs.

"You said you weren't hungry! I told you to eat a million times!"

Oh dear, it's true.

There's the food on a small table in front of her: a bowl of yellow soup, grease dotting its surface, toast soggy with butter. Television trays, these wobbly tables used to be called. The children would eat dinner off them as a treat. Sundays, yes, when they watched that program about a dog. *The Littlest Hobo*—that's it. Back when Dolly and Earl and the children were a nest of a family, cuddled under home-stitched quilts, needing only each other.

Carly straightens the blankets so Dolly can climb under. Dolly doesn't sleep in the master suite with Earl anymore. She's been put in the off-kitchen office to avoid the stairs. "I made," Dolly says, as the quilt is tucked under her chin. Beneath the material, Dolly pantomimes pushing a needle.

Carly smiles, nods. "I remember."

The nurse rattles a pill bottle over her palm and Dolly opens her mouth like a nestling to its mother. She feels lips on her temple, the warm rush of a soft exhale. It's surprising, such tenderness, but not unwelcome.

"Sweet dreams."

Carly has to leave now, and Dolly's meant to sleep until Earl comes home.

But the children are waiting.

Dolly pushes the pills against her teeth with her tongue until she hears the front door open and close and lock, and then she spits them into her pillow. She hears Jack jumping upstairs, shaking the light fixtures above her. Oh, he did that too when he first came to them: misbehaving, throwing himself around that room. But Dolly just sat and loved him through it, let him know again and again that he was safe and, finally, home. Bless him. It was that same jumping that made her investigate a few days ago—and was she ever glad she did! It was little Jack who called Dolly back to life.

Dolly was afraid, at first, mounting those stairs. She might have fallen, and then what? It would have been hours before Earl found her. But her muscles remembered with just-waking weakness as her hands grasped the banister, pulling her, cautiously, up.

The funny thing was, while the climb should have exhausted her, Dolly felt quite well. Exhilarated, even. By the fifth step her chest pushed out, her back straightened, why, she could have balanced a book on her head if she had one handy. She kept climbing and straightening, skin gathering and tightening and lifting into soft curves. By the time she stepped onto the upstairs landing, she was no older than thirty-five. She turned, following the noise until she stood in front of the door to her daughters' old bedroom.

And there they were: Jack springing from the low-set toddler bed to the twin four-post, Susan by the window, dressing her little sister in a lacy smock. Baby Carrie held up a fist of soft, downy feathers, no doubt torn from a pillow somewhere. Sunlight lit the dust that rose and fell around them, dancing in slow time to Jack's great leaps. They were hungry, they complained. Well, of course they were; it was nearly three o'clock!

Later that evening, after Earl cleaned up the mess of jam and cream cheese in the kitchen, Dolly asked if he missed the children.

"Sometimes," he said, helping her under her sheets. "But Susan's bringing little Iris around on Saturday, and it's lovely having Carrie here, isn't it?"

"And Jack?"

The knot in her husband's throat jutted from the skin under his jaw as he kissed her head. "I don't know when we'll see Jack." He turned off her lamp but stopped at the door.

"It's terrible how things change, isn't it?"

"It is," Dolly wanted to say, but she just couldn't find the words.

Alone in the dark, Dolly thought of the first photograph she'd ever seen of her son. The child had been listed for adoption in a *Keep Sweet* magazine her visiting sister had brought up from Utah. There were three children pictured: wee little Jack with the sparkly eyes, a girl about the same age as Susan, and an older boy listed as Wilf, but Dolly always thought *Wolf* because of his sharp eyes and the protective stance he took over his younger brother and sister. The ad suggested Wilf as a good fit for rural families in need of free labour, but that the little ones were sweet and playful and all three were in excellent health. The children's mother had been recently widowed.

In the section listing the reason why the Albertan government had apprehended the children it simply read: Impoverished.

Susan was already in kindergarten by the time Dolly's sister showed her the ad. Doctors had said Dolly wouldn't have another child after the difficult birth of her eldest. How could they have known Carrie would someday surprise them? *A Child Is Waiting*, Jack's caption read. The Quentin family could have him for as little as four thousand dollars. Dolly so wanted another, and the boy obviously needed a home.

"It isn't right," Earl said at first, adopting a child like they were ordering a Chatty Cathy from Sears Roebuck. But Earl had always wanted a son, Dolly argued, and little Jack was from Alberta. That meant he was already one of their own—they couldn't let him go to America or Europe or Timbuktu! So many little Indian children were being scooped up and scattered all around the world. Now *that* just wasn't right.

It wasn't until more than a decade later that Dolly heard the term "Sixties Scoop," and even then, she hadn't realized Jack was involved. Susan was the one to point out the connection during a tense Sunday dinner, when she was home from college and arguing politics with Earl over a roast chicken she refused to eat, claiming newfound vegetarianism. Voices from a news broadcast droned in from the family room.

"But Jack wasn't adopted in the sixties," Dolly argued. "We got him in 1975."

Susan shook her head. "Mom, the government adoption programs started in the fifties, but they didn't stop until after I was in high school. Besides, just think about it: you first saw him in an ad, right? In an *American* magazine? He and all his siblings were split up just because his mom was 'too poor?' In a country as rich as Canada? That's not right. This is exactly what they're talking about." She waved her hand in the general direction of the television set. "Private adoption agencies made a killing."

After that, Dolly paid attention. She started by borrowing Susan's textbook one night when her daughter was out with friends, and then, instead of switching channels when sad stories came on, Dolly started turning up the volume. There were news reports about organizations that had profiteered from child trafficking, about bewildered birth mothers finding the adoption ads of their own sons or daughters in local newspapers, and about how sometimes so many children were seized from small communities that entire school buses were filled—not one single child left behind. Dolly couldn't bear the thought of watching those school buses pull away. She felt gravel cut under her knees and heard the howl of silence in her ears. When the children are gone, a person can hear wind blow no matter the weather. The horror of it: *when the children are gone*.

Still, nothing about the situation made sense. The cost of so many children entering the foster care system was surely far higher than it would be simply to help families in need of aid. Then one evening, a reporter presented the uncovered transcripts from a speech made by a government adoption official. The speech was made in order to sell white prospective parents on the idea of adopting Indigenous children.

"As you are all aware," the papers read, "the pill, abortion, and the tendency of mothers to keep their children has virtually dried up the market for typical adoptions—and by typical adoptions I mean Caucasian, good health, and under three months."

That made it click together: the country's most vulnerable children had been used to meet a supply and demand problem when adoption markets were low on white babies. Even after residential schools had gone out of vogue, Canada had continued the transfer of children from one racial group to another and a whole industry had profited off unknowing women like Dolly, in need of another's child to love.

It just wasn't right.

So many things weren't right.

Dolly decided she wouldn't ever take a pill again.

Today she follows the staircase's worn grooves to find the children are not hungry but bored.

"Let's go to the pond!" Jack shouts. He hops from one foot to another, hands pressed together. "Pretty, pretty please?"

Carrie toddles to Dolly, arms high. Dolly picks her up and onto her hip. "I thought we might colour eggs."

Jack groans. "Nooo-ooo-ooo. We want to play."

"Alright. It's cold, though. Dress warm."

Susan stands on her bed, apart from the others, strange and beautiful and willowy. Of course she's prone to moods at her age, but sometimes Dolly wonders. The girl cocks her head and narrows her eyes. "Really, Mom? You'll come, too?"

Dolly smiles. "Yes, of course!"

The younger ones clap. "Let's go!"

Dolly turns to lead the way, but a wave of panic comes over her so she lowers Carrie to the floor. She thinks of the lipstick on her husband's cheek and blinks. *It's a difficult day*, he said. Jack's eyes sparkle as he waits. A stone drops in Dolly's gut.

She has to leave this house.

Outside, Jack cracks thin layers of ice into spidery fractals. Susan sits Carrie in her little wood sled and pulls her ahead of Dolly. Jack runs around the corner, ahead of them all.

Dolly shields her eyes. The sky is bright but deceptive. They've walked this route a thousand times, but it's not as warm as it looks. The air stings her face and she imagines blisters on her cheeks. It's too cold to be out. Where have the children gone?

Dolly walks faster, pushing her chin into the collar of her coat. She scans the neighbourhood, her eyes searching but focusing on nothing. She's told Susan a hundred times not to pull Carrie so fast. She could fall out, hit her head.

She passes more homes and comes to the street corner. Ice particles hang suspended like shards of glass in the frozen air. She's frantic, here, caught in this wide-open day. The children will freeze. Where are they?

And then, that scream.

Something shifts in Dolly's mind and memories avalanche.

Lipstick on his collar, a suitcase in his hand. Don't leave. *You can't leave!*

The babysitter who didn't show. *Karen? You're leaving us for her?*

The children and their shrieking, arguing, constant pulling. *Play outside. Just go!*

Taking to bed with medicine, crying until she was spent. *The children were breaking ice beneath her window: there were the squeaks of their boots on frozen puddles, the splintering of frozen water. Her angels were close by: creaking, cracking, lulling.*

Until . . .

That scream.

Dolly woke. *Susan—crying, retching, tripping up the stairs. Screaming, again.*

Susan screaming and screaming and screaming without break.

Mama! It's Jack!

Where is Carrie? Where is Jack?

Dolly didn't wait for answer. *Run, run, run, no time for shoes. Asphalt, ice, snow. Bare feet stinging.*

She was blind. *Too much sun.*

Where? Where? *Where?*

There: *count.*

One: Carrie. *Crying, stuck, sled tipped, face pressed into the snow.*

Two: Jack . . . *Where is Jack?*

Tiny finger, pointing, baby whimper: *Pon.*

Jack.

The child floating, facedown and still.

Jack! Dolly screamed. *Jack! Jack!*

She broke ice until she was in the water too, slipping and splashing. The cold and the pond and her housecoat slowed her so she undressed as she reached for her son, letting the robe fall away.

She couldn't reach him.

She stretched again.

Jack!

He wasn't hers to have, floating out of reach.

Jack!

His face.

He was gone.

The howl of silence.

Dolly remembers.

She remembers and she runs. There's still time. Boots slip and squeak but she flies between steps.

She's close now; they're just around the bend. That screaming. Susan's still screaming! No. Listen: laughter. Susan is laughing. But they're on the pond—Jack is on the pond!

Dolly shuffles, willing the ice not to break. But it's solid, she discovers, black where the wind has blown snow away. Carrie sucks on mittens outside the circle where the others glide, eyes lit up like emeralds in the sun. Susan and Jack jump and slip, grabbing one another for balance. *Come on, Mom!*

Dolly's knees buckle. She's older now. She bends and the children run near, crashing and collapsing into her until the cold disappears, melting away from the warmth spreading in her chest. She lies on her back and looks up at the great Albertan sky, the purity of its blueness marked only by the tunnels of laughter steaming from hot mouths. She spreads her arms and legs out wide, opening and closing, opening and closing, making angels with the children who lie near. A little boy's twinkling brown eyes smile, and the distant figures of a million people stand behind him, watching from the shore.

"I'm sorry," Dolly wants to tell Jack, but she just can't find the words.

Snow builds on either side of her face, porcelain white walls surrounding her, and Dolly closes her eyes.

A REASON TO BEND

1999

LAST NIGHT SUSAN dreamed her eyes fell from their sockets like acorns from an oak. They caught in her throat and she choked while tilling the empty spaces with her thumb. Now she tears at her lids, fingers pinching, sliding, pinching again, pulling splinters from the pupil. She blinks twice, winces, pushes the heel of her hand against the pink sting.

His frown in the mirror is as familiar as the shaving cream he forgets to wash from under his ear.

"I think my contacts are stuck," she lies.

Garrett moves her aside with two fingers and points. The case sits on the bathroom counter, sticky with dust; lenses inside, unused. Susan swallows, remembering the woody thickness of her dream. A gust of wind blows leaves from the tree outside the window until the aspen is naked.

Morning noise drifts into the silence from the kitchen downstairs. Steel on wood: eleven-year-old Iris eats cereal with raw milk, her spoon knocking a maple bowl, attention consumed by the science textbooks the homeschooler devours. From a tabletop radio, East Coast voices sing it's the end of the world.

Susan worries about that radio, its signals and waves bouncing off the walls and all around the house, mutating all their genes. Maybe that's why Susan's always changing. If it were off she would hear daisies shrink into dried fists, the universal winter only two months away.

None of this will matter, she tells her husband, not after Y2K. Capitalism will crack apart like rotten squash and the pump jack will stop, oil seeping back into the land like Earth's a great big sponge. The cosmic patterns say so, she tells him. If he only knew how close she was to figuring out those damn mysterious lines—

"You haven't been taking your meds."

"I feel fine."

"Susan."

She knocks knuckles against her forehead so he can hear her better.

"No drugs! No drugs! You know what they do!"

He holds her wrists between his thumbs and index fingers. His jaw makes Susan think of the boulder at the top of the driveway, the rock that watches and waits and means home to her in its efforts to guard those she loves. A gargoyle is locked inside that uncarved stone, powerless to ward away The Company's evil men. Susan will be sent away, and soon. What she wonders is whether she'll come home to that stone.

She starts to cry and the granite in Garrett's face softens. He sighs and she imagines his exhale blowing dandelion seedlings from her shoulder. None of this is his fault. She'd let go a thousand wishes for him, if she could.

"Remember that first summer, when my hair got caught in the spruce?" She offers him this, the moment they first met: two kids planting trees in Alberta's Boreal. He lets go of her hands and she wraps her arms around his shoulders like a vine, runs fingers through the steely flecks of her husband's greying hair. Butterfly lashes rest on his bare chest.

"Thank god you found me," she whispers.

"I don't know what to do." The knot in his throat slides against the back of her head. "Tell me what to do."

※

He plants her in the potting shed after breakfast. Susan is meant to count seeds but lets coriander spheres slip through her fingers in the same quick way dollars disappear from their joint chequing account. She lights an herbal cigarette, clove and red raspberry leaf. Iris rides in a nearby pasture and Garrett walks the perimeter of the east grazing field, noticing things. He is good at noticing. Garrett can find a stranger's fresh footprints in the soil or spot the smallest growths of invasive grasses, their seed tracked in between the thread grooves of The Company's hired boots. Garrett can see all these things, but not the lines drawn right there on the land, right in front of his face.

But it's not just him. Sometimes it's as if the cosmic patterns don't want to be read. Susan has deciphered parts of them but not the whole thing. The lines are scribbled all over, like how the Earth looks like a stitched quilt from an airplane window. They'd draw a picture and tell her how to save this place, if only she would grow tall enough to read them all at once. It's a good thing, then, that roots will soon shoot from the tips of her toes and let her head tower to the sky. She would do it for them—for Garrett and for Iris—no matter how much time it costs her beneath the bark.

Her husband kicks a post as he inspects the fence's barbs, rusted two decades earlier than their thirty-year guarantee. Hydrogen sulphide poisons everything, even lifeless metal. They both know it doesn't matter; the cattle are too ill to roam and too thin for anyone to steal. There are only nine cows left.

In the neighbouring fields, The Company's pump jack lowers its dark head to drink. Steel from the earth biting back into it, like a wolf pup eating its mother. It keeps moving just to spite her, that vicious pump jack. It knows she sees the signs. She tried to climb it once, the wind drawing lines in the snow all around it. She had to get up high to read. But the beast kept in motion and shook her from its back. Sometimes it squeals and squeaks in the night, trying to keep seers like her far, far away.

Her breath slows to the pump jack's rises and falls. She panics at the breathlessness it's caused, but Garrett breaks its control of her, walking between them all stable and sensible and strong. He greets Iris, trotting toward him on her horse. The man helps the child down from the mare and the pair face one another as the girl digs into dirt with the toe of her boot. Iris turns in the direction of her mother and Garrett looks away. But when Iris wipes her cheek with her sleeve, Garrett steps into the space between them, pulling Susan's daughter to his chest.

"This," Susan whispers to the wind, answering his morning question. *Please, Garrett, just keep doing this.*

Chop, chop, chop

Susan wakes from her nap with a start. The Company Men are cutting Susan down! The bird caught in the hollow of her chest wildly flutters.

She waits for a crash, but it does not come. She's already down, she realizes, lying on her back. She slides her left foot over her right leg and vice versa, checking for axe damage. She has not been chopped.

"Sons of bitches!"

Chop, chop, chop, chop, chop

She creeps down the stairs to find her husband pounding the old rotary phone into its cradle. Susan follows his steps to the kitchen. Iris spreads mustard onto bread at the counter and Garrett sits at the table, head in his hands. Susan pulls out the chair beside him. She sits and traces the table's wood grain with her fingertips, its alignment so familiar and yet strangely captivating. How has she not seen it before?

"They're killing me," Garrett says. "Trying to break me. They've ploughed below the creek again and fucked the whole watershed. There's nothing left."

The Company. Susan hears the catch in his voice, but the honey-coloured loops and curves of the tabletop lose her just as they begin to make sense. She must concentrate. The alignment's another part of the cosmic pattern, she realizes. If only she could follow.

"I can't do this alone, Sue," he says. "The root rot, the infections, now this. This place is bleeding us dry. If you're not here, if I have to make a decision . . ."

No, not just a pattern, but a map, she thinks—a miniature version of the cosmic patterns overlaying the farm! Between Garrett's elbows, look: four little marks, like the stillborn calves last spring. And in front of Iris's sandwich, two more lines—the heifers lost outside the barn! Susan lifts her daughter's plate to peek underneath.

"I'm just . . . done, Sue. I'm at the end of my rope."

"I've almost got it, baby," Susan says. She just needs a better view. There's something so real here, so vital and honest and ever changing. She climbs onto her chair, but when she stands the pattern just seems to stretch, as if growing along with her height. Damn it, why won't it ever let her see? Grow, she tells her limbs. Hurry up and tree. Garrett covers his mouth with his hands, steely eyes round and dewy. Iris lifts her face from her book to her mother and watches in detached study, tomato on whole wheat raised to her lips.

"The trees are always talking," Susan reminds them. "The answer will be here, right here in the wood."

Everyone is silent, better they can hear.

※

Sue sits on the toilet while her daughter washes her face after lunch. The washcloth is as scratchy as dried moss; it smells musty and used. But Iris is as gentle and sweet as the spring. Susan cups the girl's face in her hands and kisses the birthmark on her cheek. A strawberry, the doctors called it when she was born, but Susan always thought it was shaped more like a flower. Bright pink when she was a baby, now faded gold. Magic. This springtime girl is special.

"The answer's in you," Susan whispers. She notices the way thin blue veins travel from her daughter's wrist down her arm and moves the girl's sweater sleeve. "You're part of the pattern."

Garrett interrupts. He hangs a hand on the back of his neck and looks past her.

"I need to dig," he says. "Need to dirty these hands. I'll plant tulip bulbs along the driveway." His voice drifts off, but Susan knows what he would have said: they'll make a beautiful homecoming, later.

"I'll take you to town."

Susan shakes her head. She tells him he can leave her, but when he meets her eyes she can see how important this is. She's getting things mixed things up again. Hurting him, somehow.

"You could use the company, Sue."

On the drive, Susan copies her daughter's best behaviour. She stays quiet and looks out the window because, unlike Iris, she forgot to bring a book. But Garrett takes his hat off and wipes his forehead with the back of his hand, so Susan's got to say something.

"I don't want you to worry," she tells him. She knows how important this is. She'd crack in half before hurting either of them.

"The cosmic patterns are unveiling themselves," Susan says. "I've just got to grow enough to read them."

Can't he see how much taller she's gotten since lunch?

※

It's the pump jack that harvests Susan's memories, feeding them to The Company. It happens all the time: machines hypnotizing people into a kind of submissive absence, or governments painting the skies with mind-bending chemtrails to keep everyone spacey and compliant. That damned pump jack must have gotten her as they left the farm. She feels herself breaking out of its spell and wonders about all the things that must have happened between the drive with Garrett and Iris and this very minute. What did she say? What did she do? She's missed it all. Everything.

She's sitting in an office on a couch, that much is clear. A woman on a chair sits opposite her, tendrils spilling over her shoulders like the twining shoots of morning glory.

What were they talking about?

Change. Yes.

Susan would be the one to stop it—all the terrible change—if only she could quit changing so quickly herself.

The woman smiles and tells her no one can predict the future. Health is what Susan should focus on now.

Susan tries to recall how the women met, why they sit in this small room so far from the farm. Is this woman a doctor?

"I almost have the answers, but that pump jack's stopping me somehow," Susan says. "It won't let me up, so I have to tree to get tall, but then I root and when the bark spreads, well then I'm totally blind. And I'm just . . . stuck. Dormant. Garrett hates it."

The woman reaches for her hand. "That's the way it goes: up, down, up, down."

Susan nods. "Like the pump jack."

"Or a pendulum swinging from wellness on one side to illness on the other. Every time you come off your meds, it swings a little harder, further into illness. That's why you've got to keep taking the medication. We can get you right in the middle, where it's manageable."

"I've got to figure out the patterns," Susan says. "I'm the only one who can read the lines and already I'm growing berries in my hair."

The woman makes a note and Susan holds her breath. *Shit, a social worker.* The bird in her chest panics once again.

Susan shouldn't be talking like this; she got into trouble this way before. She thinks of how Iris used to rub crayons over paper covering aspen leaves, how she'd tack the pictures to her bedroom wall, adding to an overgrown collection, the spindly hands of so many trees reaching, veins exposed. They thought it was disturbing. If Garrett hadn't adopted Iris, if he hadn't married Sue . . . Acorns creep up her throat.

"My mom was stuck once, but she still took care of us."

"You've mentioned your mother. But dementia is somewhat different than—"

"No, when she was young. She was stuck in her bed, not talking, eyes open but as if she couldn't see." Susan tries to remember her mother's bedroom. Could there have been cosmic patterns on the wallpaper? All she can remember is a little fish in a frozen pond; she sees cracks in the ice and remembers the feeling of standing over him, planted heavy as an oak. Susan resists the urge to rap on her skull.

The woman shakes her head. "It's so painful for a child to witness a parent suffer. It can't be what you want for Iris," she says. "Think of what your daughter must see."

Susan thinks of the brilliant girl with the golden flower on her cheek and magic answers in her brain. Yes, Susan realizes. It *is* Iris who must see, and Susan who must teach her. Quickly, she thinks.

"I'm running out of time."

The woman leans back. She pats curls at the back of her head into place and frowns.

"Tell me, Susan, what's the truth of this belief?"

Susan closes her eyes and breathes easy again.

She's only a therapist.

Thank god.

✳

It's worse by dinner.

Susan cradles a bowl on her hip and scoops chunks of rot from her belly with a pasta fork, twirling wet fibres around its prongs, dropping the soggy mass onto her daughter's plate. She swats at termites on her abdomen, scurrying to reclaim their home.

"Do you see how the twists and loops travel like a road map?" Susan points but Iris will not read.

"Not again," the girl says, pushing spaghetti away. "I hate this."

Iris leaves the table, leaf rubbings fluttering as her bedroom door slams.

"She hates me," Susan says to the lines on the kitchen table.

The insects burrow deeper in her belly, long white bodies like pellets of glass. They could be beautiful, maybe, if not so frantic, so destructive. Susan sits in Iris's place and looks up out the window, suddenly seeing what her daughter must actually have been talking about. The pump jack has crept nearer. It has moved closer to the house, better to steal breath and rust fences and harvest memories. But Susan will not allow it.

In the dimming light of autumn dusk, Susan collects many branches and sticks. She carries the load in a wobbly wheelbarrow and makes the long walk to the pump jack, letting grasshoppers land on her where they may. "Don't snack on the leaves," she tells her little friends, pulling them from her hair. When she reaches the machine, Susan sings loudly so it can't so easily hear her thoughts.

She picks up branches and sticks one by one, throwing them at the machine, as near to its lever gears as she can get. She imagines a piece of wood finding perfect placement within a gear tooth, snapping and groaning and grinding the beast to a halt. No luck. The wood mostly hits the pump jack but does not stay, falling down into a strewn pile. Just as well, Susan thinks. She kicks the branches and sticks together near its base and, using dry grass and the lighter in her pocket, she lights the pile.

Susan does not usually appreciate fire but enjoys the glow now, its instant heat. It's a small blaze, but likely able to catch on the grease around the pump jack's bolts. She hopes it does, until suddenly she is pulled back, hands gripping her elbows. The Company Men! No. It's Garrett who is screaming at her, kicking the lit fire away from the machine and smothering the embers.

"What the fuck, Sue? What the fuck is wrong with you?"

The pump jack just squeaks laughter and nods and nods.

This is exactly what it wants.

※

At midnight, thunder claps nine times. Susan wakes from a dream that her daughter is taken from her and she screams until her tongue shreds, until the front door opens and swings shut and Garrett fully wakes her, stopping her hands from stripping the bark on her shins.

"Think of spring," he says, rocking her. "Just try and think of spring." She tries to picture a hundred springs: bovine bellows and rubber boots under floral skirts, Garrett's kisses like raindrops and the smell of rhubarb pie. It's no use. All she smells is ash and gunpowder.

"Iris doesn't know enough yet," she tells him. "She won't understand what she sees."

He holds her tight and warm for the rest of the night, but the cold moves in all around them anyway.

By morning, autumn is swept into ditches and frost ends the pumpkins not yet ready for harvest. The day is bare and grey, quiet with its annual disappointment and a sky bloated with unshed snow. It is too quiet, strangely silent, as if not a single tree speaks. Iris fiddles with a hole in her jacket pocket, pink fingertips pulling worn threads.

"Pick at it and it will only get bigger," Garrett warns.

"No," Susan tells her daughter. Susan is towering now, but still unable to focus the patterns. "Always follow all the lines. Untangle every string until you figure it out."

Behind the east field, the pump jack bends in farewell as Susan is placed in the truck. Time runs like sap from where she carved Garrett's name on her thigh and her mind begins to slow.

"Maybe I could stay home this time," she says, but her husband doesn't answer.

She presses her hand to the glass when they pass the gargoyle boulder and Susan sees the ground along the driveway is untouched.

No tulips were planted.

The day's strange silence is the absence of the cattle herd.

✳

It's a long drive to St. Paul.

When they arrive, hedges sit in front of the hospital smoking cigarettes. Moss grows from their exposed roots like hair bushing from the slipper-clad feet of old men. Nearby, saplings shiver between the cracks of the asphalt.

"Just babies," Garrett shakes his head.

The bird caged in Susan's chest beats its wings in frantic terror, louder now as the cavity walls have finally morphed from flesh and bones to thick, hollow wood.

He reaches for her, squeezes her hand. "We'll visit," he says, "every second Saturday. More, if we can."

Her fingers dry into crisps of red and orange under Garret's grip, littering the cup holder between them when he lets go. Her feet take root around the floor mat and she cries one last time, *please don't leave me here.*

But bark creeps up and covers her eyes. It's too dark when she's entombed; she can't read the lines.

"It's useless," Susan shouts. "All for nothing!" She should just crack in half.

She should just crack in half!

But they dig her out and cover her with burlap. They hoist her onto a trolley and plant her under fluorescent lamps, tapping intravenous needles into limbs, tubes dangling like vines. She is the tree from which she'd hang but they visit and, soon, Iris begins to climb. The magic springtime girl scales and sits and watches and reads. She picks at threads and follows lines and figures out every pattern. She strings lights from her mother's branches and adds new baubles on every visit. The taller her mother grows, the more this little magic daughter can see.

And while they wait for spring, Susan has reason to bend.

TELL ME WHAT YOU WANT

2002

AL'S WIFE BITES his earlobe, making that *mmm* sound as she breathes in the scent of his freshly shaven skin. He's just out of the shower and she pretends to pull at the side of his bathrobe.

"Victor Hugo would only write nude."

He pulls her hand to his groin to show his appreciation, but she slips away, winking over her shoulder, red hair spilling to the small of her back. She ushers the kids up the stairs to bed with the baby on her hip and he tries to think of new ways to describe the curve of her ass.

God, she's a knockout, always has been. Smart, too. Real bookish in college, but that didn't stop dumb jocks like Garrett from trying to get a piece. That's how they met: Pat was with Al's older brother first, but it didn't last long.

She was eighteen, her first week at the University of Alberta. That jerk picked her up at a frosh party he'd used Al as an excuse to attend. Gar was already out of school, but Al was only twenty-two and poised to graduate with a teaching degree that spring. Garrett popped Pat's cherry before falling hard for Crunchy Granola Susie Q, a hippie-chick-cum-single-mom he married only a couple months later. Pat dealt with the rejection through some pretty dark verse she submitted to the college lit journal Al happened to edit. Before Al knew what was happening, he and Patricia were going at it on top of the poems she'd written for his brother. It should have felt stranger than it did, but then again, most things should.

You'd never guess they were related, Al and Garrett. Neither Sterling son really won in the hair department. Al got their dad's male pattern baldness and Gar inherited their mom's premature greys. But despite the old-man farmer look he tries to pull off these days, Gar's brawny shoulders used to carry cheerleaders two at a time. It was hard in high school, having an older brother like that. Gar was so obsessed with tail he never even noticed the hell his own hockey team morons rained down on his little brother, pushing Al against locker-room walls before tossing him into crowded hallways half-naked.

Assholes.

Al always knew he could have bulked up a bit, but the bullying was about more than just his stature. All his life guys had made fun of his voice. It deepened a little during puberty, but not enough to keep Gar's douchebag teammates from telling everyone Al scratched it sucking dick. Whatever. No way those losers ended up with anything close to what Al's got with his gorgeous young wife. Brains over brawns, buddy. Patricia doesn't care how high his voice sounds.

Actually, she *likes* that about him. Al figured out how to work with what he was given early on and developed impersonation skills he showed off in the open-mic comedy clubs he took Patricia to when they were first dating. Janet Jackson, Courtney Love, Meg

Ryan—Al's celebrity impersonations made Patricia laugh until she cried.

"Another!" she'd beg on the car ride home. "Do another!"

He loved seeing Patricia like that: her hands clapping, face all lit up, just for him. "Of course," he'd say, with a smile. "Tell me what you want."

If Garrett passing on Patricia was the best thing that ever happened to Al, Zoe comes in a close second. Patricia found out she was pregnant with their baby girl the day before she wrote her midterms. Raised religious, Patricia couldn't bring herself to end the pregnancy, but she couldn't go back to the foster farm her mom was running either, so that led to Al putting a ring on it at city hall.

God, crazy dead-tooth Mariam *hated* Al. A piece of shit like him knocking up her holy little princess? Patricia ended up having to draw the line with that nutty grandma. If Mariam wouldn't quit trash-talking Al, Patricia and Zoe wouldn't be able to visit anymore. Well, it's been four years now and no one even knows where the old bat is—which, honestly, is probably for the best. Her own fanatical church had even cut her off, tired of her talking about the survivalist forums she frequented online and how man's sins were bringing on the end time. Mariam had worn her long grey hair in a braid since Al had met her, but around the time Zoe was born she'd started wearing this old-timey black frock too, like she was trying to pass as Amish or something.

Mariam didn't even tell Patricia she was moving; she just let her daughter find out for herself when strangers answered the front door the last time they went to visit the Northside townhouse. Sitting in the driver's seat while Patricia cried over her vanished mother in the driveway of her childhood home, Al shook his head, crossed his fingers, and hoped that whatever was wrong with Mariam wasn't hereditary. Was crazy some kind of Sterling family karma or something? Garrett's wife Susan was in and out of hospital all the time: certified paranoid.

But no, Patricia wasn't like Mariam or Sue. She was a great mom even before Zoe was born. Knowing she wanted to stay home with the kids anyway, she quit school and got a job so Al could finish the last semester of his degree. But the pregnancy must have distracted him more than he realized, because Al failed three courses.

"Don't go back," Pat begged when he told her he wouldn't graduate on time. Gar and Sue had bought a hippie-dippy organics farm on the heels of mad cow disease and were probably raking in the dough, raising Sue's splotchy-faced star child in a yuppie's paradise.

"Talk to your brother; you could work for him."

Yeah, right.

Al registered for the fall semester soon after Zoe was born, and Pat waitressed until he started teaching twelve months later.

Al takes a glass of water to his basement office and locks the door. He can't stop thinking about Patty's bite, her wink, her ass. He never imagined the thought of him being a writer would get her so hot, the little sounds she makes rubbing his shoulders, the way she pushes her breasts against the back of his head when she points out sloppy grammar. When his first column was printed she ran fresh from the shower the moment she heard the paper hit the front door. He unwrapped the towel from around her as she tore through pages, snuggled up in his lap. Patricia makes it easy to forget what he's really doing down here.

God knows it wasn't like this when he was writing lesson plans: *Hobby rockets for the combustion unit? We're not paying for those again!*

Or when he started Clan O' Nerds, an afterschool science club: *You're not even getting paid for that! We could use you around here, you know!*

He knew it wasn't easy for her, taking care of him and the house and two little kids on his thirty-grand-a-year salary. But what could he do about it? In his first year teaching the oil boom turned the real estate market bananas and their rent alone gobbled up more than half of his income, never mind what the student loan repayments took. But at least low teaching wages limited hiring competition. Al ended up landing a job at the same north Edmonton high school Patricia had once attended. It was real funny meeting Simperson, Pat's former favourite teacher.

"Is Patty still a poetess?" the old girl asked, about seven hundred love beads dangling from her neck. Al laughed when he told Patricia about that, but Patricia didn't laugh at all.

They just had to hang on until 2001, Al promised Patricia. The government promised by then teachers would be recognized for the pay cuts they'd taken '93. Livable wages, manageable class sizes, paid planning hours, and material allowances: all meagre wants were within reach. Still, Patty wasn't happy. She got so snarly every time she found Al hunched over lesson planning at the kitchen table that he started working after hours in his classroom instead.

He definitely wasn't the only teacher with the idea; with janitorial services cut and material allowances basically nonexistent, it seemed like the whole faculty spent their off-hours wiping desks and mopping floors, cutting and pasting images from magazines to the posters they'd handmade to teach kids fractions, the periodic table, human anatomy. In January, the government banned the use of furnaces after five PM as part of Education Alberta's "green movement" guise. Teachers shivered as temperatures dipped on winter evenings, and they returned in the mornings to find the ink in their pens frozen. Al would race other good-faith lesson planners/classroom cleaners out the front doors just before the late-night security alarms kicked on, and they'd bitterly congratulate one another if Simperson managed to make it without forgetting her keys.

It was tough. Al wasn't the only one in the staffroom complaining of marital trouble while chugging weak coffee. Many started calling in sick. Al tried it once—taking the day off to catch up on sleep—but when administration couldn't afford a substitute for his classes, he sucked it up and went in anyway. The mix of sleep-deprived teachers and surly teenagers was brutal, and more than once Al found himself walking away from their whiny attitudes, slamming the door behind him, tears blurring the hallway. Nerves were raw, but there was still hope. The teachers held tight to what was promised. Better was yet to come.

Until it wasn't.

Fall 2001 heralded the arrival of a new budget the government was calling "The Alberta Advantage." Patricia entered the third trimester of her pregnancy with their third child, and little Zoe got sick around the same time—weird blisters all over her face anytime the poor kid stepped outside. Strung out, Patty and Al listened to the budget announcement together but separate: she grabbing bits and pieces of the news between laundry, morning sickness, and the tantrum cries of their youngest, he through the speakers of his desktop radio while students silently scribbled answers on a pop quiz. The "Advantage" was cutting corporate taxes to the lowest rates in Canada and approving a 17.3 percent raise for provincial politicians. The province reported it had created a surplus of funds, but none would go to Alberta Education.

And Patricia fuckin' raged.

She and Al fought at the table over dinner when he got home that night, the kids covering their ears with their hands.

"Daddy, don't yell! You'll make Mommy cry!"

"They said teachers could take an extra 3 percent pay if they wanted it," Pat argued, pointing her fork as if she were the teacher, lecturing and disciplining and grading Al's response. Her other hand rested on top of her belly, the baby inside a ticking time bomb of increased expense.

Al shook his head. "They'll only give us that money if we take it from school improvement funds, and no one's going to do that. I mean, come on. What's 3 percent? You want me to be the guy who takes a raise when the fricken' gym roof is about to cave in?"

Pat pushed away from the table, chair legs scraping the linoleum floor.

"Jesus Christ, the damage deposit, Pat!"

She ignored him and waddled to the kitchen counter, holding an opened envelope above her head before slamming it back down. The landlord had raised the rent again.

"Let's worry about our own fricken' roof, eh?"

Through the faculty body, shock led to anger. A vote was held and the result decided that teachers would go on strike. Simperson, the school district's union representative, insisted the walkout not happen until after Grade 12 diploma exams. Al thought it was dumb, waiting until after tests to strike. Shouldn't they make the biggest splash possible? But Simperson was adamant; the teachers would still have clout, she argued, and students shouldn't suffer the faults of their parents' government. So the teachers waited and taught and facilitated tests and then, unified, they walked out on February 4, 2002.

The next day, teachers were ordered back to work. The education minister scoffed at all suggestions of negotiation, so the union decided it would be work-to-rule. Al felt awful cancelling the Clan O' Nerds' Telus World of Science trip, but he told the boys he hoped they'd learn something from it.

"You don't have to take crap all your life," he said. "You've got to stand up to bullies."

The next morning's classes were quiet. Clan O' Nerd members were missing from Bio 10 and Chem 20, as were kids from the photography project, the yearbook committee, the grad planning group, drama club, debate club, travel club, mathletics, the cheerleading squad, and the volleyball, football, and wrestling teams. At lunch, Al rushed from marking quizzes in the staffroom to find his homeroom empty but for Simperson with chalk marks on the elbows of a thread-worn cardigan. The kids were outside her window, she told him, blocking the road. They were out there with homemade noisemakers and makeshift signs. Giving Global Television a live interview were Al's own seven misfits, fists pumping the air in support of their teachers.

"Problems in Alberta Education affect students and teachers throughout the province," a pretty blonde with a microphone reported. Al watched the interview later that night. "With teachers now legally prohibited from walking off the job, students across the province have organized strikes of their own through popular communication websites like MySpace, Nexopia, and the internet chat service MSN Online." She turned to the Clan O' Nerd boys. "Your afterschool science club has been instrumental in organizing the student-led protest. What would you like to say to other Albertans?"

One of the students looked straight into the camera, straight into Al's eyes.

"Our teachers work hard for us. They inspire us and teach us we all have a voice. We say they're right, and we say we should speak!"

Cheers rang out behind the pimple-faced teen and for the first time since the budget, Al believed his own words.

He did have a say.

He could make a difference.

There was dignity in the job.

And if there was nothing else, there was that.

Days later, as Al locked up his classroom door after school, he heard a familiar voice blasting down the hallway. He followed the sound and found Tara Hamilton's dad pointing a fat finger into the room Simperson had taught in for over thirty years. The old woman cried in the dark, every second row of fluorescent lights removed to save money. The withdrawal of Simperson's volunteerism meant his daughter could no longer list the kayak club as an extracurricular on university applications.

"You selfish, greedy . . ." The man laughed. "It's never enough for you union folk, is it? Don't know real work a day in your life and still you think you're entitled to more."

"What are we supposed to do?" Simperson asked. "What? What?" She began to cry, her hands pulling her stringy hair. "Tell me what you want!"

She's snapped, Al thought with disgust, though he understood why. Simperson was still in hysterics as Al backed away from the scene. When red-faced Mr. Hamilton huffed toward Al on his way out, Al felt himself flinch like he used to when he was a kid, like Hamilton was one of the hockey-jock bullies tossing Al into the hall. That was when Al knew it was over. Who was he kidding? There was no dignity mentoring the children of these goons; there was no respect. Nothing would ever change. No one gave a shit. He resigned the next day, not knowing how he'd make money, just that he had to find another way.

And did he ever, Al thinks, turning the lock on his office door. He breathes deep and smiles.

Just the sight of Al's basement office makes him stand taller, puff out his chest. The chair's polished wood gleams against the deep, dark brown of the walls, painted to match the desk. There's a small dry bar in the corner, and local prints hang on the walls to inspire his work. Al reviewed this collection of erotic nudes in his first column, dedicating the piece to his wife. Truth be told, the paticularily risqué portraits have served as inspiration in other ways, as well.

Pat created this space for him in three days after he got the newspaper job. She clips his columns every week, too, and files them in a scrapbook. She knows all the gallery exhibits and local artist profiles, the upcoming festivals and canonized history and what's on the medium's horizon. She knows the paper's small readership and their wants and how to hook those old artsy types in just one sentence. She knows every word he's ever written because many of them have been her own. But what she doesn't know is . . . a lot.

She doesn't know that the column pays fuck-all. She doesn't know that despite the eight hours Al spends in his office each night, the column only takes an hour to write, and no, he's not actually working on the next great Canadian novel. She doesn't know he keeps a roll of throat lozenges on hand, or that in his real work, Al's pseudonym is Patricia. She also doesn't know how many men know about the beauty mark on her left thigh.

The night is slow to start. Al logs onto the EarJoy website and writes for a full twenty minutes until the phone rings.

"Hey, Patricia! Hot to trot?"

Al saves his work and pitches his voice an octave higher. "Can't wait!"

If he were really his wife, he'd twirl red hair around his finger right now.

The sex line's calls come in through one of the site's dispatchers. She takes the caller's credit card info and preferences and reminds them of the rules: no incest, kiddie talk, snuff, or torture. Al's specialty is the horny-good-girl routine: the doting girlfriend, the bangable babysitter, and the lusty girl next door.

Once he's logged on, the site alerts dispatch that he's available, and an EarJoy employee jumps on the line to record the minutes. Al's got to keep callers listening for at least two or he doesn't get paid, and there's a fifty-five-minute max, although a lot of callers forced off call back immediately. He makes forty-five cents a minute—fifteen cents more than EarJoy's Lonely Housewives because he's putting in the late hours, 8 PM–3 AM. The money earned is sent to a private PayPal account that he empties bi-weekly into the family's chequing account, so there are no difficult-to-answer "what's EarJoy Live?" questions on the bank statements. He does it seven nights a week and clears over five grand a month, totally tax free.

Al's early callers are mostly from the East Coast; it's later there. This time of night he'll probably get a boyfriend or two: Clan O' Nerd-ish guys who want 10 percent sex, 90 percent handholding. Those guys are usually young and try to send him gifts—teddy bears and graduation rings and hockey jerseys—but that's a big, creepy no-no. If these dudes are so set on sending presents, Al prefers cash; they can transfer extra money right to the PayPal account themselves. At about ten PM, he'll talk to a few workaholics coming down after a long day and a few lines of coke. If he's still working, these guys might call back minutes after their alarms wake them and he'll help them get ready for work.

It gets real weird after midnight—lots of pedophiles and woman-haters. Those calls get flagged, and Al doesn't know what happens next. He usually gets a frat house around that time, too, and they're fun. They just want him to tell them about his "friends" on speaker-phone while their drunken buddies holler in the background. Sexy slumber parties, naughty carwashes, steamy saunas: Patricia's done it all. And, of course, no shift is complete without a token lesbian caller—they're his favourite. If the chick's not too shy, Al can gather inspiration for the next caller and have a little fun himself (hand lotion and Kleenex ready and waiting in the top drawer).

Within seconds, dispatch hooks him up. The line clicks and the guy on the other end is already breathing heavily.

"Hey, princess."

Henry.

He's a regular. Middle-aged, white, upper income bracket—eager and easy to please. He's the kind of corporate sad sack who used to be someone but peaked at seventeen, a guy like Hamilton—the type of real tough guys who head back to their old high school to yell at their kids' teachers. Guys like Henry are already bored with their second wives and have enough time and money to call a few days a week. They're loyal to their phone actresses and always want to hear about their own cocks. Their calls are the most lucrative, too, lasting between twenty-five and thirty minutes—a perfectly respectable payout that gives Al plenty of time to take other callers, potentially meeting new regulars.

"Baby, I'm soaked," Al breathes. "I need it so bad."

It's pretty vanilla. Henry asks Al/Patricia what she's wearing, asks her to grab her tits, tells her to take her panties off. This part's easy. Al just describes Pat, imitates the way she moans. If Henry isn't too chatty, Al usually gets hard himself.

Henry ruins the mood by asking how his cock tastes. *Typical Henry*. Al tells him he's the flavour of success—nice one, right?— but the line goes quiet.

"I lost my job today," Henry says. "I worked there for twenty years. I don't know why I called. I haven't even told my wife yet."

Henry's voice breaks and it reminds Al of Patricia's when he told her he'd quit teaching. It takes him right back to the sting of her palm on his face when he refused, again, to ask Garrett for work. It makes him think of how Pat cried when he told her she'd have to go back to waitressing after the baby was born and how five-year-old Zoe blocked the door, trying to keep her mommy from leaving.

Once Al watched her close the diner from the car while the kids slept in the back seat. They had sold their second vehicle for extra cash, and he came to pick Patricia up, watching as her manager grabbed her ass as she stacked chairs. When Patricia got into the vehicle he acted like he hadn't seen anything, but she knew he had. Early the next morning he found her topless and crying in the baby's room, her milk dried up from not being able to nurse as often as she needed to.

The voice of the man he's having paid phone sex with makes Al think of the days he spent lying on top of crushed Cheerios and soured formula on the living room floor, the suffocating stink of his own unwashed body, and the incessant demands of small children. It makes him think of bad hangovers and his Joel Plaskett Emergency CD stuck on repeat, of being too sick of himself to even get up and to change the music.

Henry's voice reminds Al of how Patricia used to sleep as far away from him as possible and how desperately he needed her to look at him and how badly he wanted to not wake up at all if it meant going back to sleep unwanted. It makes Al think of how his jaw ached after she told the rest of his family, at dinner, that he was out of work. Garrett had reached for Patricia's hand when she started to cry.

"It'll be okay," Garrett said, his dirty thumb stroking Patty's porcelain skin. "I know a guy looking for a columnist and Al's got a writing background. Let me see what I can do."

Patricia wiped her eyes and looked up at him, not smiling, but not crying, either.

Remembering.

Smug fuck.

Al looked to Garrett's wife to see if she had noticed the come-on but Susan was too busy tripping out on the shape of a broccoli crown. Crazy broad. There was nothing Al could do, no move to make or plan to hatch or meeting to attend, just awful, complete desperation watching the scene in which his wife falls, again, for his big brother. He thought of Simperson, crying snot-faced. What am I supposed to do? she'd said. Tell me what you want!

Still, Garrett's column connection saved his life. He was going to tell Patricia that it didn't pay but how could he after she interrupted him, jumping into his arms like that, pressing her lips against his so hard? How could he after she led him to the basement and knelt on the unfinished floor, showing him the love he'd missed for so long? The way her eyes gazed up, searching, her lips open, finally smiling, pulling him in, the way her hands clenched the back of his thighs, claiming him, choosing him again, *him!*

Okay, maybe *that* was what saved his life.

Afterward, she grabbed a blanket off of the upstairs couch and they leaned together against the exposed beams. The worst was over. Al watched her lips as she talked about textures and colour schemes and how she'd make this space the perfect study. He told her he'd make enough for her to quit waitressing and was shocked when she believed him. He didn't know why he said it, just wanted to feel like a big shot, he guessed.

"Do you know what this means, Al?" she asked. "We'll be together, now. Home. I can take care of the kids and you can work. We're free now. Do you understand? We're free!"

She looked so damn beautiful he almost believed her. It was easy to laugh, to pull her close, to kiss her, again and again. At least that's something: the first love he made in this room was real, 100 percent.

He spent the next week glued to muted pornos, unable to sleep. One night, a chat-line commercial advertised "We're always looking for new voices!" and Al realized how he'd make the money.

"Patricia?" Henry asks, interrupting Al's thoughts.

"Sorry, baby," Al stammers, resuming his character. "It'll be okay. Don't worry, baby. Really, I'm not worried about a thing. I know you'll figure it all out. Don't you know no one can take care of me like you? You're incredible. You're a hero."

Henry coughs, choking back a sob. If they were face-to-face Al would buy a six-pack and they'd drink it in his garage. They'd play loud music and talk about asshole bosses and bullshit politicians and gorgeous girls, but instead, Al tells Henry to relax, that he's wiping away his tears, that he's kissing his neck, his chest, that he's wrapping his legs around him. Al tells Henry that he's on top and that Patricia feels so safe because Henry's so big and so strong. Al describes his wife's talents while Henry grunts and moans until Al hears the stranger cum.

Al hangs up and his skin prickles as his stomach turns. He's Patricia to as many men as he needs to be to hit his nightly $150 quota, and then he logs off, calls the dispatcher, and tells her he's done for the night.

He looks in on the kids before crawling into bed, trying his best not to disturb his wife. Naked, she throws a thigh over his, her hand reaching for his dick. She kisses his neck, trying to make him hard, but her tongue reminds him of the way the phone slips on the sweat of his skin during long calls. Give it to me, she teases.

Al clears his throat.

"Tell me what you want."

NORTHSIDE DELACROIX

2007

SOMEONE ONCE GRABBED Shannon by the ponytail and tried to drag her into the bushes in Rundle Park. She'd seen the guy in the baggy pants drinking in the basketball court as she passed, and knew he was following her after one of his buddies called out: "Rodney! Where you going, man?"

It had happened just a few months after her mom drank herself to death. Shannon was fresh out of high school and she and her mom's old boyfriend, Larry, were still living in the low-income housing apartment under her mom's lease. One minute Shannon was almost out of the park, almost home from cleaning 7-Eleven's grease traps all night, and next there was the smell of skunk and then her head snapped back, feet skidding pavement.

Not that it was much of a fight. The guy was too drunk. Shannon caught the wrist of the hand that grabbed her and spun around, snapping the heel of her other palm into the bridge of his nose. He let go and tripped, landing on his back with his feet stuck up like a dead spruce beetle, crusty and big and hard. He laughed. Shannon attacked.

Her knees told her to run but the rest of her was clenched up too tight. *Kick, punch, kick.* His nose burst the second time the rubber heel of her high top met it and he began to whimper, his hands over his face, chin tucked into his chest, "Okay, stop! Stop! I'm sorry! Stop!"

But Shannon just kept raising her knee high, pushing down hard, again and again, until he lay still, a mewing ball, spit trailing from his mouth in long red strings.

That night Shannon screwed Larry on the bed he used to share with her mom. The next morning she told him what had happened, told him what could have happened.

"Yeah, but it didn't." He pressed his nose under her jaw, traced her collar bone with the tip of his tongue. "'Cause you're bad, baby. Northside, bitch."

He crawled over her, whine-grunting when he came, every part of him limp and lazy except his dick. She lay still, shutting her mouth to his greasy hair, too numb to think of anything except skinned knuckles and the drunk's quiet crying.

Shannon's thinking about this as she drives because her sister's moaning is too much like that drunk's. Shannon turns the radio up loud to drown out the noise of Tara's overdose and Sheryl Crow sings about all she wants to do. It's almost as though they're on the way to a high school dance, what with the stink of chemical puke and Tara's sickly sweet Hawaiian ginger body lotion. Shannon's hand drifts from the steering wheel to pull at the Celtic knot ring she's worn as a pendant necklace since she was a teen. It's always been a nervous habit, fiddling with Mom's old engagement ring.

Shannon glances at the rear-view mirror. Tara's on the backseat, hair pasted to her cheeks, body shaking and curling into itself.

Where's the goddamn hospital?

Shannon hasn't been to the Royal Alex since Larry's kid broke his arm, so she doesn't really know the way. Still, she can't take Tara to the Grey Nuns, can she? Tara's a medical student there. Dr. Tara Hamilton, meth head and OB-GYN. Jesus Christ.

They pull up to Emergency and Shannon lays on the horn, interrupting the paramedics bullshitting in front. One rushes over while the other two grab a stretcher.

"What's wrong?" he asks. He leans into the vehicle. Shannon isn't usually stupid over guys but something about the question, or maybe his brown eyes, makes her wish he was looking at her.

"I don't know. Some guy said something about meth." He hadn't, actually, but Shannon knows Larry's chemical of choice.

They get Tara in quick, the guys yelling as they head through the double doors inside the hospital. Nurses meet them and jog alongside the stretcher shouting numbers and non-words. Shannon follows a few feet behind, straining to hear.

Don't tell them anything.

Tara seizes again and a yellow stain spreads between the legs of her white Capri pants, blotting and blooming like the watercolours Shannon used to paint with in art class. *Bad outfit to OD in, Tar.* Mom had done that too, she remembered, on the couch where they found her. Larry couldn't even give away the couch after; they had to pay extra to have it taken to the dump.

Tara starts gagging. A nurse is forcing something down her throat.

"Jesus!" Shannon shouts. "Go easy!"

"Get her out of here," a nurse orders, her big stupid perm like grey cotton candy on her head. The brown-eyed medic leads her out of the room as quick as he rolled Tara in.

"You look like you could use a cup of coffee," he says. "Don't worry about your friend, okay? Sandra's going to take good care of her. Look, see that Timmy's right down the hall, by the elevator?" He points to a sign and digs in his pocket. "Let me get you some cash."

Shannon shrugs his hand off her elbow and he steps off. "Do I look like I need your money?"

The girl behind the Tim Hortons counter wears an immaculate French braid and no makeup. Her uniform is boxy and nothing about her says sex, only work. Everything screams temporary foreign worker. Probably still fresh off the boat.

"Black," Shannon snaps. "No sugar."

"Yes, ma'am, one minute, one minute." The worker talks weird, her mispronounced words pitched in apology. She offers a quick smile, but drops it when she sees Shannon's face. It's another two minutes before she figures out the till and takes the change Shannon's held out the whole time.

Shannon taps her foot. She doesn't have time for this shit. She's got to get to the airport, pay the rent, the damage deposit. She could have been there and back twice by now.

"Hello? I said black." The girl flinches, spilling the cream she's poured into Shannon's coffee. Shannon turns to the man in line behind her. "Think anyone here speaks English?"

The girl's blush deepens. *Kick, punch, kick.*

Shannon's finally handed a red cup of black coffee and she heads outside for a smoke. The coffee is liquid sugar and she spits it into a flowerpot, draining the rest before chucking the cup. The whole friggin' world's incompetent. Can't blame the owners, though, not with the way those bleeding hearts keep raising minimum wage. Everyone thinks it's a good thing, the labour lobbies, everyone except anyone who actually knows anything about business. Now the only way anyone can afford to staff shops is to ship in desperate immigrants. At least you can charge them rent, make back a few of the seven bucks an hour you lose.

Modern-day slavery, that's what Lacey called the Temporary Foreign Worker program last week. She was shopping at the mall when Shannon saw her and called her over to the Cigarette Shop. Shannon could have recognized that stupid haircut anywhere, the 1991 barrel-curl bangs Lacey should have left in high school. The two had grown apart since then, Lacey getting knocked up before graduation by that Dave guy she'd always had a crush on. Three boys now: twins the first time and an afterthought two years later. Somehow they got talking about a nanny Lacey had met, a Filipina who paid back more than half of her pay to her bosses as rent.

"Well, boo fricken hoo," Shannon snorted. "Why shouldn't she pay? Chick would rather sleep outside?"

"It's not right," Lacey said. Her eyes filled up and her face got real red, just like when she'd get called on in class. "Having to watch someone else's kids while hers are an ocean away, giving back the money she should be sending home. It's sick. I mean, even if she wanted to leave . . . she's trapped, just . . . stuck."

Shannon shrugged. She'd use the program. Would charge what she was owed, too. No one's forcing them to come to Canada. People choose exactly the kind of life they want.

Sitting on the curb in front of a hospital, Shannon's only more convinced of that now. Just look at Tara: house in the suburbs, dad around 24/7, lessons at the "kayak club." Tara got *everything* and she still ended up overdosing on sleazy Larry's magic crystal. What had she said the first day she showed up? "Henry got fired. Said he can't help with rent anymore."

Shannon didn't know what was more ridiculous, that Dad still paid Tara's rent or that Tara called him Henry. Wasn't she, like, a doctor or something? Why didn't she have her own place?

"Taking some time off," Tara said. Her eyes kept closing. "Sabbatical. Working on a specialty. Obstetrics and gynecology."

Of course you are.

Lacey couldn't understand that, though, could she? Some bored housewife, buried in mommy groups and park play dates. The whole convo was a bust. It was a relief when Lacey said she had to go, had to find a swimsuit for the trip her "hubby" had planned.

"You must be, what, size 18 now?" *Kick, punch, kick.*

She had mentioned something interesting, though. Did Shannon know that the airport's Canadiana Corner was closing?

"Great location for a second store."

No shit. And a great way to get out from behind the till of the Cigarette Shop, where, for all the reading she'd done and online business courses she'd taken, all Larry wanted Shannon to do was look pretty and count the change.

The airport's committee only wanted proposals from existing businesses, but they were happy to consider Shannon's, seeing how she was the manager and all. Looked like they were going to approve it, too. Figures. Men are too easy.

Black mini skirt, heels, tight blazer, and a push-up bra: Shannon knows her way around more than just a bottom line. In the proposal meeting she cocked her head and ran fingers over exposed skin while breathing words like *demographic, profit margin,* and *net worth,* crossing and uncrossing her legs until she had all of them smiling.

She had them so dizzy they didn't even notice the typo: that "o" where an "e" should have been. *The Cigaretto Shop.* A separate establishment, the new store severed from the first, one letter getting Shannon out from under Larry forever.

Kick, punch, kick.

The only thing she had left to do was to pay the rental deposit. The money she'd get from Mom's ring would pay that and more, and it wouldn't be long before the store turned a profit. Then she'd be out, away from too-tight rows of dirty houses, half-naked kids inside ignoring the smell of liquor and sex and the new "uncle" that showed up sometime in the night. She might look for a place in Sherwood Park, like her dad. Maybe even somewhere nearby if she could stomach that much of Karen. Tara's mom is the whole reason Shannon got the short end of the stick in the first place, the home wrecker having poached Dad when Shannon was little. Dad might be business smart, but he never got wise to Karen.

People choose exactly the kind of life they want. That was the other funny thing: kids like Shannon who get left nothing except Loser Larry and a failed engagement ring but find a way to make it work anyway. "Give me a nickel and I'll make you a dollar," Dad used to say. He was always hustling, locked away in his office making phone calls no matter how late at night. That's how Shannon is too. Tough, smart, determined.

Northside, bitch.

She's about to light her second smoke when a man calls to her, asks if she'll speak with him inside. Shannon stands. "She okay?"

"Stable," he says. He introduces himself as Dr. Rhanji and asks her name, asks for Tara's. Shannon exhales all the breath she didn't know she'd been holding. He doesn't know Tara. Thank god. She lights the cigarette.

"Beats me." Shannon shrugs. "I just found her."

Rhanji frowns. His body slumps and hardens at the same time. He's tired, pissed off. "Withholding information dramatically alters the level of care we can provide."

Shannon shrugs. "Can't tell you what I don't know, buddy."

"You must know someth—"

"Like I said, I just found—"

"We know that you're her sister!"

Rhanji's bald head sweats under the hot sun, reflecting Shannon's fuck-you stance so clearly she almost scares herself.

She groans. Of course they know. Tara's probably in there right now all tears and apologies. Idiot. She shakes her head.

"Half-sister." Smoke plumes around Rhanji's face and he waves his hand to break the cloud. Shannon takes a step back. "She awake?"

Rhanji shakes his head. "Family resemblance."

Shit. Shannon rolls her eyes. Sometimes she forgets they look alike, what with Tar inheriting Karen's witchy nose.

"This is, like, a first-time thing for her. Seriously. She's, like, a professional. Real smart. I don't know what she was thinking."

"Her toxicology report suggests otherwise," Rhanji says. "There are excessive levels of methamphetamine in her system, yes, but also significant levels of Lorazepam and Oxycodone, suggesting a long-term use of both Ativan and OxyContin, prescription drugs. Narcotic, addictive. Does your sister have any underlying medical and psychological conditions? Any history of addiction? Depression, anxiety?"

Shannon blinks, shakes her head. What would Tara have to be anxious about? All she does is study and sleep. She thinks of Tara's red eyes, her shaky hands. There was that pill bottle that rolled out from under the couch. *For headaches*, Tara said. She was always complaining about headaches, about Larry inviting his buddies over while she was trying to read. *You don't understand how complicated this stuff is. I need to learn this. This is my life!*

"I cannot stress how sick your sister is," Rhanji says. "This episode has put her under tremendous strain. The fact that she is alive is nothing short of miraculous."

Shannon thinks of her mom on the couch, skin like cold oatmeal. Miracles don't happen in the Northside.

"What am I supposed to do?"

"There's an outpatient program," he says. "Free, but ineffective, a low success rate with more likelihood of Tara finding a new dealer than sobriety." The best course of action is a forty-five-day treatment centre. He recommends New Hope.

"Like, rehab?"

"In as much."

"How much?"

He presses his lips together. They're on the same team now. "It's expensive, but fairly standard, considering. The cost is about three thousand a week, but there are payment options."

Shannon's skin crawls. It's the Cigaretto Shop deposit times two.

"I think I better call my dad."

Rhanji makes a few more attempts to get Tara's name, but Shannon isn't having it. He shakes his head and says he'll leave her to it and heads back in.

Shannon's hands shake as she digs the phone from her purse. It's been a long time since she talked to her dad.

That whore Karen answers.

"Is my dad there?"

"Shannon? Is Tara with you?"

"Just put my dad on the phone."

She hears her dad's footsteps as clearly as she imagines the oak cabinets in their kitchen. Shannon hasn't visited since Dad moved out of the city, but she used to hang out at his old place.

"Shannon? Where's Tara? Is she okay?"

"Hi, Dad. It's okay. She's at the hospital."

Henry's rumbled exhale makes her think of birthday cake and training wheels. "Oh, good. She hasn't checked in for a while."

Shannon cringes. "No, I mean, she's *in* the hospital, Dad. She overdosed or something."

Silence. Shannon sits on the ground. She pulls her knees up, leans over herself, and rests her head on her own lap.

"I don't understand."

"Drugs, Dad. Meth, and prescription stuff, too, I guess."

More silence.

"What have you done?"

It's as if the ice runs through Shannon's veins instead of Tara's. She feels it cold under her skin, freezing her chest, stopping her heart. "Dad, I don't . . ."

"Six years, Shannon!"

She pulls the phone from her ear as she hears her stepmother's voice shriek. Of course, Karen would be listening in.

"Six years of schooling we've paid for. Do you know how much we've sacrificed? How hard we've worked? That's over, now, do you understand? You think she can keep her practice now that *this* is in her medical records? You think she'll ever get insurance, a mortgage, a chance at anything?"

"Get off the phone, you stupid bitch! I'm talking to Dad!"

"You should be ashamed! Ashamed! No respect! You're disgusting!" Karens voice drifts out of reach of the receiver.

"That's right!" Shannon screams into the phone. "Walk away, Karen! Walk away!"

Shannon stops shouting when she hears her father's breathing on the other end of the line.

"Daddy," she says. "I didn't—"

He inturrupts her. "She's trash now, Shannon. Do you understand? Trash. Congratulations. You've dragged her to your level."

For as cold as the rest of her is, Shannon's tears are red-hot.

"There's, like, a facility or something, but it . . . it's really expensive." She slips her index finger into the ring and presses the diamond against her lips. *I'm sorry, Daddy.*

"Expensive? Is that what this—are you asking me for money?" He laughs and laughs and laughs. "You're your mother's girl, aren't you, Shan?"

There are no words.

She's still crying when Larry's pickup pulls into the parking lot, slow and dirty, like a bad hangover. She looks away as he kneels beside her, slides a warm hand between her shoulder blades.

"Family sticks together," he says. He's sorry for everything. So sorry.

She stands and he pulls her to him, holds her so close she almost feels safe, lost in the artificial haze hanging off his skin.

"Why didn't you tell me about the airport space?" he asks. She stays still, waits for him to say more. He doesn't sound mad.

"They called the store. You spelt cigarette wrong, dummy." He gathers her hair in his hands, brushes it away from her face. "I told them we had to pass, Shan. I mean, I get what you were trying to do, but we don't need more money. More money, more people watching, okay?" The shop's really just a front for Larry's dope dealing, anyway.

The meth, though, he's done with that, he promises. Seeing Tara freak, her looking so much like Shannon—that scared him. It will get better. They're going to be themselves again, maybe have some friends over or something. It's been weird since her sister moved in. She's not like them. "I can't lose you, Shan."

Shannon holds on. She knows he's lying, but she presses against him when he wraps his arms tighter. There's no way out for people like him, no way out for people like her.

Larry says he'll see her when she gets home, and leaves. Shannon sits back down on the curb and stares into the cold clear rock flagged by Celtic knots. In the end, everyone's always alone. People like Larry and Tara just don't know it yet. She finishes the last smoke in her pack and goes in.

She walks to the room where Tara's sleeping and a middle-aged nurse smiles with nothing but love in her eyes. It's the same one as before, Shannon realizes, the one with the weird perm who told her to get out. *Sandra,* her nametag reads. Sandra whispers she'll give

Shannon some privacy and Shannon almost leans right into her when the nurse pats her shoulder, she almost grabs Sandra's hand, almost lets herself pretend it's Mom. She almost begs the nurse, *Please don't go—I am about to make a terrible mistake.*

But the nurse leaves. Alone, Shannon swallows and picks up the clipboard and pen at the end of the bed and, again, looks at her little sister.

Tara's in a hospital gown now; clean and perfect if still a little blue, just a hint of that chemical stink still on her. Shannon sits and rests the clipboard on her lap. She'll stay just long enough to explain how it's going to work, how one ruined sister will give the other the only things she has worth anything anymore: a ring and a throwaway name. Shannon will explain how Tara will get the help she needs without screwing up the rest of her life and she'll explain how much Tara will lose unless it's done this way. She'll explain how the diamond will cover most of what needs to be covered and that Shannon will figure out the rest. She'll explain that they'll never see each other again, not ever, not as long as they live, not after this. One of them is getting out and the other's back in the bushes, dragged by her ponytail.

Kick, punch, kick.

Shannon lifts the pen.

Patient Name: Shannon Delacroix

Northside, bitch.

THE COLD BLISTERS HER SKIN

APRIL 2009

THE BUSH OUTSIDE the Fort McMurray conference centre had acorns on the ends of its branches that grew straight up like it was giving the world a gazillion middle fingers. *Eff you, idling semi truck! Eff you, Tim Hortons drive-thru next door! Eff you, minivan mom with oversized sunglasses! You look like a stupid bug!*

Mom keeps talking, but Zoe pretends she can't hear. She wishes she could be like that shrub they left behind, knees crisscross-applesauce and eyes closed like a Tibetan monk on a mountaintop, hands flippin' the bird. Talk about inner peace.

"When I think about all I did for your father to become some big-shot newspaper editor. Writing his columns, proofreading, moving out to Sherwood Park . . . There's no way he would have ever moved up from that measly arts column without me, you know. And now here I am, fighting that smug cheapskate for every last . . . ugh. I could just scream!"

Mom's red hair moves back and forth at her chin even after she stops shaking her head. She used to wear it all the way down her back but chopped it off after the divorce. There was something about a lady getting a haircut and changing her life, Mom said, but Zoe liked things better before. Zoe rests her head against the passenger window and crosses her eyes. The white line on the shoulder of the road blurs and shakes and triples. Why do her parents always have to vent while driving? These days Zoe can't even buckle a seatbelt without feeling like she's swallowed a medicine ball. At least they don't talk to the boys like this.

Don't say anything to your brothers, sweetie. They don't understand this stuff like girls do.

Zoe looks out at the world they're passing by. There aren't any shrubs by the houses on the side of this highway, right smack in the middle between home and the northern town they're coming back from. No nothing except rusty cars and one red dress hanging from a clothesline. Houses in Sherwood Park always have trees or flowerbeds or rock gardens or *something*, and in the summer the city hangs flower baskets from the streetlights. These buildings look like they just popped out of the ground: small and square, weirdly spaced from one another.

Like baby teeth.

Mom keeps Zoe's baby teeth in a shoebox on the top shelf of her closet. The boys don't know about that, either. Zoe found the box while snooping, which is what she does now. The door goes click and Zoe goes zoom. Old love letters and baby clothes, college poetry and separation agreements, a pretty leather pouch with a pink flower beaded on the front (she kept that for herself). She doesn't know what she's looking for, but that doesn't stop her from checking all the hiding places in Mom's room.

Once she found a newspaper from 2002, Dad's first-ever arts column printed in the back. On the front page was a story about a girl the same age as Zoe. The seven-year-old's family had been in a car accident and everyone had died: her mom, her dad, her baby sister. The girl was the only one left and when they'd crashed, she'd bitten off her tongue. Sometimes Zoe dreams she's in that vehicle, her whole family barrelling toward some terrible, horrible accident. Mom and Dad in charge but totally out of control. Zoe and the boys are helpless in the backseat, too short to even reach the wheel.

It's not the divorce that's so hard, either. Half the kids in her class have divorced parents, maybe even more. It's the hate that's so awful. Mom and Dad both promised they'd stay a family after the split, but it's not like that at all. There's so much anger between them, and between them is exactly where Zoe has to live. Like, sometimes Mom will talk bad about Dad or Dad will tell a mean joke about Mom and Zoe can't do anything but pretend to agree or fake laugh or else they'll be like, "What's your problem, Zoe?" and try even harder to convince her why they're right and the other one is wrong. Zoe wishes Mom and Dad could be like Uncle Garrett and Auntie Susan. Her cousin's parents aren't married anymore, but when Iris visits her mom in the hospital, Uncle Garrett goes with her and sometimes even braids Auntie Susan's hair. Sometimes Zoe wonders what's worse, when one of your parents stops talking, or when both talk too much.

But mostly Zoe just feels sorry for Mom and Dad. Underneath all the meanness, she knows there's just pain. But then that medicine ball feeling sinks in her stomach again and it's like every horrible word is a foot pushing a gas pedal just a little bit harder and soon they're going to find themselves a van full of hate-filled dead people at the bottom of a frozen lake. Like, Zoe's in pain too, but she's not allowed to lip off. She has to keep a "good attitude" and "show some respect." What makes their feelings so special? She clenches her molars together. Imagine having no tongue.

Zoe's phone is dead. She wants to play the parkour app but instead just imagines the cartoon guy skateboarding over the houses on the side of the road: one, two, up-down-up-down—jump on the third Frankenstein-y one, patchy like it stole rooms from its neighbours in the night. *Ting*! Parkour guy ollies off a road sign for fifty points.

Watch for pedestrians. No sidewalks.

"Welcome to the rez," Mom sighs as music turns to static.

Zoe turns to look out the rear window. They're not stopping, just driving past, but Zoe's never seen a reserve before. She thought it would look more olden days: tepees and horses and tanning hides stretched out in the sun like the illustrations in her First Nations, Métis, and Inuit textbook. Where are the schools and stores? Don't they have any? They must. She thinks about the girls at the Young Leaders Conference, bused into town with their teachers. Zoe was the only one with her mom. So embarrassing.

It was pretty obvious the conference wasn't for Zoe. The speakers kept talking about the importance of northern youth and whenever Mom mentioned how she and Zoe had travelled almost five hours to attend, the other adults said, "Oh wow!" but their eyes were like *why?* Then Mom freaked when she heard other girls were there on bursaries and wouldn't make eye contact with the nametag lady after the lady said there was nothing she could do. When the first day began with a smudging ceremony Mom said, "I thought this was *Girls* Rising, not *Native* Girls Rising."

That was racist, Zoe thought. But she just smiled and shrugged because she felt bad. It was nice of Mom to take her to a leadership thing. Everyone knows Zoe wants to be prime minister when she grows up, but no one has ever taken her seriously before (well, Iris believes in her, but she's away at university now). But then Mom wanted to skip conference activities, to go somewhere nice for breakfast instead of eating with everyone else, to have spa nights in the hotel room instead of participating in the evening truth circles. Mom rolled her eyes reading the program guide and made fun of presentations like *intersectional feminism* and *social-economic equality*.

"I just thought it would be more inclusive," Mom said. "Less powwow, more ya-ya. Mother-daughter stuff." It really hurts her heart, Mom choked, not having a relationship with her own mother. Dad says Grandma Mariam "got sick in the head and took off." All Zoe remembers about her grandmother is a big black dress Mom didn't like to see her wearing (and maybe black teeth—but Zoe's not sure if that part's right or not).

"I never want that kind of loneliness for you, sweetie. We girls need to honour our bonds." She bopped Zoe's nose with her finger, leaving a spot of age-defying lotion behind. Zoe laughed and Mom pulled her into a bear hug.

"Because believe you me, Zozo, men will try to break them every single time."

Then it made sense what the trip was really about:

Girls versus boys.

Mom versus Dad.

And then a good attitude couldn't even be faked.

Now Zoe wishes Mom would stop staring and just drive.

"You'll get the bumps," Mom warns.

So? Zoe leans harder so more of her skin touches the cool glass. She hopes she gets so cold blisters pop on her brain.

Except her forehead is actually getting really itchy. Stupid cold urticaria. Sounds like a Harry Potter spell. Harry points his wand and Voldemort erupts, scratching hives underneath his cloak as he bends to throw up like Zoe did in Grade 3 when the teacher didn't give her any Claritin before a winter nature walk. She brushes her hair forward so it hides her face and warms the blisters with her hand. She doesn't want Mom to know she was right.

Mom takes off her sunglasses. "Night came quick," she says, fake-happy-chirpy.

"I don't even want to talk about it," Zoe mumbles. Zoe's mad because the headlights are still broken and Mom knows she gets scared riding around when it's so hard to see. Zoe told her to hurry up too, so they wouldn't have to drive at night, but Mom took forever getting ready and also wanted to buy the boys dream catchers at the hotel gift shop.

Mom looks down at her purse on the floor in front of the centre console before she starts to rummage through. "I wonder how the guys are doing," she says.

Zoe feels her shoulders tense up again. She turns back to the window as her mother reads the phone screen and hears her drop it back into the bag.

"No signal."

Mom plays with the radio dial one channel one at a time, AM to FM to AM again, pressing buttons she doesn't even know how to use and talking to herself—"Oops, let's see, nope that doesn't work . . ."—as if *trying* to freak Zoe out.

"Watch the road!" Zoe finally yells.

But Mom does not watch the road. She looks long and hard at Zoe instead.

"Watch your attitude, little miss."

They pick up a talk-radio station and Mom sinks back into her seat, hands ten and two. The host's voice is wet and phlegmy. He shouts for Canadian patriots to call in and Zoe thinks of her gym teacher, fat and sweaty on the bleachers, out of breath from yelling at all the kids to stop running like girls. "I *am* a girl!" Zoe always wants to shout back. "Truth and reconciliation gets yet another facelift," the host screams. "When does this country just move on?"

A logging truck passes and a man stares down from its passenger window. An on-air caller says missing and murdered Indigenous women are sad and all, but then his voice gets high-pitched and crazy. "How come no one cares about the war on white men?"

Mom flicks off the radio. "This is exactly why we need feminism."

In front of them, to their right, a girl appears. Mom gasps and hits the brakes to slow. The girl walks as close to the ditch as she can get without falling down the steep creek bank. Then she's right beside Zoe, face hidden by her hood, then she's just skinny jeans and parka lit up by taillights, big red bag slung over her back.

Mom shakes her head. "If I ever caught you hitchhiking!"

Zoe rolls her eyes. *Whatever.* The girl didn't even have her thumb out. Besides, once Zoe cut class to walk to the mall and three different old ladies pulled over to see if she was all right. *Sooo dangerous, Mom.* Still, Zoe watches the girl until the night swallows her up. It's a lot darker and lonelier out there now than it was for Zoe skipping fourth period. Isn't she scared?

Mom tries the dial again and finally finds music. She turns the volume high. A woman sings a few words in a different language and then her voice rings out that we're all the same. Mom says the song was a big hit the year Zoe was born. It always makes her cry, she says.

There are no streetlights out here but the moon is bright. Parkour guy zooms along the forest's treetops, pings off another sign: *Curve Ahead*. Mom rustles pens, coins, papers, her hand scrambling again at the bottom of her purse.

"Let's see if your dad managed to parent long enough to get them to sleep."

Zoe feels the van pull from the trees; the vehicle drifts.

"Mom?"

"Hello? Al? Can you hear me?"

The van crosses centre.

"Shoot. Lousy signal. Al!"

Lights flicker through the trees.

"Mom, watch—"

The trees part, headlights flash and blind.

"Mom!"

The night becomes a shake.

Light and shadow.

Mom's arm over Zoe's heart.

Grass and gravel.

Moonlight and glass.

Wild roses in the dark.

Cool, cool water.

※

Miranda stares between her feet at the border of asphalt and earth until the van's red eyes slip into darkness. She bends over, hands on knees. What kind of creep drives with no headlights? Holy fuck!

She takes a breath, swallows, and stands tall. She flicks her fingers as if fear can be shaken off like water from her hands. Kohkum's voice breaks the panic in her head. *It's never too late to turn back the way you came.* Miranda sees her grandmother saying these words from the kitchen table with needle and thread in hand, neck craned over her beading. Yeah, but when Kohkum teaches that she's talking about returning to tradition. Miranda's halfway between home and the truck stop and turning back now would be every bit as scary as going on. *It's the point of no return,* Uncle Wilf would say. He used to teach Miranda all kinds of things from his forest-firefighting days, when he'd lead his team to jump from helicopters with axes or a chainsaw to work on firebreaks in the middle of nowhere for weeks at a time. The point of no return was something he taught her right before he disappeared back to the city, so it's easy for Miranda to remember.

She scans her shoulder for pain. The van was sketchy but not as bad as the garbage-throwing logging truck before it. Thank god that pop bottle was empty. There's no soreness, no bruises or scrapes where it hit her. No lasting physical evidence of injury; just the sick-thrill grin of the semi-truck's passenger, his glinting yellow smile.

Oh well, she'll use the experience. That's how Kohkum's taught her to live. Miranda will get to where she's going and drink ten thousand refill coffees in the truck stop's twenty-four-hour diner and scribble that bottle hitting her shoulder into song lyrics until the six AM bus comes along. Someday the song will blast from that loser's radio and wipe the shit-eating smirk off his face when he hears himself skewered between Miranda's chords.

Rubber soles crunch and squeak, heel, toe, heel, toe. Glowing footsteps light the way, matching her stride. A shiver passes over Miranda and she pushes her hands deeper in her pockets. Did Mom even make it this far before she was picked up? Sometimes she has a dream of her mother walking down this highway. Miranda's own baby self calls out *Mommy! Mama! Come back!* but her mother keeps walking. She's just a shadow in the distance before Miranda remembers what she used to call her. *Nikâwiy,* she screams again and again. *Nikâwiy! Nikâwiy!*

But it's too late. Mom can't hear her now.

Uncle Wilf's old bunker bag digs into her shoulder, the guitar inside heavier with each step. Miranda wouldn't even be out here if the stupid bus people hadn't dropped the reserve's pick-up. Over the phone, the fleet owner said the rez roads were too rough for the bus to travel on anymore.

"You should tell someone to fix them."

Miranda rolled her eyes. Kohkum explained long ago why it was so difficult to get anything done around the Nation. Thanks to compound interest, the reserve's trust had more than enough to cover a lot of things, but the Band didn't have any access to the money. The Canadian government had written rules around the one-time payment they'd made upon the Nation's treaty signing with a big sketchy loophole. Before the Band was able to access even one dollar, it would have to have over 50 percent of its adult members vote yes on each individual project. Too bad less than 50 percent even actually lived on the reservation because of the way Canada had moved folks all over with residential schools, the Sixties Scoop, foster care, and just the run-of-the-mill poverty that followed things like that. Every year new project proposals are submitted for review—road maintenance applications, initiatives to cover children's school fees, plans to open a community daycare centre—and every year they are rejected because of low voter turnout. The Band has more than enough cash in the bank to cover the costs, but only the members living on reserve take the time to cast a ballot, and that's far less than half. The Band might try to rewrite the treaty terms in court too, if only they could access the money to pay lawyers.

But Miranda didn't get into it with the lady on the phone. Instead, she said thank you and hung up and sighed. Walking the highway was dangerous, but still better than two nights in Edmonton with nowhere to stay.

Right?

And, technically, she's not breaking any rules. Kohkum's rules are:

- No alcohol
- No drugs
- No boys

But she's never specifically mentioned not walking the highway before. Still, Miranda is uneasy. She thinks of the silent treatment Kohkum gave her when she introduced Grayson as her boyfriend. How mad will Kohkum be this time?

Miranda gets the no-boy rule, though, even if she's currently breaking it. Her own mom, Kohkum's only daughter, had her first baby way too young, and then that baby, Miranda's big sister Amy, had her son at the same age Miranda is now, only seventeen. It messed everything up for both of them. Or at least, she thinks it did. Miranda hasn't seen either in a really long time.

Mom went missing when Miranda was a toddler. Amy was a teenager, though, and she tried to take care of Miranda until her school figured out what was going on. Then social services got involved and the girls were split up, sent to different foster homes in the city. Kohkum tried to get them back right away, but she didn't qualify for kinship care because of the files they had on her from the seventies.

Good thing an advocate got involved. He proved how Kohkum hadn't lost Wilf and Mom and baby Jack to child welfare because of anything that she'd done wrong, but because *everyone's* kids were scooped up back then. All she was guilty of was applying for financial assistance after her husband died, he argued, and she was known to be a loving guardian. While one of her children died in care, the other two returned to her of their own volition, Mom making her way back as a teenager when she got so wild her new family stopped caring what she did; Uncle Wilf as an adult, when he was finally ready to try to face whatever pain he couldn't shake in the city. By then, Kohkum had established her own business selling beaded moccasins and medicine bags to tourists through the truck stop giftshop, was honoured as an Elder, and had brought to life the community's Healing Lodge, the last membership-approved project, in 1985. Of course, by the time a committee was actually willing to *listen* to the advocate, Miranda's big sister had already ditched her foster home. Other than one worried social worker who met with Kohkum in the weeks after Amy's disappearance, it seemed like social services didn't even care. Just like Mom, Amy was long gone.

She'd returned once, though.

"Your sister said the child's name was Courage," Kohkum said. Miranda needed help drawing a family tree for school because all the branches stopped too short. "She showed up in a beat-up Dodge with a baby not yet walking, just days before they were supposed to bring you home."

Amy had wanted to crash at Kohkum's but kinship care inspectors were coming around the house a few times a week back then, making sure Kohkum's home was ready for a little child. Besides, Kohkum told Amy, there was no reason to hide. By that point Amy was eighteen and no one could force her back into foster care. Kohkum would simply add Courage and Amy's names onto the home residents list. As long as Amy didn't have a criminal record, there'd be no problem at all.

Kohkum didn't understand Amy's refusal until she saw the news later that night. The baby wasn't supposed to be with her. Amy had left him after birth at the hospital a year earlier but had kept an eye on him and stole his foster mom's truck when the opportunity arose. Courage wasn't even the boy's legal name, Kohkum learned. There'd be no fooling social workers; Amy had no birth certificate, and his picture was all over the news.

"It broke my heart," Kohkum said, "but Amy was eighteen and, in the eyes of the law, she'd kidnapped a child. I couldn't risk them being found here. At worst she'd spend the next decade of her life in prison. At best, I'd be guilty of helping. And you were all alone and sick in hospital, the very same age as my Jack when he was taken. Nothing could risk you coming home. Amy just didn't understand."

She had left angry, Kohkum said. Angry and hurt, howling in pain when Kohkum shut the door and sank to her knees in grief herself on the other side. Later, the news reported that the boy had been returned to his adoptive mother, but Kohkum never saw her granddaughter again.

Kohkum had stopped talking then and stared into her tea. Miranda watched from the kitchen table, still slumped over loose-leaf paper. She pressed the pencil eraser against her bottom lip as she waited and wondered if it was okay to ask.

"What did the news say his name was?"

"Jude." Kohkum nodded.

Was it okay to include him in the tree?

"He's still ours, isn't he?"

Miranda left the box on the other side of her big sister's name blank and traced a line over and down. *Jude (Courage),* she wrote. She closed her eyes and sent him love and tried to imagine sunshine filling up his heart and making him warm and strong and brave wherever he was in the world.

She keeps walking, faster now. She's got maybe an hour before the highway fills with riggers heading south for days off. The Friday Fly, the girls at school call it. It's supposed to be the best time to hitch a ride, but strange men and jacked-up trucks are exactly what Miranda wants to avoid. She'd rather watch the traffic tear through the night from a truck-stop window table. The thought of high beams pointed at the back of her legs makes her shiver.

If it weren't for the early thaw she would walk the creek bed. She'd risk the forest's animals over the highway's any day. But spring came early this year and the water is running high. Better to walk fast and dry than slow in soggy sneakers, Miranda thinks. She needs to get to a phone. Kohkum will be walking home from collecting Truth and Reconciliation statements at the Healing Lodge by now. Soon after, she will be in her bathrobe, the one that matches the Snuggie she got for Miranda for Christmas off the shopping channel. *Twinsies!*

Miranda thinks of her grandmother sitting there in her chair by her photographs, listening to Lloyd Robertson read the news because her eyes aren't strong enough to see the TV anymore. Eventually Kohkum will crack Miranda's bedroom door open to say goodnight and Lloyd's baritone voice will drift in: "and that's the kind of day it's been." What will happen when Miranda doesn't say goodnight back? She imagines her grandmother's stiff hands dropping the tea, shaking as they lift the note left on the pillow, flailing as she runs around looking for a driver in their dark neighbourhood.

What have I done?

Miranda walks so fast her whole body bounces. She needs to get to the truck stop *now*. She needs to use that payphone!

I'm sorry, Kohkum. I'm sorry but I'm safe. Two sleeps and then you can ground me forever.

It's simple. The bus will get her into the city for eleven AM and then she'll take another to West Edmonton Mall for the *Canada's Got Talent* auditions that afternoon. A delivery van leaves the Edmonton terminal at eleven PM the same day, and the woman on the phone said Miranda could catch a ride all the way back to the truck stop. She'll be home by Sunday morning, five AM. Surely Grayson will pick her up, although he'll be as mad as Kohkum. Not telling him was for his own good, though. Kohkum's just starting to warm up to him. If Kohkum found out he knew about Miranda taking off, she'd never forgive him.

There's only one scenario Miranda hasn't planned for. What if she passes the audition?

Then . . . well, she can't even imagine what comes after that. But she can imagine this: album tours, folk festivals, song-writing in cafés on rainy days. The last time Grayson went to visit his mom in town, he used her internet to upload a video of Miranda singing her song "Nikâwiy" on YouTube and it got over five thousand shares on Facebook. It even made the last few seconds of CBC News. Peter Mansbridge called her a "northern star" and the next Jann Arden! Maybe even Alberta's Joni Mitchell.

If Miranda becomes rich and famous like Jann Arden or Joni Mitchell, she knows exactly what she'll do. She'll buy an Edmonton apartment with a rooftop garden for Kohkum, and if Kohkum won't move to the city, Miranda will hire a driver to bring her back and forth from home. She'll even hire a private detective to find her sister and then Miranda will move her in too—Amy *and* the baby! Okay, maybe Miranda will need a house instead of an apartment. And Jude (Courage) won't be a baby anymore.

The children in the pictures Kohkum keeps by her chair sometimes mix up in Miranda's head, the images more real than the adults they did, or didn't, become. The only photo Kohkum has of baby Jack is a grainy image cut from yellowed newsprint. In it, five-year-old Mom smiles sweetly while Jack sucks his thumb, and big brother Wilf stares stone-faced into the camera with a protective arm around each sibling. In another, Kohkum presses the baby-perfect cheek of Amy's child to her own weather-beaten face and their sparkling black eyes look exactly the same. If Miranda's seventeen now, that means Amy's kid is fourteen. Already in Grade 8.

And money doesn't buy back time.

So there's not enough money in the world to bring to life Miranda's wildest fantasies. In her greatest dreams, all the children in those photos are in the same room, all healthy and grown. Kohkum's sisters are old ladies, out of their school uniforms with their hair re-grown, braids long, black, and grey. Mom has been found and is recovering from amnesia and Uncle Wilf has made his way back, laughing and teasing and sober again. Maybe Miranda could even erase the past, make it so none of Kohkum's kids were ever taken in the first place. Amy shows up to the party and introduces her teenage son, pimply and shy, but just like her with curly hair and sparkly eyes. Even Jack, the little uncle Miranda never knew, he's there too, but a forever child, kept on Kohkum's knee. And Kohkum's hands aren't stiff anymore. They're over Jack's heart.

A horn blares and then headlights shine, lighting the trees before spotlighting Miranda. Startled, she buries her head in her hands and drops into her parka shell like a turtle on the road. What is she doing? She drops her bag and slides into the ditch, water seeping through the seams of her shoes. From between blades of tall grass, she sees the semi pass without slowing. She climbs out of the ditch and imagines the glowing, ghostly tracks sizzling out under her squishy, wet shoes. So what if she overreacted? She needs to be careful. Miranda's not following anyone's path. This journey is her own.

Up ahead there's groaning, a big heavy sound, like something settling down. Deer? Or bear? Cougar! Maybe she should run. But then she thinks about how her cat pounces right when birds are just about to fly and remembers: slow and steady is fast enough.

Curve ahead.

It's too dark to see, but there are two little white crosses on the other side of the ditch where a drunk driver hit Grayson's sister's car, years and years ago. Grayson's sister was a lot older than him. He was a toddler when she died, but she was nineteen, the same age he is now. She was going to be a social worker and was pregnant with the child that would have become Grayson's nephew. Now Grayson will never have a nephew, and Miranda does have one, but will never meet him. Weird, being on a dark road with ghosts like that. Crosses should just line the whole damn highway. Or red dresses, like the one Kohkum keeps on the clothesline to show that they've lost a woman too.

Shit. Tail lights in the ditch.

Miranda scrambles to the road sign as though the wooden pole is thick enough to hide behind. The minivan is parked, waiting for her. Clouds break and her eyes adjust in the light of the moon. No, it's not waiting. The van is crumpled, crashed, its front end sunk in the creek.

People could be hurt. Miranda can't just walk away.

A back wheel slowly spins, just off the ground, calling her like a hand waving forward.

Patricia strokes her daughter's pale cheek in the cab of the truck that has picked them up. They've been in car accident. *A car accident!* Patricia still can't believe it. She brushes wet curls away from the sleeping fourteen-year-old's face so they tangle over Patricia's own lap and down between the pickup truck's passenger seat and side door. The bumps are gone now, except for a sprinkling of angry blisters under each eye. Breathe: normal, easy, *facile*. Zoe is quiet and still, red hands tucked between her swollen face and her mother's lap like when she was a toddler. Allergy attacks have always made Zoe sleepy and that was by far the worst they'd ever experienced. Thank god this truck came along when it did.

From the corner of her eye, Patricia admires the driver, a stranger to her but serious and rugged beneath a vintage 1990s Oilers ball cap. Norm, was it? There's something to be said about the strong and silent type, those heroes who move through the world completely self-sufficient, packing blankets, extra jerry cans of gas, the tools necessary to unwrap crumbled metal from around a woman's leg. She wonders what the man sees when he looks at her.

"So, you work around here?" she asks.

"Up north," Norm says. He turns up the radio and the urgent narration of a *Hockey Night in Canada* broadcast fills the cab. Patricia shuts her mouth.

There was a time when Patricia's body in a man's passenger seat would be thanks enough, but now she feels her voice pitch too high, her smile set too wide, her eagerness come across as desperate. Is she as pathetic as she thinks? Maybe she'd just been married too long. Norm's young-ish, maybe late twenties, but she's only thirty-three. That's also young, but motherhood ages a person fast. If Zoe weren't here, would the driver consider Patricia a *girl*, or merely a *woman*? She thinks about the teenager that stopped to help on road, so thin and beautiful and innocent. Patricia made her get help. Is the driver disappointed that the woman in the cab isn't the same girl that waved to him from the road?

Patricia catches herself thinking these things and almost snorts. Why does she care? With age comes wisdom, strength, confidence. What had the girl said when Patricia told her to go flag a truck down?

"Maybe I could push the van out."

Oh, honey. Why so scared? Well, yes, hitchhiking should be scary, but this was an emergency. Summon courage, girl! Woman up! Patricia had to wonder what she was running from. Trouble at home? She runs her hand over Zoe's cheek. Some people just don't understand how to treasure a child.

Patricia scans her body, one part at a time, like they teach in yoga. Her leg is still sore but it's only a bruise. She points her toes, rolls her ankle, tests the calf. No real damage, thank goodness. But the nausea, the trembling in her hands, that image of Zoe having an attack just out of Patricia's reach . . . she closes her eyes, reminds herself to take a deep breath.

Just wait until she gets a hold of Al. Is she ever going to tell him exactly what his stingy men's-rights bullshit almost did to their daughter. Three children Patricia gave him and this is how he treats her? How he values the family they made? The greedy bastard, leaving her without enough money to get the headlights fixed; a divorcee with no resume, no pension, no credit, and now, no vehicle. Patricia doesn't know what she was thinking, ever trusting him. Except yes, she does. She was thinking he meant it when he said he loved her, when he said their kids deserved a parent at home, when he said that by supporting him she was supporting the whole family. How many steps had she taken, busting her ass at scummy diners when he couldn't get his act together? How many columns had she written for him, the hack unable to grasp even the basics of reader engagement? How could she have known fourteen years would turn into a locked office and hushed conversations over a secret phone line? Him—Baldy McGirl's Voice—cheating on her!

Asshole. Sometimes Patricia wonders how he's doing so well. Al got promoted from reporter to editor just before they broke up, but the *Sherwood Park Weekly* is still just a small paper; it can't pay well enough to support his big new house and all those toys he shows off in the double driveway. It's never made complete sense how he's made ends meet, but Patricia guesses she wasn't brave enough to ask, not when things were going well between them. Sometimes she wonders whether she should be worried if Al's up to something illegal. Selling drugs, maybe? She almost laughs at the thought. Not that wimpy weasel. Gambling? God knows he spends enough time in front of a computer screen. Online poker? Maybe. She snorts, silently, in her head. Is he even smart enough for that? He wouldn't have graduated college if it weren't for her help.

Zoe shivers in her sleep, pulls the stranger's thin blanket tighter around her shoulders.

"Can we turn up the heat?" Patricia gently asks.

The driver leans over the dashboard, closing vents and turning others so the air blows directly on Zoe. "High as she goes, sorry."

"That's perfect, thank you. You've done so much."

Patricia rubs her daughter's arm like when she was little and fresh from the bath. Blisters at the back of her baby's throat. Patricia's still in shock. It was only a matter of time before they swelled big enough to cut off the airway entirely. What if the truck hadn't come along? No. Don't think about it. Think about what *actually* happened.

What actually happened?

Clicking, or lack thereof, to be clearer. That's what woke her up, the sense that a ceiling fan had suddenly shut off. It must have been the girl on the highway, turning off the van's ignition. At first, Patricia thought she had fallen asleep on the couch. A red wine night? How much had she drunk? Everything felt slow and wet. Had she peed herself? It was too cold to be the living room, and yet there was television static. Who was rustling papers? Why weren't they in bed?

Zoe's voice, like she was talking in her sleep. "Are you dead?"

A stranger: "Are you?"

Snap. Patricia snapped out of it, just like the saying goes. Just like a flick of the wrist, fingers and thumb. The girl from the road was there just outside the minivan, looking in through the open passenger's side door. It wasn't television static in front of Patricia, but moonlight on broken glass. River water drenched her yoga pants, and the rustling was the wind. They'd been in an accident, Patricia realized, but they could sleep a while yet.

"She means missing or murdered," Patricia remembers saying mid-yawn, explaining Zoe's are-you-dead question to the girl.

Then there was silence, until: "What's wrong with her face?"

Snap. Snap, snap, snap.

Patricia's mother brain woke up and took over—clear, whole, alert. She reached over to the passenger seat and turned Zoe's face so she could see.

"Oh my god."

Her daughter had erupted in thick, white hives, her eyelids swollen shut. Patricia twisted around to kneel on the driver's seat but realized she was stuck, her left leg vice-gripped under the steering wheel.

"She's allergic," Patricia told the girl. "Allergic to the cold."

The girl got straight to work. She stripped Zoe out of her wet jeans and soaked Uggs. She wrapped her in her own oversized parka, shielding her face with the faux fur hood. Zoe stood shivering, barefoot and barelegged in the ditch as the girl yanked open the back sliding door, laying Zoe on the backbench seat, out of the wind, out of the water, stopping to call out only once: "Oh, she's throwing up!"

But still the girl climbed in and pulled Zoe onto her lap, holding her close despite the vomit. She rocked her, singing a sweet, sad song.

"I know you," Patricia said, realizing. "I shared your video on Facebook. You're Alberta's rising star, that one with the song about lost mothers. 'Niy Gah We' or something? I was like that when I was young. Creative, I mean. My teacher thought I'd become a poet."

The girl stopped rocking and looked at Zoe.

"Her breathing is . . . like . . . it sounds like she has to cough."

The hives had made their way into her throat.

But then, on the highway, a flicker of light.

Thank god!

The man pulled onto the shoulder with shelter and heat and blankets and a first aid kit, the proper tools to open the stuck glove compartment and retrieve Zoe's EpiPen.

But for such a monster of a truck, there's not much room up front. Patricia looks back at the road through the side-view mirror. She thinks of the girl's skinny legs and heavy hockey bag, her long black hair and sharp cheekbones. That parka must be wet. Patricia hopes she isn't cold. It's so dangerous out there. Why would someone put herself into such a risky situation? There's no excuse but no telling some people. Of course, the girl probably walks that route all the time, living so rural. She'd probably be more scared of the city's rush-hour traffic than a quiet highway at midnight. Funny how differently people live. Still, a line of traffic sparkles in the distance. "I feel awful leaving her behind."

"Don't worry," Norm says. "There must be fifty guys behind us. Someone will pick her up."

The game cuts to commercial and he turns the volume down.

"So, what happened to your kid's face again?"

Patricia's gaze shifts from the distant figure of someone else's daughter to her own. She's allergic to low temperatures, Patricia tells him.

"The cold blisters her skin."

NEEDLEPOINT

JUNE 2009

LIGHT CREEPS ONTO Miranda's face so she covers her head with her blanket. Her grandmother is home from greeting the solstice sun, slow steps creaking the front porch.

Step, step, shuffle, shuffle.

Miranda listens to hear the mood in the old woman's walk. If the next sounds are quiet, she'll make her way to Miranda's room and sit on the bed and stroke her hair.

Wake up, baby girl.

Instead:

SLAM. Step, step. Step-step-step-step-step.

Oh shit, Kohkum's pissed.

Miranda holds her breath but the house falls silent. She kicks off her blanket and covers herself with the Snuggie that matches Kohkum's housecoat; Kohkum always loves to see her in that. Miranda runs her fingers through her hair and walks the hallway with one shoulder to the wall, tilting her head to peek into her grandmother's room at the opposite end of their mobile home.

Almost no one meets the sunrise, only old folk squinting over the lake through transition lenses. Besides, it's not like Miranda was being lazy. She spent all night writing a song. Being grounded, it's about all she's allowed to do.

Five weeks. That's how long it's been since the *Canada's Got Talent* auditions, and that's how long Kohkum's rules have been:

No friends.

No phone.

No boys.

No nothin.'

She isn't even allowed to watch television; Kohkum moved it to the Healing Lodge and has been taking in the evening news there ever since. Kohkum's been so strict with the no-outside-influences thing she didn't even care when Miranda stopped going to school and registered for distance learning. She actually *wants* Miranda to finish Grade 12 without any friends.

Not that Miranda should complain. She's kind of happy to be housebound after the whole Edmonton disaster. She's finished ten new songs, enough for a whole album no one will ever hear. It's like the *Canada's Got Talent* judges said, Miranda just isn't what they're looking for. Just because people sang along doesn't mean they'd buy her albums. Sure, they invited her to try again at the Calgary auditions, but what can Miranda do? People want vanilla cupcake princesses warbling about sex, money, and boys, not fry-bread warriors screaming pain over missing mothers and ghosts. Besides, the Calgary auditions are tomorrow and there aren't any buses running. Miranda already checked.

The unfairness of it all makes Miranda so dizzy-tired she couldn't meet the sun even if she wanted to.

Well . . . that's a lie.

Truth is, she would have met the sun had Grayson been there. But yesterday Kohkum mentioned his dad wouldn't be emceeing National Aboriginal Day events until the afternoon because the family had to pick up a new vehicle and they'd either still be making their way home from the city in the morning or sleeping off a long night's drive. It's about time they got a new car, the way that old minivan ticks and screeches and roars. There isn't anything really wrong with it, Grayson said, except it's so loud. Miranda wonders if Grayson will get the minivan now that his dad has replaced it. She hopes so, even if she never gets to ride in it again. For Grayson, Miranda only wants good things.

She misses him so much.

He hasn't talked to her since the morning he picked her up from the truck stop all those many weeks ago. She doesn't even know if they're still dating or if the silence is his way of breaking up.

"What were you thinking?" he cried, wiping his eyes with the sleeve of his coat. "What if someone just took you? You could have been murdered. Raped."

Miranda's cheeks burn just thinking about it. She hates the R word and the thought of him thinking of her like that: naked and hurt and used. She kept her head down but watched how his knuckles paled as he gripped the steering wheel.

"I would have driven you," he said as they pulled into Kohkum's driveway. "You know she'd rather you had been safe with me than alone."

Miranda wanted to kiss him goodbye, but Kohkum was already there by the front door, arms crossed over her nightgown, in anger but also in modesty because it was too early for a bra. Miranda shook her head and slid from the passenger seat.

"You don't know my Kohkum."

If she'd known they'd be her last words to him, she would have said something different.

Kohkum folds clothes into a dusty carpetbag with her back to the door. Miranda knows she's probably donating the whole thing to the thrift store. Kohkum takes a new donation there once a week; she doesn't believe in keeping anything duplicate, unwanted, or outgrown, only things useful or loved. Which makes it surprising that the old carpetbag has lasted this long. Kohkum hasn't used it since she got Miranda back. The last time the old woman left the reserve was to testify at her kinship care application hearing, and ever since then Kohkum's said she's seen enough of the city to last a lifetime. Kohkum doesn't approve of people leaving their traditions, their communities, their families—basically, of having any aspirations at all.

"Many people at the sunrise?" Miranda asks.

"Not as many as there should have been."

"I was up late working on lyrics."

Kohkum doesn't turn around. Miranda leans against the doorframe. *Judgemental*, that's what Uncle Wilf called Kohkum when he'd found Miranda sitting outside West Edmonton Mall's Entrance 3B with the bunker bag/guitar case over her lap, her audition postponed due to higher-than-anticipated contestant sign-ups. Miranda couldn't believe he'd found her; she'd thought she'd have to spend the night alone on a bench somewhere. Wilf laughed and said the coincidence didn't surprise him at all. Hadn't he found her in that hospital when she was just little, back after her mom left and Miranda was put in government care?

"Heard you wailing from the waiting room and could have recognized those pipes anywhere! Best day of my life when that nurse said Kohkum got you home. Knowing you was home was what made me go back again myself, as long as I could stand it, anyway. Kid, I'm like your guardian angel." He raised his hands like Jesus on the cross. "Patron Saint of Kicked-Out Runaways."

Miranda laughed. She wasn't kicked out or a runaway, just trying to make something of herself. Wilf waved off the explanation with someone else's discarded smoke butt stuck between his thick fingers.

"She's too controlling, your Kohkum." He pulled a bundle from his own old red bag and handed Miranda half a sandwich. She tore into the stale white bread.

"You know she's the one who dried out the rez? Doesn't want to let anyone make their own decisions, just treats everyone like little kids and chucks 'em out when they're grown up enough to have their own say. Just look at me and Amy—both of us came back when we could, but we couldn't stay, could we?"

Miranda swallowed. "She talks about you guys all the time. And Amy—"

"I know, I know. Lots of excuses. But it's easier to talk about someone than live with 'em, isn't it? Watch yourself. Don't get big too fast, my girl."

Miranda hadn't believed Wilf, but Kohkum *has* been cold since she came back. She crosses the room to the open closet.

"What do you think I should wear today?" She's scheduled to perform at the Healing Lodge's gates, welcoming folks to the celebrations.

"Probably not the Snuggie."

Miranda takes a breath to steel herself against her grandmother's sarcasm. She turns her attention to the clothes on Kohkum's hangers, running her fingers over the menagerie of worn sweaters with kittens or cartoon characters printed on the front, buck-hide jackets and bright knit shawls reserved for days like today. She stops at the very last item, fingertips stroking scarlet red fabric.

Mom's dress.

It's the only thing Kohkum kept after Mom went missing. Mom basically lived in it, Miranda's told, fancying up the cotton shift for job interviews and dates, wearing it down with flip-flops for days at the beach. She'd even pair the sundress with work boots and black feather earrings to accessorize all edgy-like for rock concerts. Mom loved to sing. Miranda knows red is for bravery and luck. When she was little, she used to pretend the dress had powers. Her mom probably felt invincible in it, too. If she'd paired it with a hat and cowboy boots instead of wearing Wrangler jeans, would she still have gone missing on the way to Stampede?

Outside, an imposter outfit hangs on the clothesline. When the Red Dress Project invited Indigenous families to hang one for each woman they'd lost, Kohkum bought a wine-hued gown from the thrift store. To Miranda, the second-hand cloth on the line outside is the exact opposite of the one hidden away. Mom's real dress—simple, classic, bright as birdsong—stays by the mother and daughter she left behind, the ones who dream of her stepping back into it still.

There, Miranda thinks: there's a song in there, somewhere.

Miranda lifts the hanger from the rack. She's grown. Now the dress would fit.

"What about this?"

Kohkum looks up and drops a cardigan onto the bed.

"It would suit you," Kohkum whispers. The old woman walks to her dresser and opens a drawer, retrieving a deer hide sash embroidered with fine and careful needlepoint, each stitch made with a prayer of protection and love, every bead placed exactly where it's meant to be, together creating a thing greater than each individual bead, a work of small, intricate, exquisite beauty.

She hands the belt to Miranda. "With this," she says, "and your pointy moccasins."

Kohkum leaves the room and Miranda hugs the outfit to her chest. She stays beside the closet for a few beats to give Kohkum space in the kitchen. Big pain is difficult in small homes; so little room for clumsy, bulky hurt. She stares at the hide belt in her arms and notices a single bead is loose, liable to drop off and break the string, taking the next row with it. Miranda finds a needle from the box on Kohkum's dresser and pins it into the back of the belt. She'll fix it later, when there's time.

She starts to leave the room but something in Kohkum's travel bag catches Miranda's eye. A familiar design peeks out from under the discarded items.

Kohkum's matching bathrobe.

Twinsies.

Apparently, it's a thing Kohkum doesn't need anymore.

❋

A teenage girl—obviously a visitor—waves hello to Miranda as her family enters the Healing Lodge grounds. Miranda smiles back, fingers too busy strumming to return the gesture. Does she know the girl? People have been pointing and taking pictures all morning, making Miranda feel like there must be something on her face. Is her dress hiked up under the belt? She leans a little to the left and feels the sewing needle she pinned into the deer hide, so no, the skirt can't be too bunched. It's not like Miranda's in regalia, so why the interest?

The sound of community hums all around Miranda but one note rings clear above the rest. Nancy Isadore sings beside Miranada as she plays, and Miranda tries to focus on her teacher's sweet voice as it carries as high as the stars beyond the blue day, the proof of them drowned out by light but there nonetheless. It was Nancy who taught Miranda how to balance the base of Uncle Wilf's old guitar on Kohkum's kitchen chairs when she was too little to bear its full weight. Before the Edmonton auditions, Nancy asked Miranda to join her music school as an assistant teacher, but she hasn't brought it up again since. Does Nancy think Miranda's selfish for running off to the city when she spent her own life creating opportunities for the kids at home? Does she think Miranda's a hypocrite now, representing the Nation when she so recently tried to escape it?

A little girl squeals as she exits the tepee set up for children's crafts and Miranda watches as the child turns back to Kohkum, behind her, who carries a beaded keychain the child must have forgotten. The little one lifts her arms for a hug and Miranda can all but smell the wild rose water on Kohkum's skin.

Don't get big too fast.

Miranda watches a moment longer and senses she's being watched, too. The arena's been set up for local merchants and artisans to offer their products before and after the ceremonies, which will take place behind the building, under the solstice sun. People stream in and out of the arena doors. Beyond Kohkum and the girl, Grayson leans against the wall.

Miranda's cheeks burn when she meets his gaze. His face is darker than it was that last morning, his skin tanned by a sunny late spring, eyes intensified by the lines painted on his cheekbones and forehead for the dance. Everything in Miranda's body tells her Grayson is powerful and strong in the very best way. She doesn't turn away.

A drum signals the start of the celebration. Miranda tucks her guitar into the bunker bag and Nancy packs up to join the main event. It's already been decided Miranda will stay at the gate alone to direct latecomers. Visitors filter in line behind the arena from the east, mimicking the course of the sun. Dancers ready themselves for the grand entry. Grayson stares at Miranda until a red-lipped jingle dress dancer steps between their gaze and Miranda watches his hand float to the small of the girl's back. More dancers line up and when the line parts, Grayson is gone.

The people are all hidden from Miranda's view now, but the drums thunder, singers vocalizing all the world's courage and pain and victory. If a drumbeat is like the sound infants hear before birth, this procession song is the arrival of a thousand babies all at once, mothers' hearts pounding and throats crying out, fathers calling them down from the sky. Miranda imagines a baby being tricked: answering the call only to find no one's waiting around to love her, instead she's all alone and scared and confused and starts to think she's not good enough in a million tiny different ways.

It's not fair.

It's so unfair.

But it could be a song, and then it would be a little less painful.

The drumming turns to silence and then prayers ring out over a loudspeaker. Miranda bows her head and studies the wild roses Kohkum sewed onto her moccasins, beads burning so bright they hurt. She closes her eyes and lifts her face to the sun. Everything in its heat tells her she too is powerful and strong in the very best way, and Miranda doesn't turn away. Instead she breathes deep, catching the scent of sweetgrass carried on the breeze.

The smudge smells nothing like campfire, but Miranda thinks of Uncle Wilf.

He'd taken her to a lean-to by the North Saskatchewan River and insisted she rest under the only blanket he owned, bunching leaves beneath the tarp floor with the same care Kohkum used to plump couch cushions. After building a fire he played his harmonica so Miranda wouldn't have to keep up conversation. She drifted to sleep amid the sound of river waves and fire crackles and lonesome notes, waking only to recognize the song he played.

"Nikâwiy?"

"Saw your YouTube at the library, little niece. Even I've got more internet than you folk up north."

Miranda felt safe and happy, nervous but hopeful, tired but dreaming of small, friendly rooms.

When she woke again the night was dark and cold. The fire fried her cheeks and nose while her sneakered toes froze, poking out from under Wilf's too-short covers. Across the flames sat a boy.

Wilf's head began to drop, but he roused a last burst of energy to stretch his legs over Miranda's lap before lying back and disappearing into guttural snores. The boy crossed the campfire to take a still-lit smoke from Wilf's fingers, and then he sat beside Miranda.

He finished the smoke and then lit a joint and Miranda smoked some too. She laughed when Wilf yelled out in his sleep and giggled as the boy wrestled the half-empty forty of rye from her uncle's grip. She'd already broken most of Kohkum's rules, so turn by turn Miranda helped the boy drain the bottle as she watched embers glow and fly and burn out in the sky. The boy put his hand on her knee and she didn't care.

"Where you from?" he asked.

"My cousin works up there," he said, after she told him. "Or nearby, anyway. In camp. Maybe I'll drop in and see you sometime."

He tried to kiss her.

"I have a boyfriend," she said.

"Shh," he replied. "It'll be like it never even happened."

The boy's hand must have slid too high and tickled Wilf's feet because the last thing Miranda remembers is her uncle's foot aimed at the seat of the boy's baggy pants as he ran away.

The next day, the pounding of a jogger's steps on a nearby trail jolted Miranda into a morning hazy with the smoke of a northern forest fire, the sun as weak-yellow as shame. When she stood, she realized Wilf had pissed himself and urine had collected on the tarp before absorbing into her jeans. She walked to the bank of the river and threw up on the rocks before taking off her pants to wash them. When she returned to the lean-to, Wilf was still sleeping. His empty bottle lay on top of Miranda's bunker bag. She'd stolen from him, Miranda realized. She left the bottle on the grass and, remembering the way, slipped off to West Edmonton Mall.

Miranda's shoulders burned as though the bunker bag contained everything Kohkum had ever given away. Her wet sneakers squished puddles onto the sidewalk. Her face was hot and dry, and her back tensed in the early morning chill. The line to audition had already formed inside the mall, long and snaking. The competition's producers gave her a bottle of water, but other contestants kept their space. Three hours later, Miranda was next.

"Remember," a stagehand told her, "five minutes only. Go over and the buzzer will sound."

Miranda's knees shook. There was a stool to sit on, but the microphone was rigged too high so Miranda just stood, centre stage. Under the mall's large sunroof, the expressions of every tired shopper, every toddler-juggling mother, every arms-crossed teenager, and every phone-checking clerk who'd taken a rest on *Canada's Got Talent*'s folding chairs felt so near that Miranda wondered if they could smell the campfire on her skin. Her jeans had dried stiff around her legs. She tried to run a hand through her hair, but her fingers got stuck in the knots. Dried mud crunched around the sides of her sneakers. Why had she brought the bunker bag on stage? Miranda glanced to her right and saw the stagehand. Hurry up, he mouthed, finger ticking a bare wrist.

She started to sing but realized she hadn't started strumming yet. She mumbled an apology to the crowd and found the chords but the pacing was off—first too fast and then too slow. Stumped, she looked to the audience. Someone coughed and someone else laughed.

And then, from the crowd, the opening notes of "Nikâwiy."

Heads swivelled to locate the rogue musician, but Miranda didn't skip a beat. She whispered the first line in melody with the harmonica and cradled the head of the microphone as if it were the face of a tiny child and her voice contained all the love that little girl would ever need. She closed her eyes and her hands found the guitar strings and when she reached the chorus a second time more voices had joined, others clapping in time. The buzzer rang and, through tears, Miranda saw the crowd rise to their feet. The judges asked questions and were complimentary, and the crowd booed as they delivered their final decision.

When Miranda stepped off stage, Wilf was gone. She walked to the bus station alone, and, just as the boy said, it was like it never happened.

The growl of a diesel engine pulls Miranda from the memory. A large truck turns into the Healing Lodge parking lot. When it stops the world is silent again but for the arena's distant drumming. A large man exits the truck and walks to the tailgate, retrieving an aluminum can that glints in the sun. His passenger, tall and thin in a tank top and baggy cargo pants, lights a cigarette while he waits for his friend to finish his drink. The driver belches and pulls out a case of beer from the truck box after chucking the can over his shoulder. The pair meets Miranda at the Healing Grounds' gate.

"It's a dry event." She smiles in apology, nodding to the case of beer.

The large man grunts and shakes his head. He lowers the box to the grass and starts to open another can when Miranda interrupts.

"A dry community, actually. You're not supposed to drink anywhere."

"Listen to her, man," the scrawny one says, "or her uncle will kick your ass." He smiles and steps closer. "You don't remember me, do you?" He lowers his sunglasses. "Rodney?"

Miranda blushes. The boy from Edmonton. But in the daylight, he's older than she thought: crow's feet and thinning hair.

"What are you doing here?"

Rodney laughs. "Didn't I say I'd come see you sometime?" He points at the larger man with his thumb. "My cousin. It's National Aboriginal Day! We heard there was a party here."

"It's a celebration. Just, the Elders are pretty strict on alcohol."

The fat man shrugs. "Well, I'm out. Work way too hard to sit around starin' at folks on days off." He heads to the truck, calling behind him, "You comin', Rod?"

"Give me a minute!" Rodney turns back to Miranda. "Listen, we're heading south for a couple of days. Wanna come to Calgary?"

Despite the heat, a chill runs down Miranda's spine. Calgary equals auditions. The timing's too right and she knows it's not smart, but this feels like a second chance. Rodney's cousin bellows again and Miranda thinks quickly, all alone at the highest point of the year's longest day.

"Only two nights? You promise?"

Rodney smiles and winks.

Be like it never happened.

※

The backseat is like a recycling station exploded. Miranda's squished in the middle, bunker bag and guitar on one side, Rodney on the other. Cans and bottles litter the floor around her feet, some beer but mostly energy drinks and cola, used Tim Hortons coffee cups with their rims not even rolled up to check for prizes. Rodney puts his arm around her shoulders and tells his cousin to find some music.

"How far to Calgary?" Miranda yells over static of talk-radio.

The driver doesn't answer.

"Nervous already?" Rodney tightens his arm and leans in. His words are soft and slow like they mean something else, some kind of invitation. So close, too close, Miranda can see he's so much older than she thought. There's grey hair at his temples. His nose is bumpy and crooked, like someone broke it once.

"So what's with the no drinking?" the driver yells back. "You guys don't like to have fun?"

Rodney answers for her. "No, man, this girl parties! It's her grandma who's strict." He winks at Miranda. "Your uncle told me about her rules."

"Shit. My grandma wouldn't know what hit her. It'd be my fist!" The driver bellows to his own joke as if expecting a big laugh.

The chill down Miranda's spine turns into a creep all over as Rodney's fingers curl to linger at the top of her breast. Rodney leans in, lips almost touching her ear. Miranda feels his breath on her cheek.

"He's just kidding."

Outside, the highway's little white crosses come into view. Miranda thinks of Grayson and wonders how long until someone notices she's gone. The dance must be wrapping up soon; they've already driven halfway to the truck stop.

"So how you people let loose then?" the driver starts again. "You sing songs to each other?" He mocks "Kumbaya" in falsetto.

The truck passes the *Curve Ahead* sign and Miranda thinks of how she and Grayson used to cruise in his dad's minivan doing just that, singing with the radio. Would Grayson be jealous if he saw her like this? No. He'd think she was pathetic, silent under the arm of a slack-skinned, middle-aged man. Rodney puts his other hand on Miranda's thigh and tells the driver to knock it off.

"Come on, man. You never been to a round dance before? They, like, eat moose meat and bannock and stuff."

Miranda's heart races. She'd forgotten about dinner. She tries not to breathe so fast. Every time her lungs empty the hand resting over her collarbone slips a little lower. She's meant to serve Kohkum dinner. It's tradition, but who will do it now? Rodney squeezes her leg and dread swirls in Miranda's gut. There won't even *be* a dinner now, will there? People will start searching once Kohkum realizes Miranda's gone. She thinks of Nancy's angry disappointment, of Kohkum's shaking hands. She thinks of Grayson: pale, maybe even crying but trying to hide it like when he said she could have been killed.

"I think . . . I think I need to stop."

"What?" the driver says. "You didn't piss at home?"

"I just want out." She gathers the straps of her bunker bag.

"Relax," Rodney says. "There's a truck stop coming up, you can go there."

"I want out now," Miranda shouts. "Stop the truck!"

The men complain, but Miranda isn't asking permission. She reaches over Rodney's knees and pulls the handle herself.

The highway speeds underneath the open door. Rodney yells and the driver curses and cans fall out as the truck swerves to the side of the road. Doors open and the driver stands, shaking his head as he lights a cigarette and cracks the tab of a fresh beer. Miranda climbs out after Rodney and swings the straps of the red bag over her shoulder. She starts off home but Rodney grabs her wrist, pulling her back, pinning her against the truck.

"Where are you going?"

"Let go of me."

"Why? Why do you have to go home?"

He drops his head down quick and hard and she feels his teeth on hers as his tongue probes her mouth. She tries to bite but he grips her jaw with his hand, pushing the inside of her cheeks between her molars, other arm pushing her toward the open door. Gravel slides under Miranda's pointy moccasins as his hands snatch for better control at her hip. The smooth, hard flowers stitched onto her grandmother's belt press against Miranda's wrist as her hand frantically searches. Suddenly, Rodney yelps and jumps back.

Miranda runs. In one hand, she grips the straps of the bunker bag on her shoulder. In the other, the beading needle freshly pulled from between Rodney's scrawny, sensitive ribs.

✳

Despite the branches and potholes that try pull her from flight, Miranda soars off the highway, down its gravelly banks to the soft ditch and then to the forest's treeline, without breaking pace. It isn't until she feels the coolness of tree shade and hears the buzzing of mosquitoes that she dares to look back. Rodney kicks a truck tire and spits on the road before getting into the front passenger seat. His cousin laughs in that same loud bellow as before, zipping his jeans after pissing in Miranda's general direction. Then the truck starts and the radio blares and the men are gone.

Miranda sighs in relief but doesn't wait to catch her breath. With luck she can get home before anyone has noticed she's gone. Miranda pins the needle into the front of the dress and gathers the hem in her hands to keep it from the quick fingers of thorny shrubs. She walks until the treeline is too thick to navigate. Checking the road is empty first, she walks to the highway's wide-open ditch, safe in the knowledge that there's no one there to see her. The world is silent but for birdsong and her own footsteps—and *there*: there's a song in there somewhere, too.

And then, a tick and a screech and a roar.

Grayson.

His father's minivan appears through the heat lines waving over hot asphalt. Miranda climbs the ditch bank to meet the van as it pulls to the side of the road. Grayson sits in the driver's seat in near-full regalia: eyes shining, the painted lines underneath them smudged. He unrolls the window.

"There was a beer can in the parking lot and you weren't there," he said. "I almost told your Kohkum, but then the truck drove past. I saw you in the backseat, so I ran home to get the van and followed you. I didn't like the feeling I got, seeing you in that truck."

"I'm sorry. Will your dad be mad you took the van?"

"It's mine now."

"Oh yeah, your parents just bought a new one. I thought that might hap—"

"Just get in."

Miranda opens the passenger side door, climbs in, and sits.

"No one knows you're gone yet," he says. "They were still dancing when I left."

"Why did you leave?"

"I wanted to talk to you."

"I was stupid," Miranda says. "Again."

She doesn't look at his knuckles this time. She turns her head so he can see her face. "I was invited to audition in Calgary, but I shouldn't have tried to go. The guys I got in with . . . they weren't good. I don't know why I went with them."

"You tried to go because you're meant to sing. You should be making music and people should hear it. I get it. You have dreams. That's good."

Miranda shakes her head. "No, it's not worth it. I ruined every-thing. Kohkum doesn't even look at me anymore; Nancy doesn't want me to teach. And . . . you." Her voice cracks and she lets him hear it. "I really miss you."

Grayson looks over and Miranda doesn't hide the tears running down her face. He takes her hand in his and rests their arms on the console between them.

"What if . . . what if you just gave it a minute? What if you just gave the rest of us a chance to catch up?" He looks back to the road. "You're not as alone as you think you are."

He squeezes her hand and the strap of Uncle Wilf's bunker bag falls from her shoulder. Kohkum's sewing needle presses against Miranda's chest.

※

Kohkum's hands shake as they accept the plate of stew and bannock Miranda lowers to the table. Miranda kisses her grandmother's cheek and Kohkum holds her face in her palms. For a moment there is no one else in the busy dining room.

After all the Elders and teachers have been served by younger friends or family members, Miranda lines up again to receive her own meal before rejoining Kohkum's table. Grayson's father takes the podium and welcomes all attendees and speaks of the importance of family, of hope, of strength. He speaks of the wounds he suffered as a younger man, and the grief he still tends to daily. He tells the others how he stumbled after the death of his daughter and unborn grandchild almost fifteen years ago, and how he almost let that loss cost him every other good thing. And then, he speaks of the teacher who brought him back from that brink, the woman who used the wisdom in her own pain to heal others. Kohkum lifts her glasses to dab Kleenex under her eye and Miranda realizes it is Kohkum Grayson's father is speaking about.

Grayson's father asks Kohkum to join him on stage and Miranda leads her grandmother up the stairs, arm in arm. The Healing Lodge's common area is to be renamed in Kohkum's honour.

"May your life be long and your legacy continue far, far beyond it."

A ribbon is tied from one part of the stage to the other, and Kohkum is asked to cut it. She grips the handles of the large scissors with each hand and Miranda wonders if *this* could be her life's *actual* purpose, continuing Kohkum's legacy of healing.

It's never too late to return the way you came, Kohkum always says.

Miranda knows "like it never happened" is no way to live.

The women are about to leave the stage when Grayson's father raises his hand and asks them to stay. He invites Grayson and Nancy to join them. Miranda gasps as she sees the item her teacher carries, and audience members laugh. Grayson takes the stage stairs two at a time and presents Miranda with a wild rose. She covers her mouth with her hand and Grayson kisses her cheek.

"What is this?" Miranda whispers.

Grayson winks. "Just give it a minute."

Grayson's father turns to the audience. He describes Miranda's recent audition as a testament to courage, strength, and the sacred love between family members.

"It is no surprise so many were touched by the power of Miranda's performance," he continues. "All people long for truth. Truth, that day, sang into a microphone."

"Someone taped you," Grayson whispers as his father continues to speak. "It starts with you looking really nervous and then all of a sudden a guy in the audience—your uncle? He starts to play his harmonica and then you just . . . explode. It's amazing, the way he plays for you, the way you sing back. The video went crazy on social media—like, *viral*. And now . . . well, people want to meet you. In particular, people at a record label in Toronto."

"It's why you needed to finish a whole album," Nancy says, keeping her lips still and her voice low. "Why everyone's been leaving you alone to get it done."

Miranda wipes her eyes. "Well, I was also grounded!"

Kohkum murmurs out the corner of her mouth, "You were only grounded the first week. After that we just limited the distractions."

Nancy is invited to hand Miranda what she has brought up: an actual hard-shell guitar case with a soft buck-hide cover sewn to the top, beaded flowers stitched in intricate design, each one bright in the stage lights.

"So now you're really ready to shine."

Grayson holds up the keys to the old minivan. "We leave tomorrow morning. They offered to fly us but *someone* insisted we drive."

"No one's putting me in a tin can up in the sky." Kohkum crosses her arms over her chest.

The audience laughs and Miranda shakes her head. She reaches for Kohkum's hand. The words won't come strong, so Miranda whispers what she needs to say.

"You'd leave home for me?"

Kohkum pats her granddaughter's hand, dark eyes shining behind gold frames.

"My girl," she says, and smiles. "The carpet bag's already packed."

HOCKEY MOM

2011

THE MILLENNIUM PLACE locker room is like every other locker room Lacey has ever waited in. A bench wraps whitewashed walls and a narrow doorway leads to showers in the back. The digital scoreboard reads 3–2 for the home team, the time of day in smaller numbers. There's a warm stink despite the arena's chill. Lacey sits near the exit. It's her turn to bring snacks and today she's made a special treat.

The boys don't usually play Monday morning games, what with school and all, but the Kings take on the Edmonton Drillers every Family Day and the game always fills the stands. A talent scout from the University of Victoria is even visiting, which, sure, is a big deal for *all* the boys, but for Lacey's youngest it's a *very* big deal. Two years ago the twins were scouted during their Family Day game, and it's a no-brainer Denny will be picked next to join his brothers. Dave wanted to be here, but he has to take work whenever he can get it ever since the Stelmach government made such a mess of the oil royalty review. "You don't bite the hand that feeds you," is what Dave has to say about that. Dave is so smart.

Yasmin Rhanji nurses baby Suni by Lacey's side. The association mothers work in pairs and the women are around the same age, but Yasmin probably thinks Lacey is older. Most of the moms could pass as Lacey's daughters, what with their skinny jeans and straightened hair and designer scarves. They could pass for the groupies that litter the twins' Facebook pages, the girls that keep her sons too busy to visit their mom now and then.

Well, motherhood sure is different from when Lacey was growing up. Used to be that moms took care of everyone, but now women spend more time looking at their phones than they do their kids. Some even have housekeepers. It doesn't seem right; no one at home when oilmen make decent money anyhow. That's what she told Dave the last time he was home from camp, anyway.

She was putting lotion on her elbows as he came out of the bathroom with a towel round his waist and dirty laundry in hand.

"Well, nothing seems right 'til you're the one doing it," he answered.

"It's so selfish, though. These women only care about making their lives look so much better than everyone else's. Do you know Kelly Anderson went away for business for a whole week? And she gets a facial every single month!" Lacey fluffed her bangs with her palms, feeling whether or not the hairspray had kept its lift. "I haven't even changed my hairdo since having the twins. I mean, what kind of mother has time for things like that?"

"Well, at least Kelly's making money. And there's nothing wrong with her wanting to look nice for Anderson."

Lacey laughed. "Pft! What does Kelly Anderson need more money for? Her husband's a doctor, for goodness sake, one of those special brain ones at the U of A. Anyway, my mom always said a woman's number one job is her family. Not getting all done up or trying to act so smart."

Dave rolled his eyes. He threw his clothes at the hamper before dropping the towel on the floor and climbing into bed. "That's crazy talk. Lots of women handle kids and work. Why can't you be like them? It's not like we need you around here anymore. You know, you can be a bit of a bully where these other girls are concerned, Lace."

"A bully!" Lacey started to cry. "Would a bully be in charge of Pink Shirt Day at Denny's school, a day all about *not bullying*? No, no she would not!"

"You're right," Dave said, reaching for his iPad. "I don't want to fight."

"It's just so unfair!" Lacey said. "Moms do everything around the house but now we're supposed to make tons of money and look like teenagers too? Like, just give it up! Drop the yoga and find the glue gun! Put on sweats and winter weight! Make crafts, not conference calls! Be a mom, for crying out loud. I'd like to embroider pillows with those sayings and hand them out at Christmas. That would be funny."

"Yeah," Dave said. "Funny."

He put the tablet on a doily Lacey had crocheted herself and turned out the light. Lacey watched him sleep, daring herself to reach over, stroke him, wake him up. In the end she decided she couldn't stand the thought of his hands on her big hips so soon after putting that skinny Kelly Anderson in his mind.

Her face gets hot at the memory of it. She leans back against the locker room wall and hopes Yasmin can't see the blush Lacey feels. Lacey combs her fringe so it makes vertical lines over her forehead and blinks away the tears. So she looks like a mom. So what? She is a mom. Having three boys doesn't leave a lot of time to fuss over oneself. Not to mention all the work that goes into being association president. The whole team counts on her. Being a mom is the most important job in the world.

Nothing is more important than family. Not how you look or what people think of you.

Nothing.

"Someone's out to impress," Yasmin says. Baby Suni grunts, small fist squeezing her mother's breast so the skin puckers. Red and gold hoops jangle on Yasmin's wrist as she adjusts the latch. "Not so hard, sweetu."

"Sorry?"

"Snack. It smells so good!"

Lacey lifts the plastic lid and lays it by her purse on the floor. The smell of fresh-baked bread and caramelized meat veils the room's maleness. "Maple pulled-pork sammies," she says. "Thirteen hours these bad boys roasted."

Cheers echo. The women look to the scoreboard's flickering digits: 4–2.

"Woo woo!" Lacey claps.

Yasmin smiles and raises her eyebrows. "Better kiss that baby boy bye-bye, Mama."

Lacey wants to roll her eyes, but instead she fakes a smile and shakes her head. Yasmin can be such a know-it-all. She has that Twitter, too, no, a blog, *Aiding Adolescence* or something like that, and thinks she knows everything about parenting because she was a social worker before she had kids. She never mentions how she did everything backward: adopting Jude when she wasn't even married, meeting Jim when he was the National Aboriginal Day's guest speaker at her son's school, and not even getting married until after they had their real baby!

Lacey heard all about it from Kelly, and Kelly knows everything because Anderson used to work at the same hospital as Yasmin's dad. Yeah, Yasmin's some parenting expert all right. She actually *lost* Jude once. How's that for mom of the year?

Yasmin writes all these boring articles about "best care practices," "gross motor skills," and "social politics," as if teenagers care about engines or spending scandals, geez. Lacey tried to make a web blog once. *Hockey Mom,* she was going to call it, or maybe *Marvellous Motherhood*. She was going to put up recipes and household hints like how to deodorize sweaty gloves, but she couldn't figure out all those damn terms: upload, page, post, link. It made her feel stupid, like she was back in high school, just some dumb girl. *Puck bunny*, they used to call her.

Oh, Lacey *hated* high school. Yasmin was probably one of those keeners, keeping everyone late in class to ask the teacher a million questions and argue about stuff. On her blog she calls herself a *minority ally and advocate*, but really that's just code for complainer. So many complainers out there today, like that young singer with the songs about moms going missing and creepy crescent moon smiles. Like, yes: sad things happen, but it's not as if people don't do it to themselves. And how hard can life be, really, if a teenager can get famous singing songs on YouTube and an oilfield operator like Jim can get paid to speak in schools on his days off? Dave's an operator too, but he's never been on CBC or asked to lead Broadmoor High's morning assembly.

Whiners just want handouts and attention, Lace. Don't give it to them.

"You can just leave the Spring Fling plans in Jude's bag," Yasmin interrupts.

Lacey frowns. What were they talking about?

"Just there," Yasmin gestures to her son's hockey bag, the enormous diamond on her crisscross ring flashing.

The show-off. How's that for appropriate culturalization or whatever? Lacey went to school with a girl who had a diamond ring like that with the criss-crosses on the side, so she knows that design is Irish, which Yasmin *definitely* is not. But Yasmin is just the kind who's always bragging about vintage this and vintage that, as if that means cooler-than-you and not just "my-cheap-husband-got-this-second-hand."

"Or you can swing by and drop them off later," Yasmin offers. "Jim will be home. No one expects you to plan the exhibition with Denny leaving."

Lacey blinks. She hadn't thought of giving up the association. She's been planning the Spring Fling for weeks. She just made four dozen purple and gold pom-poms to decorate the lobby. It doesn't seem right, doing all that work and letting someone else take the credit. Like when the twins won Most Valuable Players at the World Juniors last year and thanked Dave on camera for coaching the Timbits team they played on as little kids, but actually it was Lacey who had coached four of the six weeks because Dave was stuck in camp all season.

"Be strange, eh? All the boys gone? Empty house." Yasmin lifts Suni to burp. "What'll you do with yourself?"

Lacey's heart thumps. Dave had asked the same thing, joking about how she can't just laze around the house forever. Talked about helping her "whip up a resume," but what the heck was she supposed to put on it? The first and last job she'd ever had was at McDonald's in Grade 11.

The thought made her crazy. Not that she'd ever tell Yasmin, but yesterday the idea of Denny going away made her tear up right in the middle of sorting laundry. For a minute, she even considered running the stitch remover over the backs of his skate laces. She always packs him an extra pair, but what if she just forgot today and the ones he was wearing bust during the game? Denny wouldn't be on the ice, not for a time anyway, and then, well, too bad for the scout.

But no. Lacey loves her son. She loves all her boys. What was being a mom without a little pain? After she dried her eyes and left the laundry room, she found Denny laid out on the couch, one of his brothers' old *Rock'em Sock'em* box sets blaring from the television: Bobby Orr on his belly before the video swiped to a rap song with the kind of 1990s graphics Lacey's father had used in his car dealership commercials. Once upon a time there would have been three guys packed like clumsy puppies in this room, four, if Dave was home. It was time to start dinner, but Lacey brought over a basket of laundry to fold and sat at the opposite end of the couch instead. It was important to take in the little things: the weight of her young son's big manly feet on her lap, the darkness of the den, Don Cherry's urgent bark: "Wasn't that a beauty hit?"

It's not fair that only Lacey has to feel this bad. Besides, what does Yasmin know about it? Her boy is adopted; it's not the same as losing your own.

"They might want Jude," Lacey says. She thinks of Jude's silly hockey hair, the girly curls bouncing out from under the kid's helmet. "Good goalies are hard to come by."

Yasmin shakes her head. Cradling the baby, she bends low and digs through her diaper bag. "My kids won't be raised by agents."

The Tupperware's hot on Lacey's lap. "Well, they're not *raised* . . . I mean, Denny's almost seventeen . . ."

Yasmin snorts and waves a breast pad. "You don't have to defend yourself, Lace! I didn't mean it like that. It's just, we've got, what? A year left, maybe two? It's just different priorities. You guys value wealth and fame and all that, and for us . . . Parenting is just more of a spiritual experience, you know? We try to stay true to Jim's culture. His community honours personal growth and respect above all else. Collectivity, like . . . putting the family first. Besides, our Jude . . . well, he was already given up once, you know? That terrible choice his birth mother had to make—well, that's enough for one lifetime! He deserves a real family. That's what matters most—to us, anyway. It's different for everyone!"

Lacey coughs. It's all she can do to keep from laughing. L-O-L, as Denny would say. As if Yasmin knows anything about family. The fake. The phony. Lacey knows all about her priorities. She heard all about them from Kelly, just last month.

They'd been sorting the bottles collected after the association's Christmas party. Lacey asked Kelly if she'd had a good time and the woman let out a wail so long and loud Lacey thought she'd cut herself. "I cheated on Anderson!"

Rye and butterscotch schnapps, she said, that was what did her in. Burt Reynolds, the drink was called. The party's designated clean-up crew—Kelly and Yasmin and Coach Norm—got into the leftover bottles before tackling the hall. They woke up the next morning a butt-naked ball of late-thirty-somethings spread on the dance floor, nothing on any of them except for Coach still in his weathered old Oilers hat. Each scrambled for their clothes before scrubbing tables and passing a broom over the hardwood.

"Where'd you tell Anderson you were all night?" Lacey asked, whispering in disbelief.

"He didn't know I'd been gone! I tripped over Ty's hockey gloves when I tried to sneak back in, but Anderson thought I'd just come in from taking out the trash. It was garbage day."

Kelly wiped away tears and Lacey just shook her head, not knowing what to say.

"You won't tell anyone, will you, Lace?"

Lacey promised she wouldn't say a word. How could she? Imagine: a three-marriage-wide blowout. Poor Anderson. And Jim! God, Jim, he'd do anything for Yasmin, so exotic and him with those buckteeth. And all those kids . . . awful! To break up a family . . . wow. That was the worst thing you could do. And for what? Lacey couldn't understand it.

The intermission buzzer makes Lacey flinch. Nickelback screams through the intercom speakers and Yasmin stuffs the breast pad into her bra, jerking layers of clothing over her chest. Lacey yanks her sweatshirt so it doesn't cling to any wobbly bits and runs her fingers through her bangs again, lifting them this time to keep from looking too done. The boys don't give a hoot what she looks like, but she'd never want to embarrass DenDen.

Skates chop down the hall like an anthem. God, she loves that sound: blades against rubber, the thudding steps of healthy boys, cheeks rosy and the ice's chill all around them. O Canada! It makes her think of Dave back when he was Midget captain, about how they'd fool around after practice, her up against the wall, him teetering on skates, hockey pants around his knees. Back before the boys or the rig or the association or him losing his hair.

Al Sterling, editor of the *Sherwood Park Weekly*, enters the room first. He comes in backward, pointing a camera down the hall. Al had been married to a girl Lacey knew from school until they got divorced a few years back. So many broken homes. Sad!

He crosses the room with a series of clicks and whirls, tipping his hat and winking like he's some kind of playboy rock star. "Ladies," he says, in that girly voice of his. Yasmin looks at Lacey and lifts an eyebrow. Lacey tries not to laugh.

The boys barrel in, all laughter and shouts and barely hushed obscenities. A mustard smell stings Lacey's eyes as they crowd her. She cranes her neck to find Denny.

"See the scout?" Yasmin asks.

Lacey can't see anything but the bodies of boys blocking her view. "They make better walls than windows," she mumbles.

Then: flashes of blue, rich and dark. Gold trim. Vike's colours! Lacey cocks her head. There's the scout, talking to her Denny!

"DenDen," she calls to him, lifting her hand to wave him over. Her son turns and scowls before shifting his attention back to the scout, adjusting his stance so she can't read his lips.

The gaps between the boys close. Lacey tilts her head to the other side. "Excuse me! I'm trying to see."

Suni begins to cry in that tit-stinging, gut-cramping way. The room is too hot, too musty, too loud.

"Can you just—"

She reaches to move a player, but her hand finds sweat-drenched flesh above his waistband and under his top. She pulls away, fingers soaked and warm.

"Sorry, just—"

They're stealing all the air. Spit pools behind Lacey's molars. She's dizzy. Sick. Why are they so close?

"Wait, just—"

A boy spits tobacco chew into an empty water bottle, brown slime dangling from his mouth. Lacey's stomach turns and her throat tightens. She can't see. Can't breathe. The boys crowd nearer. Wait, she tells them. What's happening? Where has Denny gone?

She feels a push, a few pushes—the boys all crowding around and bumping into her like she's nothing more than an old hockey bag on the floor. A grabby hand snatches at the sandwiches on her lap and Lacey jumps up. "FUCK OFF!"

The words bounce off the walls like a hit off the boards. The container falls from her lap, a moist splat on the floor.

The air is much cooler, standing. Except for Suni the room is silent, frozen, all mouths open, eyes wide. Like musical statues, Lacey thinks. It's laughable. She could laugh. She does laugh. The boys laugh too, grinning at each other, leaving her out of the joke.

Making her the joke.

Kelly Anderson's boy smirks and pretends to cough into his hand, eyes darting to his teammates. "Psycho!"

"Mom," Denny starts. Too late. She did it. It's done.

The handprint shows up quick and red on Ty Anderson's cheek. A line of blood appears where Lacey's pinkie nail caught the head of a crusty pimple. Slapped the smirk right off his face, Dave would say. Would he say that? Suddenly Tyler looks very young, tears dropping on his skates. They all do.

Yasmin leads the kid to the other side of the room, the boys parting for them to walk through.

So Lacey's the bad guy.

"He shouldn't have," Lacey whimpers.

There's a click and a whirl. Al has taken a picture. He looks up from the camera to Lacey's face and steps back from her glare. The room blurs.

She doesn't want them to see her cry, but Lacey can't see anything at all. She turns to leave, but slips in the pork, falling hard on her knee.

"My sammies."

Her voice sounds so pathetic. She hears her brother's voice in her head.

Dumb little girl.

Cry baby.

Why are you so emotional?

No, it's not just her brother's voice, it's her dad, too, and Dave and all her sons and every gym teacher she's ever had. She pushes herself up, hand on the bench, meat falling from her knee as she plunges into the hallway.

The double-wide lobby doors are down the hall. She'll go home, that's what she'll do. Keep her head down, get outside, start the truck, call Dave. Denny can find a ride. Lacey will never have to see these people ever, ever, ever again. She reaches for the purse strap on her shoulder. *Idiot.* She's left her bag in the dressing room, keys and phone inside.

A door swings open: Kelly Anderson.

Oh god, Kelly.

She steps into the hall, clip-clip-clipping as she flounces toward the dressing room. "Hey, Lace! Just going to give Ty a thumbs up. DenMan's killing it out there!"

Lacey quickens. Pain shoots up her knee. She tries to push her shoulders back, tries to walk with purpose, but everything's against her now. Screw it. She runs at a limp, Quasimodo fleeing Notre Dame like in that Disney movie baby Denny loved, her elbow knocking Kelly's scrawny hip.

"Ow!"

The lobby is warm, familiar. Fathers, grandfathers, and uncles stand with hands jammed into pockets, a contest for who can laugh the loudest. Women wait beside them in side conversations, fingers hooking the coat necks of children trying to crawl on the dusty floor, ruin the ski pants meant to last a season. Older kids hop foot-to-foot in concession lines, impatient for paper plates of steaming poutine. Girls huddle, fuzzy mittens hiding blushing faces as boys from the B teams flirt. *Puck bunnies,* Lacey thinks. Stupid, boring, useless. She wipes her eyes and runs her fingers through her hair.

An hour ago she led these people. Thirty-five years in places like this, the hours of her whole life counted on scoreboards while she sat still and cheered. But soon those doors will swing open and the story will be passed like a puck, each and every one of them handling it, shooting it on to the next, skimming over the slippery truth of all Lacey had done before she had done what she had done.

Psycho.

Then what? Would Yasmin take over? Would Denny talk to her again? Would Dave even bother coming home?

Why can't you be like them?

Nothing seems right until you're the one doing it.

You don't bite the hand that feeds you.

Psycho.

No! How dare they? How dare they judge? It was Lacey who did everything right. Lacey who stayed home, who never stepped on toes, who never got shrill, who never did anything for herself! How dare they! How dare they! How dare they!

"Lace!"

Jim. Yasmin's Jim, his arms stretched open in that old-fashioned fringed jacket of his, a concession-stand hotdog in one hand.

"Don't you worry, Lacey. DenMan's got it in the bag!"

He hugs her, a homey, sweetgrass hug. Lacey thinks of that week last June when Jim taught Aboriginal Sports to Denny's gym class. Lacey was at the school helping supervise the hot lunch program. Jim is so good, so kind. How wonderful he was with the children: assertive, gentle, championing their every effort. Lacey sinks into the hug. His loveliness takes her right back to the dark den of her big house, to safety and family and *Rock'em Sock'em* Don Cherry.

"Jim—"

The buzzer signals the end of intermission and the lobby empties, the crowd returning to the rink.

"Something happened . . ."

Jim frowns, tilts his head. "You okay, Lace?"

". . . at the Christmas party."

Wasn't that a beauty hit?

FAITH

2012

SNOW FLIES IN the dark outside Jim's windshield like he's crashing through space and dodging asteroids, a suicide mission at warp speed. Nothing or anything could lie beyond the metre of coned illumination his headlights cast: deer, moose, oncoming vehicles. Might be safer to pull onto some back road and wait out the whiteout, but three weeks in Fort Mac has his back crying out for its own bed. He checks the fuel gauge but snow's not going to stop anytime soon and he'd run out of gas waiting for it to, anyways. He slows his speed and keeps on keeping on, come what may.

Beside him, his phone's screen lights up the cup holder. Yasmin. One eye on the road and one on the phone, Jim lifts it to his face.

A photo. Caption: *Guess who got Daddy a special present?*

His wife and kids stand in bathing suits and toques in an outdoor hot tub he's never seen on his property before. Yasmin smiles big, one arm raised stiff like Vanna White on *Wheel of Fortune*. In the other she balances little Suni on her hip, their baby girl's serious eyes considering the water warming her toes. Behind them stands seventeen-year old Jude, arms crossed. Who wouldn't pout, his mother half-naked and posing sexy in a red bikini? Jim's jaw sets. How long has it been now since he took the kids back home? He's missing everything, working so much. Jude will be grown before he knows it. What'll the kid know about culture and history and tradition if Jim's only able to take him south once a year?

He thumbs a response.

We should be trying to save.

Oil might be strong now, but Jim's been an operator long enough to know better than to put much confidence in barrel prices. Year to year, Jim's as likely to be working double time as he is to be unemployed, and the truth is, right now neither option sounds great. Some days the only thing worse than change is everything staying the same.

He drops the phone back into the cup holder. Sometimes Jim wonders what's the point of even having a phone, everyone's obsessed with feeling connected through texts and tweets and Facebook messages even when they're so obviously not. Sure, there are days when it feels like the only thing that keeps him going are Yasmin's photos of the kids, but then there are times he wonders if it would be better to just be *gone* when he was gone, not at his wife's virtual beck and call. Might be good for Yasmin to get a taste of life without him. He knows he's not supposed to think like this. It's not "generous" or "expansive" or "recovery-oriented." It's been a year since he found out about her cheating and the couples counsellor says they're supposed to be in the "rebuilding" phase now. Truth is, they're both just motoring toward the sunset, hoping and pretending time will make things right, like a quiet sheriff in an old western. Really, Jim can't see a horizon for them to drive off into at all. Their whole life's a friggen' whiteout right now, the horizon don't even exist.

The only thing worse than change is everything staying the same.

He grips the steering wheel with two hands and shrugs his shoulders down and back. Perk up, man. So work's been busy; that's not so bad. Three years ago the patch was so slow he spent most of winter 2009 broke and visiting classrooms, letting kindergarteners run their fingers through the fringe of his moose-hide jacket while teaching older kids to play Aboriginal games: kick ball and cling ball, ring the stick. Well, the downtime wasn't all bad either—leading a school assembly, he met Yasmin while she was parent-helping in Jude's Grade 9 social studies class. A whirlwind romance led to Suni's conception just seven months later and only a couple weeks after her birth they tied the knot, Jim legally adopting Jude in the same ceremony.

So that rough patch was worth it, he thinks. Is this one?

This highway always gives him too much time to stew, Jim tells himself, nothing on the air but a racist, yammering talk-radio show. He thinks about his kids, biological and chosen, both loved the very same. Yeah, of course they're worth it. They're worth everything he's got.

Jim hits the brakes as a deer appears on the side of the road and then he realizes, no, it's a person. The hitchhiker turns and extends a thumb, walking backward while clutching on the hood of their heavy coat with the other hand, fighting against the wind and snow. Jim straddles what must be the centreline to give them wide berth as he passes, but then thinks about how bone-cold it must be to walk in the storm.

In the middle console, Yasmin lights up his phone again:

Come on, we can afford to take a little risk.

She's right.

Jim pulls over.

Parked, the asteroids disappear. Outside the windshield it's just miserable winter again, heavy snow littering the dark road like campfire ash kicked up in the wind. He waits for the hitchhiker to approach.

The interior light's yellow glow fills the cab as the door opens and the hitchhiker leans in, pushing back their hood. A young woman, cheeks freckled and acne-scarred. She glances at Jim and then scans the truck. Looking for what? he wonders. Weapons, rope? A man wouldn't need anything extra to harm her if that was a thing he wanted to do.

"I can give you a ride," Jim says, "but that's all. I don't want anything from you. Where you headed?"

"Just going to the truck stop, up the road."

"Okay."

The woman pulls herself into the passenger seat with the truck's top handrail before slamming the door.

"What are you doing out walking in this?"

"I was visiting friends. Gotta get where you gotta go, right?" She rubs her hands to warm them before bringing one to her face, scratching at the scabs on her cheeks.

Jim grips the wheel, suddenly aware of nervousness he doesn't often feel. A few weeks ago a trucker was left nearly dead on this same road. A girl he'd picked up convinced the man to turn onto a range road where her boyfriend was waiting. But what are the chances of two people getting hurt on the same road? Not so likely. Except, of course, they never did find the girl. The chances of the same person doing something like that twice? Out of the corner of his eye Jim checks his passenger out. Well, that's a different story.

He clears his throat, asks the girl her name but doesn't pay attention to her answer. Jim went to school on a reservation just like the one this girl was visiting except his was down south, past Calgary. His parents were born and raised in the community but left to buy a nearby cattle ranch. Out in the sticks with no transportation, people hitchhiked all the time. It was harmless, mostly. Harmless, he thinks, except for Doreen. It was a full nine months before foothill hikers found Doreen's body. Folks must have skied past her every day, whoever put her there burying her so deep in the snow. Nine months, Jim thinks, that's how long he waited for his own baby girl: singing to her and praying, imagining what Suni would look like and what day she'd arrive. Doreen's mama felt those nine months twice, he realizes: once with joy, the other in despair. The guilt almost flips Jim's stomach. He sits straighter in his seat. There's a reason he tries not to think about Doreen.

But he'd never heard of a driver getting hurt before. That trucker's story was a one-off. Besides, Jim's trained for dealing with strangers in small spaces. On days off he delivers homeless folks to the shelter in the Hope Mission van. He knows not to get taken in. Last guy Jim dealt with was a dreadlocked fella way bigger than this little white girl, and crazy as shit to boot. The guy told Jim he could read auras and see into the future and even gave him a "personal prophesy."

"Oh, it's coming for you, man," the fortune teller said. "But you'll be okay."

It was just gibberish, really.

Then again, maybe this girl is "it."

A chill runs over Jim's arms.

He shouldn't make assumptions. God knows enough are made about riggers like him. Gentler folk believe all oil workers to be hurtin' Albertan cokeheads screwing desperate women in oilfield housing. Swimming in the big bucks while the wives at home spend it on Escalades, Prada bags, and antibiotics for reoccurring venereal diseases. That's the joke. And maybe Jim's met a few shitheads like that but, truth is, most of the guys he knows are just so damn tired, just so damn homesick, just so damn determined their kids won't do without in a province with a cost of living so high it's near impossible for a man to make a living.

"So where you going?" Jim asks the girl.

"Truck stop."

"No, I mean, are you catching the bus? You from the city?"

The girl shrugs. "Just waiting to see what turns up, I guess. See who's around."

Jim nods. He's heard the crew laugh about women who work truck-stop parking lots.

"How much did your truck cost?" the girl asks. Jim looks over as she plays with the truck's buttons and dials. Under the centre interior light, he can see thin blue veins under the skin of her neck, the track marks on her inner arm.

The muscles in Jim's shoulders tense. "Why?"

"Just wonderin'." She leans over the centre console to read his dash. "Looks like you need to gas up, anyway. I know a real private spot if you wanna hang out."

Jim shakes his head. "I got family waiting at home."

"Shit," she laughs. "Who doesn't?"

He stares straight ahead and they drive a little longer in silence. Light reflects off a *Curve Ahead* road sign and Jim slows down, unsure where the bend is without the painted lines, asphalt, or even tires marks visible in the fresh powder. He follows the thinning patches of grass, only visible where the shoulder shelters the sparse blades. Of course this woman has a family; everybody does.

Doreen's mom used to volunteer in the classroom when Jim was in elementary school, just like Yasmin did for Jude. He wonders how things take such a wrong turn. Somehow, Doreen's house had turned into a party place by the time they were in junior high: uncles staying with them in and out of jail, strangers over all the time, lots of drinking and drugs. A kid didn't have a chance, growing up like that. In Grade 10 Doreen got her front teeth knocked out by a cousin and, embarrassed, she stopped going to school. She got a reputation for messing around with guys for money or rides or pretty much anything else, so Jim did his best to make sure everyone forgot about the time he held her hand at the Friendship Centre dance. But after his parents gave him a car for his sixteenth birthday, Doreen started acting like his girlfriend, asking for rides in front of his friends. The guys joked they were a perfect fit, Doreen's gummers leaving lots of room for Little Jimmy's buckteeth.

Doreen, Doreen, wants Jimbo's peen!

Jim didn't want to be seen anywhere near her.

On the night she went missing, Jim had turned the porch light off on her and left her standing in the dark. She was near beating down his mom's door at almost midnight, yelling how she needed a ride into town, how it was an emergency. But his parents weren't home, and Jim didn't believe her. She was looking to score, he thought, she just wanted a lift into town to party or buy drugs—who knew what she was into? He found out later that her little brother had been airlifted to the children's hospital that same afternoon. The kid had rolled his quad and there was swelling in his brain. Doreen had just wanted to see him; she just wanted to hold her mom's hand in a waiting room while the little guy went under. She was just scared of losing her brother.

So she found a ride elsewhere, and her little brother lost her, instead.

"Does anyone know you're out here?" Jim asks the girl. "Do you have a phone? Any way to protect yourself?"

"Who do I have to protect myself from, man?" She laughs and takes out a small pocketknife, flipping the blade to clean under her nails. "Little things can do a lot of damage, you know?"

Jim tries not to swallow. "I'd feel better if you put that away."

The girl cocks her head and smiles at him.

"Yeah, I bet you would." She stares a minute longer and then shakes her head. She slips the knife back into the pocket of her coat and laughs.

"Man, you gotta have a little faith."

Jim pulls into the truck stop parking lot and parks alongside the gas pump.

"You sure you don't want to hang out?" the girl tries again. "It don't cost too much." Lit up by the overhead light he sees the gap in her front teeth, so wide it's like she's missing a pair. She's younger than he thought, blue eyes shining like all the world's still new and exciting, like she hasn't done what's she's going to do near long enough to know any better about it.

Jim shakes his head.

"Listen," he says. "Whatever you've got to do to be safe, just do it, okay? Don't even hesitate. You be safe, and I'll get me some faith."

The girl's smile fades. "Yes, sir," she whispers.

She opens the door and Jim watches her walk to the truck stop's front entrance as he fills his tank at the pay-as-you-pump. She turns and flashes him a peace sign. Jim nods in return.

Snow-blind, he thinks of faith as he pulls back onto the highway. Faith in people, faith in the patch, faith in two people trying to hold their world together, faith that the road will be clear. Faith that doing the right thing won't hurt too bad, or maybe that it just won't hurt too bad for too long. Faith to keep on keeping on because there isn't any other way, or faith that whatever happens is meant to happen, whether a person likes it or not.

450 to Edmonton, a road sign reads.

He reaches into the cup holder to let Yasmin know how long until he's home but the phone's not there.

He thinks of the girl, just that little bit safer.

A consequence of faith, Jim thinks.

One he can live with.

WHAT IS BROUGHT BACK, WHAT REMAINS

2013 / 1990

KAREN BREATHES INTO her hand in the privacy of the beach house's kitchen. Laughter howls from the living room, but Karen isn't having fun. She sniffs her palm, confirming the putrid smell that's plagued her for weeks. How embarrassing. She slides an oak drawer open and shakes Tic Tacs into her mouth before pulling a fresh bottle of rosé from the wine fridge. She'll arrange a dental visit once she's back in Sherwood Park. Until then, mints, Chanel No. 5, and a few drinks will have to mask the stink.

She uncorks the bottle and pours wine into her empty glass, relieved to temporarily escape the inanity of her company. The executive oil wives' weekend is well underway and all the women are lubricated by both drink and the sex appeal of the lock-haired tarot card reader. These weekends have a habit of quickly devolving, the second-wife attendees (some of them not even wives yet, merely girlfriends) turning into animals when out from under the supervision of much older husbands. Golden retriever puppies, that's what they make her think of. The big blondness of them, their eager, bouncy breasts. Karen's the only first executive wife left.

And yet, that's not true. Karen is no longer a first wife but a first widow, the second anniversary of Henry's heart attack having passed last May. She only hosts the annual event because of her own reluctance to forfeit her seat on the otherwise all-male executive events coordination board. A weekend with obnoxious slush puppies and the obligatory fifteen grand annual donation isn't much to pay for access to powerful men cycling through marital experiments. These curvy young blondes don't know, but Karen's tried all their men on for size and all that's left to do is take her pick. For what thin, dark, fifty-three-year-old Karen lacks in youth, she makes up for in keen sense of humour, chic style, and a sharper sort of sex appeal. In the end, every man wants a woman who'll take control.

She slides her shellac-nailed fingertips over the vacation home counters. But for the marble, this kitchen is downright nautical, a lavish translation of the shiplap-sided lake shack Karen grew up in. Karen had been smart then, too—too smart, her mother complained. Mother called her *conniving*. Thank god for simple, gentle Nana, her warm, jiggly arms stretched open like a blanket big enough to cover the world. When Karen is at her worst, she still imagines the comfort of her grandmother's arms. Sometimes she thinks she must be misremembering it. How could it be that any person loved her so well?

They left that lakeside home after Nana died. Karen's uncle turned up a week after the funeral and sold it from underneath them, splitting the sale with the pro-bono realtor Mother ended up moving in with afterward. Karen got a job elsewhere as a live-in nanny but never forgot the lesson. She and Henry would leave the entirety of their estates only to each other, trusting one another to divvy it up correctly among surviving relations. There'd be no absent family members coming out of the woodwork so long as Karen was at the helm. No broke sibling or ne'er-do-well nephew turning up for a handout. Clever Shannon, Henry's long-estranged daughter— the product of an earlier, disastrous relationship—could take a long walk off a short dock before she got a penny. It had been Karen and their daughter Tara who had made Henry's life so rich. It was Karen and Tara who deserved the whole of his love.

She walks to the window above the kitchen sink and flips a switch. Plank flooring heats up under her socked feet. Had it done that the last time she was here? She doesn't recall. It has been so many years. What had brought her back, a little bit of heartache? Well, where better than Vancouver Island for that? It feels like the end of the earth here by the ocean, an in-between space in the autumnal fog, perfect to remember or to forget. She thinks about her childhood by the lake, how by morning the waves would always have brought to her a thing someone had forgotten: a note in a bottle, a sandcastle bucket, a floating flip-flop left at the shore.

Glass in one hand and bottle in the other, Karen returns to the ladies. She walks the circle made around the psychic's wobbly little table, refilling glasses. The group's token non-executive wife (only invited because the executive husbands wanted her field-operator husband to bring their three National Hockey League sons to their annual golfing retreat) lifts a giant Tim Hortons paper cup and beams a smile just as warm and homey as the coffee.

"I've got my double-double, but thanks, Karen." The woman tilts her head to the side, but her 1990s feathered bangs don't move an inch.

What was that old joke? *The bigger the hair, the closer to God?*

Karen pats her shoulder. She's always had a soft spot for women like Lacey, round and thick and a little boring. Sincere people make the nicest company, their happy-go-luckiness a salve for the jaded-but-glamorous. Karen's given Lacey the second-best bed in the house. Let a girlfriend sleep on the pullout.

"Your turn, Kar," a blonde says, getting up from the card table. Karen refreshes the woman's glass and begs her off—"I'm just here to make sure you have a good time!"—but the others insist. Karen sits on the chair opposite the psychic and places the wine on the floor by her feet. The man closes his eyes and Karen makes a tight-lipped smile to her friends as he rings a little bell over the deck. Well, that's a nice, spooky touch.

She was right to fly him out from Edmonton. He came right on time and really set the mood: incense and candles, yogic music, and salt spread in the four corners of the room. She'd found him during a shopping trip to Ascension, a kooky bookshop her daughter's therapist girlfriend, Theresa, had taken them to. Theresa collects the type of woo-woo panaceas that comfort patients whose lives are out of control: meditation tracks, healing stones, essential oils meant for calming. A lapsed Catholic (and rural Canadian Frenchie to boot), Theresa's endearing penchant for the superstitious is nothing but good, girly fun. Really, Karen couldn't see how she could love Tara's girlfriend more. Now that Henry's gone, the girls are all Karen has.

The storefront clerk told them there was space open if the women wanted a reading with the house psychic, but Tara wasn't interested in that sort of thing and Karen really didn't care, so they let Theresa take the offer and accompanied her to a tiny bead-curtained room. For her question of love and career the psychic pulled a tower on fire and three swords through a heart.

"You must be brave," he said, accented words dripping with sex. He placed his hand over Theresa's. "And be kind."

"*La gentillesse est comme la neige*," she said, and smiled. "*Elle embellit tout ce qu'elle recouvre.*"

"Kindness is like snow," Tara whispered to Karen, translating Theresa's French. "She embellishes everything she covers."

"*Oui*," the beautiful man said.

Seeing those big sexy hands and hearing that "*oui*," Karen knew she'd found the entertainment for the wives' weekend. Who wouldn't enjoy such a hunk? And think of how much more fun the experience would be with a little wine thrown in. Tara could be such a stick in the mud with the sobriety kick she'd been on since that Shannon got her into trouble years ago. The little upset had really changed Karen's daughter. She'd chopped all her golden hair off and dyed it into a dark pixie cut. Easier for work, Tara claimed, but Karen considered it a sin. Staining natural blond? She was *blessed* to inherit her father's gorgeous colouring. Take it away and all Tara had left was Karen's hooky nose.

And oh, Tara was so *serious!* When they were leaving the store Karen spotted pretty little pentacle necklaces with the words *Always With My Sisters* engraved on the back. Theresa just about died when Karen suggested that each of them get one.

Tara just rolled her eyes.

"Really, Mom? What do *we* know about sisters?"

Oh well. That's the way it is sometimes, the strangeness between mothers and daughters. Karen is eternally proud, regardless. Her Tara, the doctor! She'd gotten herself out of that rebellious stage she'd gone through and now—finally away from Shannon—she's doing great. Thriving, even, working on boards and committees to introduce gay-straight alliances in high schools during her spare time. Tara's coming out had surprised Karen far less than her choice to partner with a woman so much older, but Theresa really is a dear. Still, a decade's difference? At first Karen worried Tara had mommy issues. But no, she tries not to think about that. In the end, Karen is just happy her daughter is finally making some demands of the world, as she should. Thirty is a very empowering age for a woman. Of course, Karen completely supports Tara even if they don't share current politics. She and Henry had always considered themselves socially liberal if fiscally conservative, anyway. They even made a dinner party joke out of it:

Civil rights at all costs! (except financial ones)!

Well.

She realizes she's daydreaming when the psychic knocks on his deck, waking her from the memory. Come back to Earth, Karen.

The psychic pulls three cards, lips mumbling a chant. He lays them before her on the table: a thief tiptoes from camp with seven stolen swords; the dead rise to an angel captioned *Judgment*; a woman and child journey into the sea, knives caging them within their vessel. Karen watches the act and wonders if he keeps a collection of "readings" to randomly employ. What's the script this time? Be brave and kind, like he read to Theresa? Or maybe, if he's interested in a bit of late-night vacation fun, you will meet a tall, dark, and handsome man?

The psychic's eyes flash. He sits still and stiff, nostrils flared, gaze fixed just above Karen's shoulder.

"You hold money not yours to keep."

Giggles teeter into confused silence.

"What did he say?" Lacey asks.

"She holds money not hers to keep," someone whispers.

"An inheritance is owed."

Inheritance? Whose? Tara's? He's not talking about *Shannon,* surely. Henry hadn't seen the girl since she was fifteen years old.

Chairs nervously squeak. Karen smiles and narrows her eyes. "I'm sorry, I don't . . ."

He slides his dark hand over the table and covers hers. Suddenly, Karen is very tired.

She's had too much to drink, she realizes. The room has started to spin. Outside, ocean tides swirl under a full moon and things are being brought back in waves. And this house . . .

This house is just as it was . . .

Back then.

✳

Karen pulls the framed photograph from Tara's suitcase and holds it up for the nine-year-old to see.

"Aren't you glad I packed this?"

The girl looks up from the bed and shrugs. Daddy shouldn't have gotten so mad, Karen tells her, but Tara shouldn't have left her brand-new Discman on the floor, either. The girl has no idea how lucky she is; most adults don't even have such expensive toys.

Henry should not have called their daughter spoiled, though. That was mean and untrue and, of course, it opened the gates for Shannon to swoop in and snatch his attention, pulling Henry from the broken Discman to the wingback chairs on either side of the rental house's chessboard. Why her husband thought it was a good idea to bring the fifteen-year-old on Karen's surprise thirtieth birthday getaway, she would never understand.

Karen studies the photo before handing it to her daughter: Tara and Henry, each in a red kayak, raise a paddle at Rundle Park. It had been Karen's idea for them to join the water-sports club. An excellent provider, Henry lacks in the more hands-on areas of fatherhood. He's always so busy with his work. Karen can only imagine how much the quality time means to Tara. The little girl had tripped over with thanks when she tore wrapping paper off the frame, the gift tag marked by Karen *Love, Daddy*.

"Why don't you show him you brought it?" Karen asks. "Go on, he'll see that you're sorry, that you *do* care about the things he gives you."

Tara moans and drags herself from the bed and into the living room. Karen crosses from the girls' bedroom to the kitchen. She watches the scene as she puts away the groceries they collected at a funny little market with goats on the roof. The girl hands her father the photo and sits beside Shannon, who wiggles over to share the big chair.

"Mom packed it."

Henry smiles and holds up the frame, but Shannon interrupts. She fidgets with the diamond ring at the end of her necklace. A ridiculous thing for a child to own. Really, it should have been returned to Henry after he broke off the engagement, but apparently Shannon's mother didn't see it that way. The man is altogether too soft where previous relationships are concerned.

"Remember when we went paddle boating at the zoo, Dad? When that goose hissed at Mom?"

Typical. Karen interjects, calling Henry to the kitchen. God knows they hear enough about Shannon's boozy mother without inviting her into vacation conversation.

Henry's seat groans as Karen pours them each a tall glass of Long Island iced tea. Shannon's interest in chess lost, the girls play a hand stacking game: palm over palm over Tara's knobby knees.

"She was heartbroken," Karen whispers to her husband.

"Who?"

"Tara! You shouldn't have gotten so cross. She didn't mean to break the music thingy."

It would be nice if he spent a little bit of time with her, Karen says, just one-on-one. It's hard for polite little Tara to get a word in edgewise with Shannon here, what with the elder so loud and jealous and in-your-face all the time.

"I could take Tara for a paddle," Henry suggests.

Karen brightens. "Great idea, honey."

They'd found the two-seater kayak in the rental cabin's garage upon arriving. The cabin's last guests had returned it to the wall hang without wiping it down and a starfish was found slowly decaying on the vessel's hull. Look, a sea urchin, Karen pointed out to Tara, holding her nose against the rotten smell of it. She pulled the fish from the boat and tossed it into the bushes lining the driveway.

Mo-o-om, Tara had protested. *It's an echinoderm, actually, and it wasn't even dead!*

Karen waved her off, annoyed. *Whatever. It is now!*

Henry takes a sip of the cocktail and smiles. "Ah." He starts to speak but the girls are too loud, Shannon shrieking like a banshee.

"What?" Karen asks over the noise.

"I said, can we . . . ?"

"Sorry?"

That awful laugh! *Slap.* "Ow! Mo-o-om!"

"For Christ's sake! Shannon, what are you doing to her?"

Karen surprises even herself with the severity of her voice, but she doesn't let it show. She strides to the chessboard, hands on hips. The girls freeze, mouths hanging open before laughter blurts out.

"It's okay," Tara says. "She just missed my hands."

A handprint reddens the skin below the hem of Tara's jean shorts. Karen points at Shannon. "Unacceptable."

When Karen turns back to her husband, Henry catches and squeezes her upper arms, holding her, calming her.

"I was just going to say," he says into her eyes, "can we finish this drink first? Sit. I have something for you."

He leaves to the master suite and Karen waits on the couch, patting the seat beside her for Tara to join. The girl snuggles in close under her mother's arm and Karen plays with the girl's hair, admiring its golden sheen in the sun. Shannon, hair as brassy as her personality, leans into the wingback, legs spread as if to claim as much of the room as possible. She pulls a bottle of pink nail polish from her shorts' pocket and paints her nails. Tara shakes her head away from her mother, tying her long locks into a tight bun.

Henry returns with a white box the length of his arm.

"For the woman who 'stole' my heart," Karen reads. "Oh Henry, it's a fur!"

A beautiful blue fox. Karen smiles at her husband and feels a shiver of excitement when he winks back. Weeks ago they'd seen a film in which a woman strip-teased down to blue fox fur for her Italian mobster boyfriend. Karen slips the stole around her shoulders and rests her cheek on the softness of the pelt. Tara squeals at the cuteness of the little creature and Karen lets her slip its paw between her palm and thumb. Karen lifts the animal's wee face and pretends to give Tara kisses with it.

"Look, Dad!" Tara says.

Karen unwraps the stole from around her shoulders and passes it to Henry for his appraisal, certain it was his secretary who'd picked it out.

"Can I see?" Shannon asks, bubble-gum nails wet and glistening.

"Sure." Henry passes the fur to his eldest but Karen grabs it just in time. Shannon barely contains a smirk as Karen packs it back into the box.

"Thank you, darling," Karen says. "But you two are going to lose both daylight and the tide if you don't get going. Tara, Daddy's going to take you kayaking. Put some sunscreen on your nose."

Shannon's mouth falls open. "I want to go!"

"I'll take you tomorrow, Shan."

"You and I will be just fine here," Karen tells the teen.

"Yeah," she interrupts. "Girl time. Right, *Mom?*" She rolls her eyes and stands.

"If you're going to unpack, take this with you," Henry tells her, passing Tara's framed photo. Shannon groans and stomps away, slamming the door behind her.

Shannon stays in her room for another hour but that's fine with Karen. She finishes stocking the fridge with collected goodies from the Coombs market: a wheel of Quebec brie, smoked salmon, artisanal garlic hummus with a pretty little maple leaf made of red pepper flakes garnishing the middle. Tara will get a kick out of that.

Finished, she gives proper inspection to the room she and Henry will be sharing, stretching over the down duvet, the cool satin sheets underneath. She finds a home-stitched quilt in the cedar truck at the end of the bed and pulls it all around her. There's a homey, dusty smell to the blanket that makes Karen think of hot chocolate and tobogganing and the laughter of little children. Karen once worked for a woman who made quilts like these. It was her first nanny job; she'd been hired to mind three small children but made fast friends with the mother and spent much of her time cutting squares while Mrs. Quentin worked the machine. Dolly was quite the seamstress. Karen holds the heavy material a moment longer, face pushed into the smell, the memory bittersweet. She lays the quilt over the bed.

Well, this is a treat . . . or would have been, she realizes. Tara is usually in bed by eight PM, but Shannon will want to stay up until at least ten. She wonders if Henry will even be awake enough for sex by then. Goddamn it. Maybe she can sneak him away for half an hour's "nap" once he and Tara return.

She changes into a black two-piece and platform wedge sandals and takes her glass of wine through the bedroom exit to the high wraparound deck that connects to the living room's sliding door. Karen watches her husband and young daughter cut along the shoreline, sunlight sparkling in the ripples they cause with every stroke. Beneath Karen, bikini-clad Shannon sashays onto the lawn with a beach towel and a *Teen* magazine she must have picked up at the market. Even from a distance Karen can make out Courtney Love's image on the cover, the messy white hair and blood-red smile. So that explains what Shannon's got on her face. Crimson lips in the day at only fifteen years old! Now what does *that* say to the world?

The girl lays the towel on the grass and then runs the length of the dock, standing on tiptoes and waving to the kayakers. Tara almost drops her paddle as she waves back and Henry blows her a kiss. Shannon pretends to grab it from the air, pulling it to her chest, bending a knee.

The flirt.

She knows what she's doing, Karen thinks. That girl is bad news. She takes another sip of wine and watches Shannon return to her towel and sit, applying baby oil to her tanned shoulders and small, high breasts before flipping through the glossy pages. *Too smart for her own good.* Oh, Karen knows.

Karen had only been two years older than Shannon when she took up with Mrs. Quentin's husband. The family had been bedridden with a flu Karen avoided and Earl had been the parent to recover first. Too weak to work but too well to sit in bed, Earl helped Karen with the caregiving duties and the pair got to know one another serving chicken soup to toddlers and massaging vapour rub onto little feet.

She was good at being a mother, Karen realized. She liked deciding what the children would eat and when they would bathe and what jammies they would put on at bedtime. It was as if she were the powerful captain of a great ship, her care steering the family through each passing moment of every day. It was nice to be soft *and* strong, to envelop others in the same way she so often craved to be held. On the third evening of the sickness, Karen caught Earl watching her rock baby Carrie while he lay beside little Jack, the nursery children too feverish to sleep.

Later, after it went too far and all was ruined, she would take solace in the fact it had been Earl who kissed her first, on her lips and then just under her ear, Dolly asleep upstairs. But she couldn't quite lose the truth of this: that night, when he watched her as she rocked Carrie, Karen hadn't looked away. She had known exactly what she was doing.

And it had cost sweet Dolly so, so much.

But Karen has always been brighter than women like Dolly.

The tide begins to turn, the water giving way to rocky beach, puddles and starfish left in the wake. Karen pulls herself back to reality. Shannon might be manipulative, but Karen's the woman in Henry's life. And it's not like she's some thick old hag, for god's sake. She looks down, inspecting her body with the detached appraisal her husband applied to the blue fox. She is thin and rich and gorgeously tanned, skin loose only where the C-section scar puckers. She'd add a bit of oomph to her breasts if she could, but those plastic balloons everyone else is going under the knife for look so trashy. What Karen lacks in curves she makes up for with trim, smooth abs to display the Italian leather belts she sometimes leaves on for Henry to grip. She should get the stole, she realizes. A contrast of fur and nakedness—what's sexier than that?

She tops up the wine glass on the way to retrieve the garment and then arranges herself on the sun lounger, the animal draped around her just so. On the grass Shannon applies oil until she shines like sunlight on the water, but Karen ignores the burn her stepdaughter is procuring and rests an arm above her head, closing her eyes as though she's asleep. Henry and Tara pull up to the dock.

The peace is interrupted by adolescent squeals. Karen squints open one eye. Shannon's thrown herself around her father and he's piggybacking the girl up the deck stairs while poor Tara struggles to carry both oars in her too-big life jacket.

Karen resumes her pose but Henry doesn't stop to greet her, Shannon driving him like horse. "Onward! To the kitchen, for a snack!"

Oh for god's sake.

Karen unwraps the stole and follows them inside. They won't know what to eat and will end up just making a mess.

"I'll make something," Karen says, stepping between Shannon and the open refrigerator door. The girl shrugs and grabs a carrot from the veggie platter. She bends over the island counter with Tara and Henry as Karen gathers ingredients for a Mediterranean charcuterie board. Put some damn clothes on, Karen wants to say.

She opens the hummus container but realizes the plastic security ring has already been broken off. Inside, the pretty maple leaf has been destroyed, scooped out, marks left in the purée like a three-finger swipe.

"Were you in the hummus?" Karen asks Shannon.

Shannon snorts. She swallows air and sticks out her stomach like she's had too much to eat. "What was your first clue?"

Karen doesn't even know what to say. She shakes her head and looks down, brings her thumb and middle finger to her temples.

"It doesn't matter, Princess," Henry says. "Do we have salsa?"

"Out," Karen says. "Everybody out."

She cuts tomatoes and garlic and green onion for the salsa, but of course they have no cilantro. She wasn't *planning* on making salsa. And now, thanks to Shannon, they'll be eating it with pita bread instead of chips.

Karen walks to the sliding door, her arms full and body unbalanced by wine and the platform sandals. No one rises to help her; Tara and Henry distracted, laughing. What's so funny? There's

Shannon, Karen sees, sashaying the porch in the fox stole, wrists limp and pursed, painted lips grazing the fur around her shoulders.

"Who ate my hummus?" Shannon mocks.

Karen pulls the door handle and kicks it the rest of the way open.

She drops the food on the ottoman table and yanks the stole from around Shannon's neck. The fur is greasy and wet with baby oil, fibres clumped and separated, stained red where dark kisses have marked.

"Look what you've done!" Karen shouts. She holds the stole to Shannon's face. "Look!"

Shannon presses her lips together, eyes shining as if trying not to laugh. Karen shakes her head and heads back into the house. Behind her, Henry comforts the girl.

Karen's going to scream. She could pull her hair out. She walks, needing to pace. She turns and steps into the girls' room. Tara's bunk is neat and tidy and Shannon's is already unmade, clothes thrown all about. Henry smiles from the framed photo on Tara's nightstand. Karen grabs it and looks, that beautiful moment she orchestrated and captured and printed and wrapped and gifted, and then she puts the framed photo quietly on the floor and presses the thick heel of her platform sandal into the glass. She feels better with every quiet crunch and crack and she grinds shards into the glossy picture, stripping the paper of her daughter's face. And then she goes to the master suite and wraps herself in the quilt and cries.

When Karen finally comes out from her room, Henry is in the office study and Shannon's still in her bathing suit on the deck, Tara bored and alone in front of the television.

"Get something to read," Karen tells her daughter. "I packed a new Archie comic in your suitcase."

The girl pulls herself from the couch and Karen waits. And then: "Mom!"

Karen takes a breath and meets Tara in her room. The girl looks up, kneeling in front of the broken glass.

"Tara! After the Discman? Your father's going to be so upset."

The girl starts to cry. It wasn't her, she promises. She found it like this!

"Well, if you didn't break it, who did?"

"Shannon?" Tara offers. "Maybe it got knocked it over while I was kayaking."

Karen nods. "I believe you," she tells her daughter. She extends her hand to help the little girl stand and she pulls her into a hug and dries her eyes.

"But we have to tell your father."

Karen follows Tara into the wood-panelled office where Henry sits stooped over a file. Tara bursts into tears as she reports the broken frame and promises him, too, "It wasn't me!"

"It's alright," Henry says. "Thank you for telling me."

Karen tells her daughter to go and then lowers her voice to her husband. "It was no accident." She tells him how the glass scratched the photo, Tara's face snuffed out.

"It's creepy, Henry," she says. "From now on, you visit Shannon on your own time. I have to protect my child."

Karen's words fall on her husband like waves on rock. He looks past her as she speaks but nods when she asks if he understands.

"Do you want me to send her in?"

Henry shrugs. He looks at her, finally, and sets his jaw. "Well, it's not up to me, is it? Nothing's up to me."

Karen turns to leave, expecting to be told to stay. Instead, he asks for privacy, tells her to close the door on the way out.

"I have a phone call to make."

She shuts the door and quietly leans against it, eyes stinging with tears. Behind her there is a clicking noise, a lock turning, and then the sound of Henry's heavy footsteps back to his desk. She waits a moment longer and hears his deep voice murmur, *Hey, princess,* and Karen knows he's called that dirty phone line again.

The last hours of her twenty-ninth year will be spent alone.

She collects herself and walks into the living room, stroking her daughter's cheek to remind herself why she makes such decisions. Then Karen grabs the blanket from the trunk at the end of her bed.

She finds Shannon on the porch, sunburned skin shivering in the cool of twilight, the ocean spread endlessly before her. There's no reason to be merciless. Karen is captain of this ship, deciding who stays aboard and who is peeled away like a corrosive urchin from the hull. Bratty Shannon is already five fathoms deep; there's no way Henry will visit the girl on the other side of the city without Karen and Tara in tow, not with his schedule. Karen slides the glass door open. She covers the blinking teenager's goose-pimpled legs, smoothing the blanket with a warm, sincere smile.

The psychic snaps his fingers and Karen returns to the howling laughter of the room.

"Where did you go?" someone shrieks. "Were you hypnotized?"

Karen shakes her head and blinks. What? Where's Henry, the girls? Karen's life floods back and the psychic stares into her eyes.

"Give back what is hers," he tells her. "Or rot from the inside out. It's happening already, the decomposition. I smell it on your breath."

Karen covers her mouth and the women shriek with laughter.

"He's got you there, Kar!"

She feels her cheeks burn and stands to leave. The wine glass by her foot tips over and breaks into a million pieces on the hardwood floor. The blondes hoot and squeal and pile over one another. Screw this, the woo-woo witchcraft and the dumb lot of them, Karen thinks. She pulls a toonie out of her pocket and drops it onto his table. "Thanks for nothing," she says.

Come back, the women holler, but Karen waves them off without turning. She closes the door of the master suite and takes in the room, aching for the young woman who'd once slept here. Behind her, the laughter gets louder. Ingrates. It's the last time she's ever funding one of these excursions, that's for sure. There's Shannon's money, Karen thinks. She can have next year's fifteen grand, if Karen even manages to find her, that is.

She walks out onto the deck, the sky dark but the water lit by the light of a bright moon. She shivers in the cool air and looks up at all the stars. She considers asking them if Henry is with her at all, considers begging, like Earl told her Dolly had done: *Don't leave us. You can't leave!*

But Karen has always been smarter than women like Dolly.

She knows everyone is alone, always.

She wraps her arms around herself.

Behind her the door opens and there's kind Lacey, holding a quilt. The woman drapes the blanket around Karen's shoulders, smoothing the material as if warming a towelled child, fresh from a bath. She asks Karen if she's okay and Karen nods.

"I'm sorry," Karen says.

"Everyone is," Lacey says under the bouncing fringes of blond hair. "Everyone's sorry for something."

"No, I mean, I just need to be alone."

The sound of the party blares through the door as Lacey turns and leaves. Then, in the quiet, Karen walks the cedar stairs barefoot to the cool, wet lawn and then to the thick, cold sand. The tide is low, the moon's pale light illuminating black puddles and left-behind seashells. Karen walks very far, until she stands at the water's edge. A thick, recognizable stench fills the air and she brings her palm to her face before seeing a dying urchin at her feet.

With both hands, Karen lifts the rock the creature clings to. Her blanket trails behind, the carefully stitched squares collecting sand and silt and salt water. She walks until waves strip the quilt from her, until the ocean kisses the scar Tara's birth left on her belly, until the tentacles of the starfish begin to lift, wavering in its return to home. The creature is already dead.

Gently, Karen releases the stone.

ASCENSION

2015

SUNDAY, SEPTEMBER 6, 10:45 PM

Tara follows the Yellowhead Highway until she's the only vehicle on the dark road. From the dashboard speakers, a girl croons about crescent yellow smiles. Tara presses the knob, silencing the sound. She could use the quiet.

She thinks of someone she met earlier in the week. Tara had been manning a menstrual cup distribution table at a homeless shelter on Wye Road and a woman had pulled a chair up and remained there for the day, body hulked over a small notepad as she crossed lines through items on a long-running list. She really liked what Dr. Hamilton was doing, the woman said, her dark eyes sparkling above a bright smile. She also liked to help people. The woman held up the notepad. "See? Look at my list."

To Do:

Visit lady doc

Drop off cans

Open doors for folks at Sally Ann

Amy, she said her name was. Amy Ascension. She'd got the last part of her name from a shop that sold crystals and cards and books on reincarnation. Ascension meant climbing, or rising up, like an angel watching over the world. That's what Amy was, she said, an angel-in-training.

Tara asked if she would like a cup, and explained to the woman how to use it. Using a cup meant she wouldn't need to spend money on tampons or pads again, and the product wouldn't need to be replaced for at least five years. "That is, as long as you have somewhere safe to keep it when it's not in use?"

Oh, yes, Amy laughed. She didn't live in the shelter but had only come to visit.

"I'm not homeless. I live in my car."

It wasn't a perfect situation, Amy admitted. The back window had once been busted out, but it still gets her to and from work every day. And the busted window isn't really a big deal. She just keeps it covered with a garbage bag and duct tape, a blanket in the winter.

"I feel terrible for these people," she said, shaking her head. "They really have nothing. So I come here to cheer them up sometimes, share my smokes and stuff."

Tara didn't realize how much she hurt for the woman until she felt her own hand press against her chest. She thought of Amy's large body cramping in the too-small space of a driver's side seat, dashboard vents blasting to fight the cold slipping in from outside.

"Why are you so good to others, Amy? Are they good to you?"

Amy smiled. She was always on the lookout for a baby she'd had to give up, she explained, except now he'd be grown. She tried to be a good mom but didn't know how to do it and ended up giving him back to the people taking care of him. It was hard to give him back for two reasons: one because it broke her heart, and two because it was hard to do without getting into trouble. In the end, she parked near where he'd be found, and hid herself nearby, waiting and watching until someone came across the baby, safe but sad and all alone in her car. That was how the back window got busted out, so many years ago. After her son was safe and taken to people who'd help him, she had slipped back into the car with no one watching and driven away to lie low for a while. By the time she got back to the city the boy's other mom had moved houses. Amy has half kept watch since, not really looking for him, but looking out, just in case.

So that's why Amy believes in doing good deeds, she explains, because she knows it's so important to be brave and kind. She pours out all her kindness one person at a time, hoping it'll trickle down to her lost little boy the way raindrops connect in tiny streams on the windshield. A nice note stuck to a waitress's bumper might make her so happy she serves a teacher extra fries and he might feel so good he stays after school to help the boy Amy never stops thinking about.

"Do you have anyone like that, lady doc?" she asked. "Someone you miss? Someone you never stop thinking about?"

Tara presses on the gas as she considers Amy's question. Why, exactly, is she risking so much to perform a rural home visit in the middle of the night? When it comes down to it: yes, her reasons do match Amy Ascension's. Tara does have something to prove, a wrong to right. There is someone to pour love out for, someone lost from her life.

Someone Tara still talks to, in her mind, when she's scared.

Say something, she asks the memory of her sister.

Remember that time in the river valley, after the freezing rain?

I was too close to the edge. I fell over the bank and you jumped down after me.

And then we were stuck, but we were stuck together.

⚜

Friday, September 4, 3:00 PM

Tara doesn't usually offer home visits, but Mennonite women don't usually ask for abortions, either. When Tara entered the clinic's examination room, she found Leah flanked by two little girls with perfect golden braids and shin-skimming sack dresses, each an exact image of their mother, as if the trio were a group of unpacked Russian nesting dolls. Leah spoke to the children in Low German and the girls covered their ears.

The young woman explained that opioid detox had taken her last pregnancy and would surely take the child inside her now. Tara nodded in sympathy; it wasn't uncommon for addicted patients to seek sobriety upon pregnancy only to experience spontaneous abortion due to muscle contractions and severe fever as toxins left the body. For this reason, many addicted mothers-to-be felt no option but to continue using—the better of two terrible choices. It was for this reason that Tara had become certified in methadone maintenance treatment.

"I'm three months gone," Leah explained, but Tara guessed by the swell of the woman's belly she was closer to five. "My husband went back to work this morning and it'll be three weeks until he's home again. He took all our . . . stuff." Leah looked down at her dusty lace-up shoes. "I still have nightmares of the last child boiling inside me," she whispered. "My fever that high. I won't let another baby suffer like that. If you don't take this one fast, I'll do it myself."

Leah looked up then, as if challenging the doctor, searching for surprise in Tara's face, but there was no shock to show. In the scope of Tara's gynecology career there had been no class or faith or culture Tara had not seen represented in her waiting room. Besides, she had recently watched an entire miniseries on Amish drug trafficking. Only one year earlier, the province had found an Old Order farmer guilty of the distribution of cocaine. But Leah's situation didn't include secret meetings with a cartel or the mapping of underground trading routes. Leah had simply been overprescribed oxycodone following the emergency caesarean of her youngest child. Tara frowned as Leah explained the makings of her addiction. Every physician in the province practised the privilege of prescribing addictive substances, but few assumed responsibility for treating the addictions they contributed to. Of the hundreds of doctors Tara considered her contemporaries, she was one of only ten qualified to administer methadone.

For someone who had never so much as tasted a drop of alcohol, the opiates in the tired young mother's system felt like an answered prayer. When her husband hurt his back falling from a rig soon after the baby was born, Leah explained, she offered her pills to him and soon they began using recreationally, trolling clinics and emergency rooms with the kids in her father-in-law's loading truck after the day's chores were done. Doctors got wise to Leah, so her husband started making private purchases at the oilfield camp he worked at, sharing when he was home but letting her go weeks without when he was away. Leah knew how it went: he left today, so she'd be sick again within hours.

Tara nodded. It was all she could do not to wrap her arms around herself, her own skin prickling remembering the on-fire sensation of withdrawal, the deep, sharp churning of the stomach, the all-consuming, knife-edged fear.

"Leah," Tara explained, "pregnancy termination is a safe and routine procedure, and one that is your medical right. But would you still want to abort if there was another way?"

Methadone could save both Leah and her fetus, Tara explained. The drug was safe for pregnancy if administered carefully, and all Leah would have to do is come in for supervised daily doses. After she gave birth, Leah would be weaned from the medication and detox symptoms would be minor—like a bad cold or mild flu. The whole process would be entirely confidential.

The woman shook her head. "I don't drive." Leah lived almost an hour away and her cousin had brought her this time but wouldn't be able to every day. "You can write me a script and I will refill every week or two."

Tara bit her lip. She wanted to help and believed the woman's intentions hinged on the well-being of her child. Still, she knew neither good nor bad existed in the throes of disease.

"I can't give you more than a daily dose," she said. "I'm sorry, Leah. It's just too dangerous."

The young woman crossed her arms. Both children continued to cover their ears, Leah's eldest staring up at the doctor while the younger girl leaned forward to look past her mother to her sister. Leah waited for the next offer, her long blond braid and narrowed blue eyes so familiar Tara made an almost-impossible promise.

"I can come to you," she said. "Over my lunch break, every day. It'll mean dropping half of my afternoon appointments, but I'll do it if you're serious about getting clean."

Leah opened her mouth to speak but closed it again. She leaned away from the doctor, as if to better take her in.

"Why are you helping me?"

Tara paused before answering. She thought of the ice bank in the river valley, of her sister's sharp blue eyes, Shannon's hands cradling either side of Tara's face.

Tar.

The doctor leaned in and touched her patient's knees, echoing her sister's words, spoken so long ago:

"We've got to lift each other up."

<u>Sunday, September 6, 11:15 PM</u>

Tara flicks her headlights onto high beam. Shannon's pitched laughter rings in her head.

We couldn't climb out, the rain made the bank like glass.

Tara remembers her big sister kicking the snow, so quick to anger. Bad news, Mom used to call her. Shannon wasn't a nice girl, like Tara. Shannon was Tara's half-sister, on their father's side, and Tara's mother had no time for her. The day of the ice bank incident would be the last time Shannon was allowed to babysit.

We were like puppies, Tara tells the voice in her head. Like we were jumping at a door that wouldn't open. I wanted to play dogs, remember?

I said, "Tar, this is serious." We kept trying to get out, but we just kept sliding back down.

A ringtone fills the Jeep's interior. Tara reaches for her phone and hears her wife's fury.

"*C'est quoi ton problème*? Are you crazy?"

"It's a new moon," Tara tells Theresa, changing the subject. Theresa believes in new moons: in beginnings and rebirth and forgiveness. Hope, in the darkness. "It's a beautiful night for a drive."

"You promised me."

"I promised her, too."

"*Tu me brises le coeur.*"

A sob rips through the speakerphone and Tara feels a pull in her chest. She can almost see Theresa, so soft and so warm, still in bed, midnight black curls weaved with silver and wild with sleep, the lines between her brows deep in shock to have woken up alone.

"You're not safe. I'm calling the police."

"I'm fine!" Tara laughs to exaggerate her safety. Hear the softness of my voice, she thinks, feel the calm of this road.

"I'm calling 911."

"Baby, you can't . . ."

"*Je suis!*"

"Babe . . . you don't even know where I'm going."

Silence.

Click.

Theresa has hung up.

Shannon's voice laughs again in Tara's head.

Kick, punch, kick.

Shut up, Shan. It's not like that.

No. You're "nice." I know.

※

After walking Leah and her children out of the examination room and closing up the clinic, Tara had come home to find a police officer sitting opposite her wife in their living room.

Threats had been made, the constable explained. *Albertan Renegade*, an alt-right site evolved from a now-defunct shock-jock radio show, had published a story on Tara and Theresa's plans for a government-funded women's addiction and hospice centre. The site's audience, a mostly male Caucasian fan base who referred to themselves as "patriots," was as furious about the project as they were about most things since the recent election of the female-led, left-leaning NDP.

At first Tara thought it was a joke. In the last year, more Albertan lives had been taken by opioids than by car accidents and no one had suffered as much as addicted mothers and their children. The centre would fill an enormous gap: it would provide space for women at risk to care for their children while getting clean, and it would keep children out of an already bursting-at-the-seams foster care system. A former mental health resource worker and addictions rehabilitation worker, Theresa would serve as program coordinator and on-site therapist; Tara would serve as the centre's general practitioner and methadone treatment provider. They'd already discussed partnership with a young psychiatrist friend of Theresa's, the child of one of Theresa's earliest patients, Susan. Iris would assist with the chemical imbalances that contribute to self-medication. The space would also offer reproductive health, long-term care, and terminal hospice services in alternate wings, freeing room in other hospitals. Ground had broken on the project last spring and it was set to open in the fall. The couple was already interviewing nursing staff.

Then Theresa held up her laptop for Tara to read.

The article bounced from describing the centre as a lavish penthouse for junkies to a squalid den of child abuse. Tara was labelled a baby killer. Her cheeks burned as her patients were described as leeches on society and any resources spent on their recovery a waste of taxpayer dollars. These were reasons why she should be sharing her own sobriety story, Tara thought. She could be a poster child for recovery, dispelling ignorance and discrimination around those who suffer addiction.

And lose everything, she imagines her sister's voice saying.

Besides, you made a promise.

Theresa scrolled down past the article to the comment section. As Tara read, her hands gripped the sides of the computer, liable to snap it in half. Each added comment was as vicious as the last. Addicted mothers had always faced an exquisite kind of hatred, their illness singled out by the public for more sharpened abuse. The AR website was simply capitalizing on that outrage, monetizing abhorrence through banner ads and digital traffic. Tara scrolled to the top of the page and found a female byline.

There's a special place in hell . . .

"She calls us radical feminists and professional protestors and militant lesbians," Theresa said. "But the hysteria at SheSober is much worse."

That *was* the worst. Theresa had spent three years creating SheSober.com, a recovery program and virtual community for women seeking recovery. The platform was meant to be inclusive and honest and safe. Tara turned and placed the laptop on a counter to navigate to the site, covering her mouth as she read the threats of violence directed to her in the comment section.

"Have any members shared identifiable information?" Tara asked.

Theresa wiped tears with the heel of her hand. She turned to the officer standing behind them and cried, stomping her feet.

"*C'est ridicule!* What are you going to do?"

The constable shook her head. "There's not much we can do about online content," she apologized. The RCMP was documenting all legitimate threats of violence, and additional threats should be reported, as well. "For now, the best course of action may be to take down the site until everything blows over. These people won't remember the story in a week."

"No," Tara said. "People need this site." There'd be no hiding, and no abandoning SheSober. Tara would take care of moderating comments and blocking malicious users. She'd stay up all night if she had to.

"Well," the constable offered, "additionally, we can provide you both with a security detail for the next few days."

Tara snorted. "Now *that* sounds like a waste of taxpayer money."

Tara walked the officer to the apartment building's parking garage and waved goodbye before heading to her Jeep to make sure she had locked the doors. An unopened beer can sat beside the vehicle's front tire like a gift and she eyed it for a moment before telling herself not to be so stupid. What did she think it was, a pipe bomb? She picked up the warm can and placed it in the trash by the elevator door. As she stepped into the shaft, her eye caught the glow of a cigarette just as the steel doors began to close. Someone sat behind the steering wheel of an old car in one of the visitor stalls, watching.

Her sister's voice piped up in her head.

Tar, you gotta be more careful.

※

<u>Sunday, September 6, 11:20 PM</u>

Tears blur the highway. Tara leans back against the headrest with her chin up. She reaches into the console beside her and finds the shape of a secret pack of Player's Light. Tara doesn't drink, overeat, cheat on her wife. She hasn't messed around with pills or even taken more than a Tylenol since hitting rock bottom eight years ago. But sometimes . . . sometimes Tara just needs something bad in her mouth.

A little phallic for your tastes, Tar, don't ya think?

The doctor ignores the inner voice. She puckers up and sucks.

You wanted to try to walk across the ice, remember? I was scared you'd break through.

I thought a wolf would come and eat me if we stayed in one spot.

You were crying.

It was dark. And cold. I was scared.

I was too.

Tara opens the window and holds the smoke like a tribute to the night. She stares at her reflection in the driver's side mirror: red eyes emphasizing the angle of her nose, short, spiky hair pointing out from her head unstyled. Everything about her feels painfully sharp. But the image disappears into the shining headlights of unwelcome company. Tara slows and turns onto a range road running parallel to the highway. The time glows green on the dash's digital stereo and Tara counts back the hours to when Leah's last dose should have been administered. More than eleven hours overdue. Leah must really be suffering by now.

Tara leans more heavily on the gas and hopes the car behind her isn't a cop.

※

Saturday, September 5, 12:30 PM

"Sorry," Leah said as she switched off the pot of boiling water. Mariam and Isaac don't believe in coffee, so she isn't allowed to keep it in the house.

"Is tea okay?"

Tara yawned and nodded, watching Leah's large German shepherd sniff and lick her toes. The dog had the thick coat of an animal that frequently slept outdoors but was polite enough, having been pulled into Leah's trailer so to not alert anyone of Tara's arrival. The animal's name was Phoebe, Leah said with affection, after Leah's grandmother and after the moon, although it wasn't supposed to be named at all. Mariam and Isaac don't believe in pets, either. Here, every creature has its place, and every place is like a very small box.

When Phoebe grew tired of sniffing Tara's toes, she lay below the kitchen table and Tara leaned back in her chair. She had guarded SheSober against AR's keyboard warriors until the wee hours of the morning and could barely keep her eyes open now. Outside the kitchen window and across a dry grass field, ravens made a meal of garbage bags thrown onto what must have been Mariam and Isaac's porch. The birds reminded Tara of the online trolls, relentlessly cawing and eating up trash and shitting it all over the place. She didn't know what was worse: the crudeness of AR's Patriots, or the fact that newspapers had ripped a favourite wedding photo of Tara and Theresa from Tara's private Facebook profile and printed the story front page.

Theresa cried when she found the daily sitting on their doormat that morning. What photo would they hang in the entrance now? But perhaps worst of all was deleting SheSober member stories to protect author anonymity. Women silenced to appease the anger of men, what else was new? The night had been nothing but defeating. Until, that is, a new SheSober sign-up: plainjane_95.

A profile photo of a pink Alberta rose sent Tara a private message: *There's a computer in the barn. Mariam forgets to lock it sometimes.*

Leah had found the site's address on the business card Tara's receptionist had given her, and she'd sneaked online to thank Dr. Hamilton. She apologized if she was rude earlier, she said. She was just so scared.

But I'm going to be healthy now. Fresh and clean and wise, just like my own mother. Through your help and God's grace, I'll change everything around me and about me from the inside out.

And I can't wait to meet this baby.

It was almost enough to heal Tara's beat-up heart.

With shaky hands, Leah cleared crochet hooks and yarn from the kitchen tabletop to a basket on the floor. She placed Tara's mug in front of her, spilling only a little bit of tea onto the placemat. "Did you find the place alright?"

Tara smiled. It was standard, the niceties patients clung to, but the doctor never ceased to find them sweetly amusing. "I did," she answered. "But I must say I'm a little concerned leaving my vehicle on the side of the highway." She'd been told to park there and follow a foot trail through the trees and past the barn to Leah's trailer's side door.

Leah glanced out the window beside Tara, to her in-law's mobile home. "I'm sorry, but they'll know you're here if you park in the driveway. I'm not supposed to have visitors when my husband's away," she said, closing the curtains. "Mariam says females get unnatural ideas when left alone."

She blushed and turned back to the dishes in the sink.

In her sleep, Phoebe groaned.

"That's not . . . I mean . . . your community doesn't traditionally feel that way, does it?"

"No," Leah said. She pumped more soap into the dirty water. Where Leah grew up, women were friends and men weren't sent away to make money. Everyone worked together to raise children, farm the land, preserve the harvest, and staff produce stands. "I was a schoolteacher," she told Tara, turning from the soapsuds to see if the doctor believed it. "For the little ones. Before I was married, of course."

She wiped the last dish clean and unplugged the sink. "My parents wanted me to wait longer before getting married," she confessed. "But I was so in love." She and her mother and father had met her future husband at an area conference of Mennonite churches when she was only seventeen. It was a rare occasion for Leah to leave the colony.

"When I first married," she said, "I used to wonder if my parents knew what Mariam and Isaac were like."

She fell silent, watching the basin empty of its water before turning to the raw roasting chicken on the counter and picking up a set of kitchen shears. The dog hurried to Leah's feet and sat, panting.

"Then the babies were born, and I knew they didn't."

Mariam and Isaac weren't at all like the Old Order folks Leah had known growing up. They didn't even let her go to church but for Isaac's living room Bible study under Mariam's supervision. Sometimes Leah wondered if her parents-in-law were truly brethren at all. Mariam wasn't even her husband's real mother; his biological mother, a real Mennonite woman, had died when he was a child. Mariam was "English"—Canadian-born and from the mainstream world. She met Isaac through an online chat forum for religious folks and he'd brought her to the farm when Leah's husband was a teenager. The couple was strange, even stranger than the most traditional people Leah's parents had known. Mariam, especially, was histrionic, paranoid, aggressive, and cold.

Leah snipped the wings off the roasting bird and fed them to waiting Phoebe, the animal's daunting jaws accepting the gift with a gentle mouth. Leah wiped the blades of the scissors over her rounded belly, leaving faint pink lines across her white apron.

"It's Isaac who makes the rules," she said. "But it's Mariam who keeps them."

Tara shook her head. "Leah, why do you stay?"

Leah worked a moment longer, silently patting dry and seasoning the chicken, lifting it with expert hands before dropping it into the large slow cooker. Tara wondered if perhaps she hadn't heard the question. Finally, Leah paused and lifted her head, staring out of the small window above the sink.

"There's nowhere else for us to go."

She shook herself from thought and turned to Tara, crossing the room with jaw and blue eyes set, once again the image from the exam room: a woman strong and stony and the incarnate of a ferocity Tara had once known so well.

"I mean it, doctor. There's nowhere else. My parents have six children still living in a four-bedroom home, and me and the girls and this baby would make four more. They can't take us in. We're better off here. Mariam and Isaac won't live forever. We just have to stay faithful, stay sweet. No one can ever know why you're here."

Leah held her stare until interrupted by the cry of a small child from the back room. Leah held a finger to her lips as Tara opened her mouth to speak.

"If they don't hear you, they'll think you don't exist."

She excused herself to the back quarters and Tara waited, peeking through the window's yellowing curtains to better investigate Mariam and Isaac's property.

But for the ravens in the garbage on the porch, the barren landscape between the houses was still as bleak and arid and motionless as it was before. But no, Tara realized, that wasn't right. There was movement behind the barn now; the black wings of more ravens, strangely curved and slow moving. Suddenly, Tara realized it wasn't birds at all. A woman stepped from behind the barn into view, her black dress grazing her ankles as the afternoon breeze caught the material, swelling the skirt. Locks of steel grey hair slipped from the old woman's long braid and whipped around her face as she wiped her brow with her wrist.

Mariam.

Tara squinted and leaned closer to the window. On the woman's hand, scarlet shone in bold contrast to the washed out, dusty yellow filter with which the afternoon sun had painted all else. Was Mariam bleeding? Tara watched as the old woman bent toward whatever she had been working on behind the barn. When she stood straight again, her hand clutched the legs of three headless roasting birds, their blood dripping into the earth. The old woman raised her face to look across the field, to Leah's home. Tara dropped her hand to let the curtain fall, unsure whether she had been spotted.

"All right, they're back to napping," Leah whispered as she returned. One hand supporting her expanding belly, she leaned over the kitchen table to close the linens tight before opening her palm to the doctor. Tara placed a pill into Leah's palm and Leah lifted her hand to her mouth, throwing back her head and shivering, the sleeves of her cardigan pulled to her knuckles.

Tara cocked her head. "You think I don't know the pill between the fingers move?"

Leah rolled her eyes and shook out her sleeve.

I was only going to break it in half, she said. Just in case.

In case of what?

In case you forget about us.

Not going to happen. We have to trust each other.

I won't put my baby through that.

You won't have to.

If you forget . . .

I won't.

I promise.

※

<u>Sunday, September 6, 11:25 PM</u>

Trees light up as headlights turn, high beams tailing Tara on the dirt road.

Shit shit shit shit shit

It could be nothing, Tara thinks. Could be a local, a scenic-route aficionado, a near-sighted granny uncomfortable travelling at highway speeds. A drunk avoiding check stops.

A drunk, looking for fun.

Tara slows and hangs right, back onto the highway. She seeks her sister's voice as distraction.

It was so cold I didn't even know my hand was hurt.

There was blood on the snow.

And that tree root, jutting out of the bank. If I could just reach it . . .

I thought we were going to die.

It was so stupid I couldn't believe it. We needed that root. It was right there.

From the range road, the stranger's car horn blares and Tara tightens her grip around the wheel. She tries not to think about what she found pushed into the crack of the Jeep's driver side door: the newspaper image of their wedding photo, cut from the front page. Someone had read the story and knew which building they lived in and which vehicle was Tara's. Who would do that? And why? Tara had dropped the square of newsprint and then picked it up again, tearing it into a million little pieces.

"I think we have a stalker," Theresa had said the night before, but Tara just laughed it off. A faceless chalk angel had been drawn on the condo's entry steps.

"Babe, it was just some kid's sidewalk art."

"Just be careful, okay?"

I just kept thinking, how did this happen? How did we get stuck down here?

※

<u>Sunday, September 6, 10:15 AM</u>

Theresa refused their weekly jog when they woke up that morning.

"I think you could use it," Tara said.

Theresa lifted her brows. "*Excusez-moi?*"

"For the jumpiness, I mean." Tara laughed and wrapped her arms around Theresa's waist. "Babe, you're perfect. I just mean . . . I know you're anxious. Exercise is good, right? Get rid of that energy?"

Theresa shook her head. "Tar, we've barely slept in three days. And besides, there's been a weird car hanging around." A lady on the floor below theirs had mentioned it in the elevator. "A beat-up old thing. I'm not going anywhere, not for a few days at least."

Tara thought about the visitor's car she'd seen in the parking garage, a lit cigarette held in the shadows, and told her wife to go back to bed. Tara would bring in coffee and breakfast. With a break to administer Leah's MMT, they could hibernate and watch Netflix all day.

She was lowering the handle of their French press when Theresa shouted her name, calling Tara into the bedroom.

"*Regardez!* It's her! On the *Alberta Renegade* article!"

Theresa held up the laptop from the bed and Tara scanned the comment section.

plainjane_95 wrote on 08/08/2015 at 12:13 PM: *And if she profane herself by playing the whore, she profaneth her father: she shall be burnt with fire—Leviticus 21:9*

"She wouldn't have written that." Tara shook her head. "She must have forgotten to log out."

Theresa put the laptop on the duvet and crawled onto her knees, stroking both sides of Tara's face between her hands as she stared into her eyes. "No, *mon ange*. Look at the time. This was written from her computer *while* you were there."

Tara's stomach churned. Isaac? Mariam? Had one of them been in the barn when she'd walked past it down the foot trail from the highway?

Theresa began to cry. "You can't go back."

"Baby, Leah's next dose is in less than two hours."

"You can't." Theresa shook her head. "Send an ambulance instead." She raced to the front door and grabbed Tara's keys from the rack, clutching them against her chest. "I won't let you go. *Non, non, non.*"

Tara opened her arms and took her wife into her embrace. She kissed her fingertips and eyes and lips.

"*Ce n'est pas ton problème,*" Theresa whispered. "It doesn't have to be you."

Tara nodded and brought Theresa back to bed. She held her and thought about parking in ditches and dogs as watchful as the moon and little girls with immaculate braids and how few places there are for a mother to go. Tara stayed like this until Theresa fell asleep, counting down the hours, feeling Leah's pain with every extra one.

And then, quietly, Tara lifted the keys from her wife's pillow, and left.

❋

Tara hangs back. She exhales as the vehicle travelling parallel passes her own: a dodgy old car, a taped-up garbage bag covering its broken back window, the edges of its thin plastic fluttering in the night breeze. Its taillights flicker through the willows that separate the range road from the highway. Tara is not being followed. Why the car honked is anyone's guess.

Tara is close to Leah's now so she slows and crosses the centreline, easing into the ditch to park. It's too dark to see the trail without headlights so she leaves them on but turns off the ignition and takes her keys. Reaching for the medical case on the back seat, she realizes the car on the dirt road is looping back to the exit.

Shit.

Tara grabs her phone and presses 9 and 1 and then leaves it like that, her thumb ready over the last digit. She wraps her keys in her fist, pushing the largest between her middle and index finger in case the driver wants a fight.

She makes her way through the trees but stops near the barn at the sound of low growling. Rapid-fire barks bombard the silence of the night and ring through the sky as Tara hisses Phoebe's name. Finally, the dog hears Tara's voice over the sound of her own canine warnings. Phoebe trots close to lick her palms but her barks still echo in the clear night. The ground behind Leah's trailer is suddenly cast in a yellow glow. Mariam's porch light has flickered on.

Shit shit shit.

Quick but quiet, Tara opens the side door to Leah's trailer and calls her name. No answer. Tara lets herself in, Phoebe slinking through the doorframe ahead of her.

The kitchen is bright but dirty, the light left on over the table where the children's meals are crusting, a Crock-Pot still greasy by the sink. There is silence from the back room where the children sleep, but at the front: a moan.

"Leah?" Tara calls. "It's me. I have your medicine. I didn't forget."

The doctor walks to the master bedroom to find Leah at the foot of her bed, hair loose and plastered to her face in fever, sweat, and vomit. Phoebe walks to Leah, sitting at her feet confused, distressed by the copper-sick smell of the scene. Leah lifts her face, body trembling and hands hidden by the long sleeves of her nightgown, clasped tight between her knees. Lines of blood run down her legs and over her ankles, painting scarlet footprints on the carpet under her feet.

"You made me," Leah sobs. "You forgot about us! You did this."

She lifts her hands, scarlet palms clutching a crochet hook.

"I didn't let her suffer."

Oh Jesus.

Leah cries and cries, keening into herself, arms wrapped around the swell of her stomach. "I'm sorry, baby. I'm sorry. I'm so sorry."

Tara hits the last 1 and the speakerphone option and puts the phone on the floor beside her. She lifts Leah and lays her shivering body on the bed, pushing apart her knees and shouting directions to the dispatcher over the noise of Leah's grief.

She needs light, a bulb or a lamp. She exits the call to bring up her phone's flashlight app, surveying damage until interrupted by the slam of a door.

"Murderer! Pervert! Witch!"

Startled, Tara scrambles to her feet but trips and falls. When she looks up again. she's met by a wide yellow grimace, black-toothed in front. Mariam is manic, crazed, in a long nightgown. Wild grey hair frames her bulging eyes. Phoebe barks in competition with her shrieking, the dog's howling high pitched and constant.

Again and again Mariam screams. She calls to God with hands raised and trembling, a terrible, horrifying prayer. Tara scurries to stand as Mariam turns and rushes to the kitchen. Tara follows in time to see her snatch shears from the counter.

"No!" Tara shouts, but the old woman flies. The doctor stands in front of her patient's room, one hand on the door handle and the other raised in an attempt to stop the blades.

"Stop! No! Stop!"

There is nothing in the world but eyes and hate, slicing fire and thick-furred yelps: the splitting of flesh where shears enter Tara's body. Her arms and cheeks and breasts burn again and again. The shock of it sends Tara to her knees, but she does not let go of that door.

Finally, Mariam drops the scissors and raises her hand to her mouth. The old woman takes in the horror of her work before backing away in stumbling steps. "I'm sorry," she mumbles, and then she turns away, running into the night. Tara falls onto her hands, sucking air and coughing blood. She has to get outside.

She crawls and gasps, but air doesn't fill her lungs. She spits blood onto the carpet. Weak, she looks up, panting. Leah's small daughters look down at her, eyes full of fear between sleep-mussed braids, the small hands of the two little girls clasped tight.

Sister holding sister, all alone, together.

※

The night air is cool. There's gravel under Tara's palms and a stranger standing in the shadow of the barn, smoking a cigarette.

We couldn't do it without each other, Shannon says.

The driver from the road steps nearer.

I needed you and you needed me. Not one without the other.

Tara feels herself lifted and held. She is cradled like a baby in the smell of tobacco and the comfort of soft arms and a warm body: a mother who is kind and alive and well and strong. Phoebe whimpers at the doctor's side, sniffing the stranger, licking up the mess of Tara's blood.

There was blood in the snow.

"I'm cold," Tara whispers.

"I got you," the voice promises.

Shannon? Shan?

"I got you, lady doc. I got you."

I told you to be brave. Said I'd hold you up so you could grab the root. I told you you'd have to fight until it broke from the ice and I promised not to let you go.

"I don't under . . . I didn't know what to do."

"You did anything anyone ever gotta do, lady."

If you could lower the root to me, I could climb it. I could push us higher, over the bank.

"I was scared."

"You were brave. You were kind."

Tara closes her eyes. Life is no more than the night sky and warm arms; the sweet, fading song of the woman holding her, a tune so familiar and sad: a lost woman and a lonely road, her steps unceasing. *Nikâwiy.*

"My sister's song," the woman holding Tara whispers.
We have to lift each other up, I said.
We have got to lift each other up.

HAVE A NICE LIFE

2016

JUDE DRIES OFF with the towel he keeps in his backpack. It's a wet day to walk to work but city transit is always a nightmare. He rubs the terry cloth over his face and checks under his T-shirt to make sure the pouch he wears around his neck isn't as drenched as the rest of him. All good: the pouch is soft and dry and Jude tucks it safe back under his shirt again. Zoe gave him the beaded bag only a few nights ago. In it, she placed the dried petals of a rose he'd given her.

"For you to give back to me another time. When we're ready."

Dad said the medicine bag looked pretty authentic—made of deer hide and stitched with sinew. Somehow Zoe had come into possession of it when she was a little kid. The wild rose beaded on the front symbolized life, she told him; she'd looked it up online. Jude was touched, but his own research claimed Alberta's official flower stood for sacrifice and mourning, too.

Checking his reflection in the washroom mirror, Jude pulls his wet curls between gelled fingers to keep them crunchy and straight. He tosses the hair gel into his bag, folding the towel so it won't wet the passport inside. Remembering the thin blue booklet, he lifts it out and feels its perfect edges under his thumb. Today he's got an important decision to make, and three options to choose from. He thinks of the list he made the night before:

To Do:

Go (and let her break your heart)

Stay (and break it faster yourself)

Propose (maybe convince her not to leave at all?)

He lets the passport fall open to where the pages separate: a diamond ring pushed into the booklet's spine. Jude's not ready to get married but he doesn't want to lose his girl. Both of them know long-distance relationships never work; they've already talked that option out. If she's in Ontario and he's stuck in Alberta it's hello friend-zone while they focus on their studies—which is basically the same as goodbye.

A girl like Zoe Sterling is not going to stay single for long.

She's coming to pick him up at the end of his shift and they're supposed to be travelling with some friends of hers to Kingston, Ontario, for a concert, a four-thousand-kilometre one-way trip that will take them into the States and back up again, ending with her catching a bus to Ottawa and Jude alone and sad in the back of a hippie van for another four thousand kilometres home again. He doesn't even know Miranda and her boyfriend, Grayson, just that the girls found each other on Facebook years ago after they were involved in a car accident or something. He tries to imagine the awkward drive home: strangers in the front seats, heartache in the back. Ugh, nope. No go. He just can't do it to himself. He imagines, instead, getting down on one knee in the parking lot of the

Hamilton Women's Recovery and Care Hospice, all the patients and staff watching from their windows.

Zoe Sterling, will you marry me?

Then he can imagine the trip —there *and* back, both ways together. It could be like a practice honeymoon. Now that's the way to do it!

He stares into the ring's diamond as if it were a crystal ball. His parents would freak if they knew what he was planning. Four years divorced, they'd given him Mom's old engagement ring on the understanding he'd pawn it for tuition since Dad was laid off and couldn't help with school costs. But just because the ring was worth something in 2008 doesn't mean it will sell now. More than forty-four thousand oilfield workers are out of work; everyone is selling big-ticket items dirt cheap. Jude would be lucky to get two grand and that wouldn't even cover his last year at the University of Alberta, where at least he can live in Papa Rhanji's basement suite, rent-free.

No, if the ring is to be used for anything, it makes the most sense to put it on Zoe's finger and ask her to stay in that basement suite with him, just one more year. She's only a second-year student anyway, and the University of Ottawa's political science department will still be there after Jude graduates in the spring. So what if she has to give up the scholarship? Next year, they could make the move to Ottawa together. By then, she'd be entering year four and he'd be a recent grad, ready to support them both.

He tucks the ring into his pocket and buries the passport back inside the bag. Pulling his phone from a smaller compartment, he sees Zoe's texted a selfie. It's a mirror shot: her smiling in a black tube dress, *The Future is Female* etched in white font stretched against the front. Long red hair spills over her shoulders.

Packing!

He replies with a thumbs-up and a smiley emoji with hearts for eyes:

Can't wait!

He rereads his words after they're already sent. What is he thinking? If she says no to the ring—and that's a major possibility—then Zoe's packing for a solo trip and she doesn't even know it. Should he tell her he's having second thoughts? He feels guilt pang in his gut. God, he doesn't want to let her down. But he doesn't want to let her go, either.

If it weren't for the prospect of his heart being stomped on after the concert, there's no way Jude would even consider missing this show. He's obsessed with Gord Downie and all of Canada is poised to celebrate the iconic band's final concert after their front man announced his terminal cancer diagnosis four months ago. Besides, Miranda's not *just* Zoe's friend; she actually earned a spot to perform as one of several acts in the afternoon before the evening concert. How cool is that? Her video entry into the concert contest won the performance as well as four tickets and the invitation to hang out backstage and meet everyone. Jude's never met Miranda before, but they do have a bit of a weird connection. Jude's dad, Jim, is one of the reasons why Miranda's sort of famous. Jude and Jim were at West Edmonton Mall during some *Canada's Got Talent* auditions a few years ago, and it was Jim's video of the then-nervous teenager that went viral. Now Jim jokes about being owed royalties anytime he hears one of her songs on the radio.

Anyway, being a part of this concert . . . well, it's a pretty huge deal. God knows Miranda won't need Jude ruining it for her when it's time for Zoe to say goodbye.

So:

~~Go (and let her break your heart)~~

Stay (and break it faster yourself)

Propose (maybe convince her not to leave at all?)

He underlines that last one but is still kind of unsure. Whatever he decides to do, he's got eight hours to figure it out. Not that he'd admit it, but Jude's the kind of guy who believes in signs: numbers noticed or feathers found, a song you can't get out of your head until you realize its lyrics are the exact answer to the problem you're trying to solve. Maybe it's just superstition, or maybe Dad's actually right. Maybe our ancestors are always with us, guiding and watching out for us in ways we don't know. Jude drops his phone into the empty pocket of his scrubs and grabs his Bluetooth earphones before heading to the staffroom to start the day.

I'll take a message anytime now, he thinks, a silent prayer to who-knows-who.

"Hey, Jude." Sandra smiles as he enters the room. She lifts her bifocals off her nose, letting them hang on the gold chain around her neck. Dr. Iris—Zoe's cousin and Jude's primary reason for wanting this job—sits opposite the nurse, cradling a mug of coffee in her palms. Jude places a hand on either of Sandra's shoulders, bending to kiss the top of her white curls. Sandra is his grandfather's best friend, and Jude's known her all his life.

Sandra pats his hand and passes him a cupcake from the plate on the table. "It's my birthday," she tells him.

"Happy Birthday, Nana," he says. "Time to retire?"

The old lady laughs. "Not on your life. When it's my time to go, I'll just tuck myself into one of them beds down the hall."

Jude turns to hang his backpack on a coat hook and feels the women watching him as he grabs a mug from beside the percolator. Laughter erupts as he fills it with tap water.

"What?" he says. "You know I don't drink coffee!"

Sandra reaches over the table as he sits and squeezes his arm.

"So young. You will, honey. You will."

"Well?" Iris asks. She winks, lashes resting on the gold-coloured birthmark on her cheek. Zoe once said that splotch was Iris's own "cutie mark," like the pictures on the back of Suni's My Little Pony toys.

Jude frowns and shakes his head. "I don't know what you're talking about."

Sandra smacks him. "You brat. Come on, fess up—are you leaving us?"

"Think hard," Iris advises. An alumnus herself, it was on her recommendation that Jude was accepted into the U of O psych department for his last year. Back then, when he'd first got that acceptance letter, only a couple of months before oil prices went to shit, everything seemed perfect: him and Zoe going together, starting a new life in a new place where they'd study and explore and keep one another sharp, keep each other safe. "Tomorrow's the last day to register for classes. The connections you'd make there would pave the way for your whole career. You could make some real changes, Jude. It's important, the work you want to do."

Jude tries to swallow the knot in his throat. He can't mention costs or Sandra will say something to Papa Rhanji. He thinks of how Dad cried the day he'd been laid off from work. Jim had given

Jude everything he could ever ask for in life and still he thought he'd let his son down. Papa Rhanji's financial involvement would only shame him more and Jude owes Dad way more than that. Besides, Papa Rhanji's retired now and he already helps Mom out with groceries and rent and stuff. It's not like he's made of money.

Theresa, the centre's co-founder, interrupts the conversation. Fresh from leading the morning recovery circle, she sings bonjour to all and kisses her index and middle finger before pressing it to the portrait of her late wife. Dr. Tara Hamilton smiles in the photograph, thin lips pinched under a prominent nose, short, dark hair framing far-and-away eyes. It's as if she sees something in Jude— maybe in everyone—he hasn't yet found himself.

"How's Ms. Delacroix?" Theresa wants to know, pouring herself a coffee.

Sandra shakes her head. "Not long with us. We drained fluid last night and the GP's recommended a shunt, but she's not having it. Been demanding doctor-assisted death since Global News broadcasted the legalization. Says Iris needs to 'get her shit in a pile and off her already.'"

"Ah," Theresa sighs. She shakes her head. "*La mort n'a peut-être pas plus de secrets à nous révéler que la vie?*"

"What does that mean?" Jude asks.

"It means Delacroix's in a big hurry to get nowhere," Iris says. She wipes cupcake crumbs off her hands with a napkin. "Besides, she won't be around long enough for my licensing approval. Come on, let's see what we can do."

Jude slips a headphone into his ear so he can listen to the Hip while he works. He's happy to shadow the doctor. Iris is the whole reason Jude is changing bed sheets and spoon-feeding old ladies when most of his third-year classmates are interning for pay at private practices. Alberta's youngest licensed psychiatrist, Iris has made significant strides in introducing the holistic elements of her hippie-kid upbringing to her pharmaceutical-based professional discipline. It's a medical revolution Jude feels primed to join. As a child who first learned to read sounding words out of Papa Rhanji's medical textbooks, and one who's spent the last four summers learning Elder Medicine in the community near where his dad grew up, Jude imagines himself pioneering a new modality: a marriage of western and traditional wellness, something that might result in a truer sort of healing, something that might be accessible to all of Canada's people.

Right now, Jude is mostly just a glorified candy striper, but he's also one who gets to host drum circles and brings Dad in to lead weekly smudging ceremonies and co-facilitates Theresa's group talk therapy sessions. He's also been given reprieve from entry-level duties whenever anyone has to deal with Ms. Delacroix. The end-stage lung cancer patient can be difficult, but she likes "the Kid." He reminds her of someone she used to know, though who it is Ms. Delacroix can't put her finger on. Whoever it might be, Jude likes Ms. Delacroix, too. He finishes every shift with her, watching the six o'clock news.

"You sit with me," she tells him every day when his shift ends, patting the chair by her bed. "Stay. When you're here, I don't have to think about this shitty mess, dying all alone."

"Opiated" growls in Jude's left ear as he and Iris enter Ms. Delacroix's room.

He centres himself, forcing his lips to curve upward as he says good morning. It's getting harder to visit, watching Ms. Delacroix go. Sunlight breaks through the clouds outside and spills onto the wasted woman, highlighting the crevices and hollows that make someone still so young look so old. She isn't even forty yet, younger than Jude's mom. He crosses to the window and adjusts the blinds the way she likes: closed.

"Syrian refugees have created a thriving chocolate business in Nova Scotia," he says. Jude reports three happy headlines a day, an effort to convince her to stay on the planet just a little longer. "And nearly three hundred million dollars has been raised for Fort McMurray wildfire victims."

"But no jobs for the rest of them," Ms. Delacroix croaks, reaching for the tissues. Black speckled Kleenexes litter her bed. "And no jobs in Fort Mac either."

"Okay, but the Connecticut squirrel with the cup stuck on his head has been rescued by paramedics."

Ms. Delacroix coughs. "Okay, kid. You got me. That is just stinkin' cute."

Her inhales come in desperate wheezes as she struggles to slow herself.

"Shannon," Iris says, drawing a syringe, "it looks like you're experiencing shortness of breath, and I know that's really frightening."

"Gee, doc, med school paid off."

"I'm going to give you morphine to turn off that feeling of suffocation, okay? Hold on, it'll take a moment to kick in."

Jude almost reminds Iris of the patient's addiction history but remembers Ms. Delacroix doesn't have enough life left to abuse. He and the doctor wait and watch as Ms. Delacroix holds a crumbled Kleenex in a grey fist to her chest. Slowly, the woman lowers her hand and the tissues fall to the floor, breath winded but slow enough that they are able to take vitals, check for bedsores, chat. Mid-sentence, Ms. Delacroix drops into a daydream, face turned to the window. Jude squeezes her hand before he leaves.

"Tar?" she whispers, her eyes locked to some distant place above his shoulder.

"It's Jude, Ms. Delacroix."

Ms. Delacroix's eyes focus back into their usual steely, sharp blue. She touches his arm. "Open the blinds, kid. What would I do without you?"

In the hallway, Iris rests her hand on Jude's shoulder. It's time for her to do rounds and for him to make beds and wash bedpans, change patients out of gowns that have been soiled in the night.

"Shannon isn't going to last two weeks," the doctor says.

He shakes his head, looks at his feet. "I wish there was more we could do."

"No, Jude," Iris stretches the words. "Keeping in mind any road trip plans, you need to understand, Shannon isn't going to last *two weeks*. If you're leaving us today, make sure you say goodbye."

She watches his face until he swallows and nods. "I can't afford to go." He looks at the toes of his tennis shoes. "I was going to . . . I'm thinking of asking Zoe to stay, just one more year. What do you think?"

Iris frowns. "You know," she says, "Zoe's mom had to make a choice like that, between being someone or belonging to someone. It ended pretty bad."

Jude nods. He knows all about the divorce.

"So you think I should just let her go?"

"I think you should interrogate your intentions before encouraging someone you love to risk her future for yours."

She turns to her work, leaving him alone in the hall. Jude raises his hands to the back of his head and interlocks his fingers.

A bittersweet strum starts to play. "Bobcaygeon." He thinks of Zoe singing along that night they couldn't get into Man Machine Poem's Rexall show and had to squeeze onto a sports bar's last barstool and watch the Marathon Tribute on Much Music instead. She swayed with her eyes closed, the sprinkle of white scars on her cheekbones illuminated by a neon Molson Canadian sign, revealing themselves just like Downie crooned, one star at a time.

He knows Iris is right. Asking Zoe to put her life on hiatus is selfish. She's so excited to study right on the doorstep of Parliament Hill. Besides, who does he think he's kidding, expecting her to say yes? She's already said no before.

Jude had shown up a few weeks ago with the rose on the steps of the Alberta legislature where Zoe was working as a summer tour guide. He told her he loved her and asked for one more year. It was supposed to be the big romantic gesture, like in a movie that ends with lovers kissing in the rain. But Zoe pushed him away.

"You want me to stay? I barely know you!" she said. "I could be working for Trudeau!"

She had told him everything about herself, she said, the weird allergy that caused her scars, her driving anxiety, her embarrassingly ambitious dream of becoming prime minister, the snooping obsession that had manifested during her parent's ugly divorce. But he was so closed off and private and detached. He made her feel like a weirdo, like he was normal and healthy and she was some clichéd sad girl, a broken little doll for him to fix. Well, if he wanted that, she said, he should look for someone else because she was doing just fine and love worked both ways and he didn't seem that healthy himself, so scared to let her in.

She was right, Jude realized. He was a coward. Even on that "Bobcaygeon" night he'd panicked and tried to play it cool.

"These men are geniuses," Zoe had whispered, tears trickling over stars.

"Some of their stuff's okay, I guess."

Idiot.

"Listen," she said on the steps, petals dangling at her knee. "It would take a lot more than a flower to stop me from going, but I'd love it if you were the guy I thought of every time a Hip song played. Let's go to the concert together—one last perfect date. And if you want to share your weirdness with me, I'd probably love that too."

There *was* a kiss...but no romantic rain, and no good news either.

He's stuffing urine-soaked sheets into the washing machine when Sandra asks for help lifting a patient. He follows her to a van marked Great Plains Nursing Home where they meet a practical nurse in printed scrubs, a silver angel-wing necklace shining on her neck and the name *Carrie* etched on her nametag. The nurse opens the van doors and together they help an elderly man as he lowers himself from the vehicle. Behind him, a woman with long, thin hair sobs in her seat, arms raised as if she were a tree, praying to the sky. The necklaces around her neck look like the kind kids wore in pictures of Woodstock, back in the day.

"Come on, love," the man gently says. He turns to Jude. "She's a little scared."

They'll need to carry her, Sandra says. Jude introduces himself to the old woman and apologetically lifts her up and out of the van. She startles and then clutches his shirt, whimpering into his chest like Suni when she falls off her bike. As Jude walks, the old woman's grabbing hands find the medicine bag tucked under his scrubs and T-shirt. Her fingers follow the leather drawstring and pull the pouch to view.

"Jamie," the old woman keens. "Jamie, Jamie, Jamie!"

Jude stops, confused, and the old woman's husband leans over to see.

"Well, I'll be . . . yes, love. It's just like our Jamie's." The old man's mouth falls slack as he shakes his head. His eyes glisten. "That bag . . . they could be one and the same. Now that's something I hadn't thought of for a long time."

Jude resumes his careful steps, carrying the patient into the hospice as she presses the bag's beaded rose to her lips. He places her on her bed and he and the old man leave to let the nurses clean her up; she had an accident during the trip. The man introduces himself as they wait in the hallway.

"Simperson," he says, extending his hand. "Thank you for your help."

"Jude," he replies. He tucks the bag back under his clothes. "It must be hard for you to see her like that."

"It's not easy."

"We could have called you after admittance. You could have come in once she was settled."

The man shakes his head. "Where she goes, I go, son. That woman has led me all 'round this globe. We've lived and loved in England, in Ecuador, for a short while, even on a hippie commune in Vermont!" He chuckles. "That bag you have around your neck, it reminds her of one a friend made after we lost our son, back when

we lived up north. That woman . . . she's made my life a journey—
an adventure, that's for sure. I'll not leave her to travel alone yet.
Not ever."

Carrie calls Mr. Simperson into the room and Jude looks in after
him. Iris scribbles notes on the counter by the sink while Carrie
and Sandra prop pillows behind the old woman. In the midst of
the busyness, the old man sits on his wife's new bed, cupping her
wrinkled face with his weathered hands, wiping tears away with his
thumbs. There's pain in Jude's chest, like he's looking into a beautiful
and brutal future, one he wants and one he's scared of.

One that would be worth all the brilliance and all the fear.

Where she goes, I go . . . she's made my life a journey.

Goosebumps shiver up over Jude's arms and legs. The sign!
That's what it's all about: adventure and risk-taking, travelling the
world, moving through life together. Just like Zoe's invited him to
do. Almost resolved, Jude looks in again at the elderly couple. But
adventure isn't in that room, only sacrifice. It's a man covering his
love's feet with blankets to keep them warm, arranging knick-knacks
on a bedside table to make a frightening place feel like home. It's
someone putting aside his own wants to ease another's pain.

It's like what Iris's father, Garrett, does when he comes to
visit Susan.

It's like what Papa Rhanji did for Mom when his wife passed away.

It's what Dad did, adopting and raising up a son that wasn't his.

It's what Jude is doing for lonely Ms. Delacroix.

Stay. What would I do without you, kid?

Shit.

That's what *her* life is about:

Two weeks.

Jude's heart hits the floor. He's not going anywhere. As Carrie and Iris leave the room, Jude pulls the straps of the bag over his head and unties the pouch's drawstring, smoothing the ruched material. He stares at the beaded wildflower a moment longer before turning the soft bag, emptying its contents into his palm and pocketing the petals. Inside the hospital room, Simperson strokes his wife's face as her grip softens on the blankets under her chin. Jude extends his hand and slides the pouch into Simperson's as they shake goodbye.

"She needs this more than I do," Jude says. The old man smiles and tucks the pouch into his sleeping wife's palm.

Jude is blinking back tears when he meets Iris in the hall, the tall, thin doctor holding the smaller, mousier Carrie close to her side with one arm. She reintroduces the nurse as her aunt.

"So, you're related to Zoe too?" Jude asks, coughing away the tightness in his throat.

"Other side of the family." Carrie smiles. "Susan's my big sister, room 52? Iris's mom!"

"Room 93, actually." Theresa appears from the front office and opens her arms to gather Carrie into an embrace. The centre had to move Susan, Theresa apologizes. It was a space-making issue.

"It's fine." Carrie's smile is tinged with sadness. "Was probably the most she moved all year."

The women chat a few moments more and then Iris asks Jude to help Carrie find Susan's new room. The pair walk in silence.

At the end of the long-term care wing they find near-vegetative Susan sitting in room 93, locks of hair littering the floor around her bed.

"Sue," Carrie gently scolds. She sits by her sister's side and touches Susan's head, red, raw, and patched. "What have you done to yourself?"

Jude grabs a garbage bag from the counter cupboard and scoops strands like he's clearing leaves. "I sure wish you were an evergreen, Sue," he says. "Then again, maybe you'll change. People never stop changing."

Susan's silent lips curve into a small smile.

Jude and Carrie work together, applying ointment to the wounds on Susan's scalp. They turn her over and wash broken skin with saline and redress bandages. This is what staying in one place looks like, Jude thinks. This is what happens when you don't move.

Jude waits in the hall as Carrie says goodbye. He pushes his hands into his pockets and fiddles around with what's inside before realizing he's been fidgeting the ring like a worry stone all day long. He really ought to put it back in his bag.

At lunch, he unpacks cold chicken salad and finds he's missed a text from his mom.

Home for dinner, sweetu?

He stares at the screen.

Yes. Probably. What else am I gonna do?

The concert?

Jude sighs. *Not going,* he types before deleting it. *Not sure.* Delete, delete.

I don't know.

There's a long pause before Yasmin's reply.

Be brave, sweetu.

Yeah, yeah. Be kind.

It's the same advice Mom always gives, the words Jude's bio mother scribbled onto a napkin she left behind the day he was born. Mom acts like they apply to everything, but what do they mean when staying isn't brave and going isn't kind? Through Jude's headphones, Downie screams he can get behind anything. Well, that certainly doesn't help.

Be brave. Be kind.

Jude repeats the phrase like a mantra as he shovels cubed chicken into his mouth.

He opens Snapchat and an old hockey teammate scores from the centreline of a sold-out arena, the crowd going wild, again and again, Denny's three-second-clip set on automatic repeat. Jude pushes his lunch away and puts his phone down on the table. So he stays, what happens next? Another year living in Papa Rhanji's basement, another two or three more until he gets his master's degree and is even qualified to work as Iris's junior? Between then and now, a lifetime of Instagram photos: Zoe at school, at concerts, on the prime minister's campaign trail, finally tagging some guy—a new boyfriend—in one of the photos. When does Jude's life get to start?

Be brave. Be kind.

Advice from birth, but what the hell is it supposed to mean?

A tiny woman knocks on the staffroom door. She's half hidden by sunglasses and an old-fashioned scarf. No, not a scarf, Jude realizes, but an old fox fur. The woman lowers her dark glasses and looks up over the lenses. Could he point her in the direction of Ms. Shannon Delacroix? Jude walks her to the patient's room but doesn't mention Ms. Delacroix's never had a visitor before. The woman covers her mouth with her hand when she thanks him and moves to step inside but temporarily freezes, stepping back.

"I'm sorry," she says. "It's just been a very long time."

She summons whatever courage she needs and enters the room, pulling the door closed behind her. Sandra catches Jude by the elbow on her way past.

"Was that Mrs. Hamilton?"

"Who?"

"Theresa's mother-in-law. As in, *the* Dr. Hamilton's mother?"

The pair try to spy but can't see through the door's frosted glass window.

"I wonder what she wants with Ms. Delacroix."

While the MMT rehabilitation patients are in a group session, Jude chips dried rice cereal from a high chair in the living quarters' empty kitchen. Suddenly, he sees the tiny woman again, this time rushing down the hall as if she were being chased. She stops at a locked corridor before turning around, pressing her fingers against her temples. Jude presses the pause button on his ear bud.

"Mrs. Hamilton, are you lost?"

"Oh, god, you know my name! Please," she begs, her hands shaking toward him before she catches herself and raises them to her lips. "Please don't tell Theresa I was here."

"I won't," Jude promises. "Why don't you let me get you a cup of tea?"

Mrs. Hamilton asks him to call her Karen. He asks how she knows Ms. Delacroix and the birdlike woman searches his face with sharp eyes before lowering them to her teacup.

"Shannon is my stepdaughter."

Theresa had mentioned a dying patient over dinner the night before, Karen said, and she recognized the name of her estranged stepchild. But it was clear Theresa didn't know the patient was her late wife's half-sister. Why Tara never told Theresa, Karen has an idea.

"My Henry, Tara and Shannon's father, he did alright for himself," Karen explains, blowing steam off the hot tea. "Or he did when oil was good, anyway. But Shannon was always bad news, just like her mother. Junkies and winos—if they get their hands on your money they'll kill themselves with it and then they'll still want more! Tara knew that. Of course she did, working with these kinds of people." Karen spreads her arms wide, gesturing to the empty dining room.

"But I also know that Theresa has a heart of gold," the woman continues. "I think that was why Tara didn't want Shannon in their lives—Tara didn't want Theresa to be taken advantage of. I want to honour that. Theresa can never know, not about Tara's sister, or that anyone kept this from her. Please, Jude. Theresa is all I have left."

She purses her lips into a thousand burgundy lipstick wrinkles and locks her eyes on Jude's. Jude nods but looks at the floor.

"Well, regardless," Karen says, "I came here today to make things right. I've been holding onto Shannon's inheritance for some time now, not really knowing where she's been living. She'd probably have drugged herself to death with the cash anyway, but, well, that's not going to happen in here, now, is it? And yet, the woman's still impossible! I mean, you must know how she is." She wipes her eyes with the fox fur and shakes her head.

"I don't think I've been called a whore since 1977!"

She puts her sunglasses back on and thanks Jude for the tea, swears him to secrecy again. Seeing how the old woman continues to shake, he opens his arms and she melts into a hug before pulling away to cover her mouth.

"I'm sorry," she tells him. "I have a dental problem. The breath, it's so embarrassing."

Jude shakes his head and laughs. "I . . . I'm sorry, I don't smell anything at all. Perfume, maybe? It's nice."

She cups her hand over her mouth and nose and exhales.

"Well, what do you know?"

He walks her to the side exit of the living quarters and closes the door after her. Here he'd been thinking that Ms. Delacroix needed him, but family walks back into her life and she doesn't even care. Well, Jude *does* know how she is: nasty, manipulative, mean. Jude thinks about how she acted when the Man Machine Poem tour was featured on the news and he told her he was thinking of going.

"You're going to leave me here alone for that leftist propaganda?" she snorted. That's what she called Downie's life's work. The woman can't see any good in anything, only her own self-inflicted bitterness. He shakes his head and checks the time on his phone. 5:45. Jude is done, defeated. He's going home. Zoe can drop by his mom's house if she wants to say goodbye. He presses play and "New Orleans is Sinking" starts his heart racing in time with the beat.

He heads to the staffroom and grabs his backpack. He puts his jacket on and leaves the break room, heading down the hall and to the front door.

"Kid," Delacroix's gravelly voice calls.

"I'll see you tomorrow," he shouts back.

"I might not be here tomorrow."

Jude stops and closes his eyes, takes a deep breath through his nose.

Be brave. Be kind.

He lowers the volume on his earphones and takes a slow exhale and turns on his heels, heading into Delacroix's room. An oversized manila envelope sits on the counter by the door with *Shannon* scratched on top in red ink. He picks the heavy package up and carries it over, places it on Ms. Delacroix's lap.

"Sit down," she says without moving to open it. "News is about to start."

Jude glares at her a moment before sighing, giving up. He drops his backpack and sits in the chair by the bed as she points the television remote, so large in her frail hands, at the screen across from her bed.

"Have a visitor today?"

"Uh huh," she says. "You taking off with that girl of yours tonight?"

Jude shrugs. "Dr. Iris tell you that?"

"Yup."

He leans back, locks his fingers behind his head, and tries to ignore the pain in his throat. "Well, I'm not. Sometimes you just want what you can't have. Not that I'd expect you to understand."

Ms. Delacroix laughs. "Ouch, kid," she says. "Kick, punch, kick."

She starts to cough again, a long attack until she spits bloody phlegm into a new tissue. "Shit, you don't know nothin' about wanting yet."

The news hour starts up with a scene from the Hip's final Manitoba concert, played just the night before. "It's a Good Life" twangs and Jude swallows hard.

"Now, if I know you," Ms. Delacroix whispers to keep from setting off coughing again, "I bet you've been searching for hippie-dippy messages from the universe or some bullshit, trying to figure out what to do with yourself about school and the concert and that girl you're so messed up about." She taps on the envelope on her lap and coughs into her tissue again, the scarf covering her scalp slipping low over one eye. Reluctantly, Jude leans over to fix it.

"Well, kid, here's your sign."

She looks up from under the white scarf, her face as soft and peaceful as he's ever seen. He opens the envelope and looks inside before putting it down again, wiping his face with his hand and looking back to Ms. Delacroix.

"What is that?" he whispers.

"Fifteen thousand in hush funds." She winks. "You think they take oil money out east? 'Course, this means goodbye for you and me."

Jude shakes his head and then leans over, looking down, letting the tears he can't help but let come hit the ground between his shoes. Outside, a vehicle's engine screams. "You can't give me that," he says above the noise, voice breaking. "I can't leave you here by yourself."

"Get a grip, kid," Ms. Delacroix says, voice cracking. "Your girl's here."

A large van rolls to a stop in the lot outside Ms. Delacroix's window. Its side door slides open to reveal Zoe, laughing, inside.

"If I go," he whispers, "I won't get back in time."

"Go on."

"I'll never . . ." He tries to clear his throat. "I won't ever forget you."

"I know, kid."

He wipes the tears from his face and tries to leave but just can't get it together. He pushes his hands into his pockets, feeling too small, too clumsy, too young to know what to do. On one side his hands crunch rose petals, on the other his finger drifts to the silver ring. Jude pulls it from his pocket, slipping the Celtic knot onto Ms. Delacroix's cold hand and kissing her knuckles again and again and again.

"You're not alone," he tells her. "When it happens . . . if I'm not here . . . I don't want you to think you're alone."

Shannon stares at the ring, blue eyes no longer sharp or steely. Bottomless.

"I'm not alone," she whispers. She looks up and strokes the side of Jude's face, the ring smooth against his cheek.

"Kid, have a nice life."

Jude kisses Ms. Delacroix's forehead one last time before rushing out the door with his bag, passport inside. He hits play again, and behind him he swears he hears Ms. Delacroix whisper a name between opening bars of the next track.

Tar?

He strides into the parking lot to where Zoe sits on the floor in the back of the van, her flip-flop feet sticking out, the hem of her long skirt wet in the sleeting rain. She frowns, eyes pink around their rims.

"Only a backpack, eh? I had a feeling this might be good—"

"I have something to tell you," Jude interrupts. "A lot of things, actually, because I want to be brave and be kind and give you what you deserve. So listen. I don't want to fix you, Zoe. You're perfect. I just haven't told you enough about me because I really like you and you make me really nervous and I really don't want to screw anything up."

He drops his bag to the ground and Zoe stands, seeing the tears in his eyes. She pulls him away from the van and into the warm summer rain, lifting a hand to the guy in the driver's seat, asking for just another moment longer. The brunette in a red dress beside the driver nods and smiles at Jude with bright eyes and sharp cheekbones, her bare feet on the dash as she plays with the guitar on her lap. A dream catcher hangs on the rear-view mirror between the couple, and the woman wears a smile so familiar that looking at her is like coming home. Miranda, Jude remembers. He smiles back with a slight wave and then returns to Zoe's eyes.

"Okay, like, I freaking love the Tragically Hip. I don't just like them—I love them. I know every song Downie's ever sung. I listen to him all day long, and I mean, some Sam Roberts and Joel Plaskett too, but I really, *really* love the Hip. Here, listen."

He pulls a bud from his ear and presses it against Zoe's, linking them together with a long white cord.

She nods, her mouth a perfect O. "Okay, well more reason you should come—"

"I mean, I would lose my mind to be at one of their shows, or at any show with you. I don't know why I didn't tell you this before. Oh! Oh, and my weirdness! Okay! My parents' divorce was really hard, too, and they were actually pretty cool about it, so I can't even imagine how difficult your parents' must have been for you. And that snooping thing you went through? That's nothing compared to my thing. I mean, okay—I was so messed up after my parents split, I actually started calling a phone sex line. Yeah, phone sex. In the age of internet porn! Weird, right?"

She inhales and shakes her head unconvincingly no, shrugs.

"Yeah, no. It's super weird. It is. But it just made me feel less lonely, you know? And that's not even the weirdest part. I got obsessed—*obsessed*—with the girl I liked to talk to. I'd call just to say goodnight. Her name was Patricia. She had this amazing voice, like nothing I'd ever heard before. And, I mean, I could tell she'd been doing the sex line thing for a long time, but she was really nice to me and I started to think about her all the time so I sent my old hockey jersey to the address of the place that billed me and then the next thing you know an operator tells me I'm blocked. At eighteen! At eighteen years old I was that weird and pathetic and lonely and sad that a sex line blocked me. I mean, my god. Zoe, that was only, like, four years ago."

Zoe presses her lips, holds air in her cheeks like a chipmunk hoarding seeds.

"Oh, and then today? Okay, I guess I'm still messed up, because today I wanted to keep you here so bad that I was even going to ask you to marry me."

Zoe leans away, eyes wide. Jude laughs.

"I know! How insane is that? We're not ready to get married!"

She shakes her head no.

"But I was thinking about that, and I told you all about this, because I just want to be with you. I want to be with you so bad, Zoe, because I'm so in love with you. And maybe I've said too much now, maybe you don't want anything to do with me, but—"

She presses a finger to his lips and reaches with her other hand to sweep the wet hair from his forehead, all the gel from the morning running slick down his face.

"Your hair is curly when it rains."

"Zoe, I want to come with you."

"You do?"

"I do. Yeah. And I want to stay with you. And I have to call the U of O, like, *now,* to register for classes. Because Zoe, I love you and

I want the best for you and, hell, maybe if I'm lucky, someday—far, far in the future—maybe I'll even get to be the prime minister's husband."

Zoe laughs. She throws her arms around Jude's neck and stands on her tiptoes, pulling him to her. He presses his forehead against hers and can't even hear the music playing until he's holding her face in his hands, his thumbs on those glorious scars, his lips on hers.

A song about courage.

EPILOGUE
TO DO

1994

THE BABY KICKS her bladder one way and the steering wheel pushes the other and now Amy has to wear the too-tight sweatpants. She has to leave the car parked where it was, hidden deep in the parkade from nighttime security guards, unless she wants to drive in a warm puddle of pee.

Her belly bumps against the gearshift when she reaches to the backseat. She tosses clothes around until she finds the only other pair of pants she can still get into and double-checks the parking lot before opening the car door.

The morning air steams off her wet legs as she changes out of her track pants and into the sweats. Her thighs sting as she pulls up the too-tight pants. She wrestles the waistband up over her bum and it snaps under her belly, digging deep into her hips. She stretches her top down until the Cigarette Shop logo flattens her boobs but it springs right back up when she lets go and a roll of fat sticks out below her shirt.

Amy hangs the wet pants over the steering wheel to dry. She'd rinse them if she had a bottle of water, but she doesn't so she'll just have to wash them later. She walks around the car and sits in the passenger seat to make a list. Amy messes up without lists. She does stupid stuff like filling her gas tank when she's out of cash, and then people yell at her and she has to drive away and hide so she doesn't get caught. But if she writes lists she's all organized and in control. And it feels so good to cross stuff off. She doesn't put a checkmark beside things once she's done them, like some people do. She puts a line right through, like a sword.

Today her list says:

To Do:

1. Lock car
2. Brush teeth, hair, wash face
3. Grab a smoke
4. Sneak a puff
5. Work
6. Call Rodney
7. Taco Tuesday!
8. <u>Wash sweatpants</u>

She underlines that last one because it's important, except she'll have to get the pants after work so Shannon doesn't smell them in her backpack. Amy counts the money in the bag's top pocket and writes:

9. $10.38

Then she makes sure everything she needs is packed and she starts to leave. Oh, wait:

10. Entrance 3B

It's easy to forget where you've parked at West Edmonton Mall, the biggest in the world.

Amy's gut feels tight, so she hurries to get to the washroom. She sits on a lemony toilet seat and tries to go but can't, so she just washes up and leaves real fast. If she gets to work before Shannon, she can poke a hole in a cig pack from the back of the shop and sneak out for a quick puff. No one's noticed the missing smokes yet, and she can always blame the torn-up edges of the packs on mice. Besides, it's so much nicer smoking in the morning when there's no one around to stare. Last week she got in trouble for smoking on her lunch break.

"Not in uniform," Larry said, pointing at her baby belly. "Makes the Cigarette Shop look bad."

Dammit. Shannon's already there, bent over the magazine rack like a page three SUNshine Girl come to life with her tiny crop-top and perfect body. She pulls and twists the shiny ring on the chain around her neck, mouthing words to a song Amy can't hear, her earphones plugged into a black Discman. Shannon is Larry's girlfriend, and since he owns the Cigarette Shop, she doesn't have to wear a uniform or work weekends or anything.

"Holy camel toe, chubs!" Shannon eyes are little slits, sparkling like the glitter on her cleavage. Amy lifts the section of counter that flips up and turns sideways to shuffle in. She tries to look at her flip-flopped feet and wonders when she cut her nails last. *Camel toe?*

"Your pants, pity fuck. Not leaving much to the imagination."

Amy glances down into the warped steel of the counter in front of her. It's true, the tight pants show everything, and man, is she ripe. She's been real thick and heavy between the legs for weeks. It hurts, the fullness there. She thinks of when Mom was pregnant with Miranda and wonders if she had the same problem, except

Mom was always skinny and beautiful, not big like her. Flat ass and fat ass, that was what a kid at school once said about Amy and Mom. Amy came home crying about it and Mom was so angry she was going to get Uncle Wilf to give the kid a talking to until Amy begged her not to make it worse. Instead, Mom sang a song to make Amy feel better.

Mom always sang.

And Amy always felt better.

She wishes she knew where Mom was now.

Shannon won't stop giggling, her head cocked as she stares at Amy's crotch. Amy's face gets red-hot. Her stomach cramps up again.

"I'm just going to go to the washroom," she tells Shannon.

"You better not sneak a smoke!"

Amy visits the bathroom three times that morning but just can't go. It feels like someone's turning a corkscrew in her gut. She pushes until her legs shake but nothing comes out.

The fourth time it happens she's counting Player's Light cartons in the back, and the pain makes her fingers clumsy. "I'll be right back," she says, picking dropped packages up from the floor.

"Okay, soft shit, do what you gotta do," Shannon snorts. She winks over the till at a guy at the counter, the first customer of the day, buying an *Edmonton Sun*. He's older than Amy and Shannon, maybe mid-twenties, but good-looking—wearing those low, baggy pants Rodney likes. Shannon leans over the counter like she's whispering, but she's not. "This is, like, the eighth time she's gone this morning."

The guy laughs. He glances at Amy real quick and then eyes right back to Shannon's tits as she counts his change. Amy decides not to go to the washroom then and tries to ignore the pains. Then writes down when they hit:

9:08

9:19

9:31

At 9:42 she says, "I think I'm in labour."

Shannon rolls her eyes and stares back down at her magazine, licking her middle finger before flipping the page. "Whatever."

"I get a pain every eleven minutes."

"Bullshit." Shannon looks up, her lips soft and pouty but her eyes as sharp as broken glass. "I've been right here all morning and you haven't said shit. This is, like, reverse discrimination. This is why I told Lar not to hire a preggo. You don't get to just take off when you don't feel like working."

Amy's mouth opens and closes, but no words come out. She hates it when Shannon's mad at her, but Amy doesn't say anything because Amy knows Shannon's mom died last year and she must be really sad. After the baby's born, Amy is going to come back and say hi and Shannon's going to be so surprised. They'll probably end up being pretty good friends, actually, two daughters, no mothers—they can take care of each other. Rodney and Larry will get along too, and they'll party together at those clubs Shannon's always talking about.

"I didn't mean I have to go right now. I was just—"

"Whatever."

Amy shuts up and sits down. What is she supposed to do? Breathe, she thinks. Right. She's never been to any of those birthing classes, but she's seen lots of movies. She writes down:

In, out, in, out

Huh huh huh

Hee hee hoo, hee hee hoo

Hoo hoo hoo, hoo hoo hoo, hoo hoo hoo

She doesn't make a big show of it, but practices breathing when the cramps hit. Then Larry shows up with lunch for Shannon and hears Amy breathing and he tells her to go home even though Shannon sighs real loud.

"Last thing we need are her guts on the floor."

So this is what Amy does:

To Do:

Get food

Call Rodney

Tuesdays mean taco meal deals at the food court, so Amy gets two tacos, deluxe Mexi fries, and a diet iced tea. She still has seven dollars and she only needs twenty-five cents to call Rodney, so she buys another taco meal deal just in case she gets hungry later. She gets paid in a couple of days anyway and she'll be at the hospital tonight, so there's no reason not to spend the money.

She's stuffing the food into her backpack when Shannon comes hurrying up to her, waving a folded piece of paper between her fingers.

"Hi," Amy tries to say, but another pain hits and the only sound she makes is *mmmm*, hands pressed to her lower back.

Shannon sees the pain this time and Amy sees how her forehead wrinkles up, like maybe she actually cares. "You forgot this," she says, handing Amy her morning list.

"Thanks." Amy tries to smile but her stomach is too rock-hard. She wraps her arms around the beach-ball shape of her belly and exhales a small whimper.

"My mom used to make lists like that," Shannon says, looking at the floor. "She'd write down everything. I thought yours was one of hers for a second." She looks up at Amy again, right in her eyes, this time.

"Anyway, you're going to be a better mom than she was. I know it. Your kid will be really special."

Amy is speechless. She tries to say something nice back, but Shannon turns and stomps back to work, all rush and skin and attitude. Amy unfolds the paper and reads the list: she's parked at 3B. Walking makes the pain so bad. It's like her hips are falling apart, like the baby's trying to dig out of her back. She carries her bag in front, imagining her crotch getting fatter with every step.

She stops at a payphone and her stomach turns all fluttery like the baby's rolling around, except it's not. It makes her head hurt, dialling his number. What if his phone is out of service this time? Last week she heard a click, like someone picked up, and then there was this shuffling and another click, like maybe he wanted to talk but chickened out. Maybe today he'll answer.

Amy lifts the black receiver and pushes the buttons and holds her breath. Her stomach drops because the call goes right to the answering machine.

"Hi, Rodney, it's me. Amy. I think the baby's coming. I keep getting pains, but not too bad, though. It kicked me when I dialled your number. Feels real weird, the kicks, kinda gross. But it was cute this time, like it knew I was calling you. Anyway, I'm probably gonna go to the hospital soon. Bye."

And then: "I really wish you were here."

She blinks and blinks and tries to breathe. It's warm out now and she forgot about this morning, so the smell of pee surprises her when she opens the driver's-side door. She wants to cry when she remembers her comfy pants are still wet, but she figures the hospital must have extra clothes.

Amy leans against the side of the car and tries to figure out what to do. It's too early to go to the emergency room, but people will stare if she's moaning all around the mall. She looks down through the car window at the junk all over the backseat. She's not going to show up at Rodney's smelling like smokes and piss and fast-food grease so she grabs her pen and writes on an empty Mcdonald's bag:

To Do:
Fold clothes
Throw out garbage
Empty ashtray
Clean up pee

She turns on the car radio and a man sings a song about courage. She wants to laugh because maybe that's what she should call the baby. Instead, she crosses the chores off her list as she cleans, but the driver's seat is still wet so she sprays it with the Febreze she keeps under the back seat and puts a blanket on top. The air freshener smells like Rodney. He'd spray it in his bedroom whenever they smoked weed or had sex so his grandma wouldn't know what they had been up to.

"Like it never happened," he'd wink, hipbones sticking out over his shorts. It was awkward, sometimes, him so scrawny and her so thick, but he was so strong when he was on top. She always felt proud to be his girl.

It takes a pretty special guy to love a girl for her insides, to not care what she looks like or where she's from. He was the one who taught her how to drive, too, that time he got drunk after playing basketball. He liked it when she drove, liked to tease her, try to make her crash, his hands between her legs. She feels as warm as chocolate left on the dashboard when she thinks of Rodney like that. That's love. That's what he's going to feel like when he sees her with his baby.

She doesn't even blame him for being scared. She should have been more careful, should have made him wear a condom. She rang the doorbell of his grandma's house every day for weeks after she found out she was pregnant, but no one would answer. Then one day she noticed the kitchen light on through the window when she showed up, but when she left it was turned off. That's when she figured out what was going on.

She would've had an abortion if he wanted her to, but how was she supposed to get to the clinic without a ride? The bus didn't stop anywhere near the clinic and the girl on the phone said Amy wouldn't be allowed to leave alone anyway. Her foster mom, Mariam, thought abortion was so bad that people should go to jail for getting one, and Amy's real mom was gone and Kohkum didn't drive and all her old friends were up north on the rez and Amy hadn't seen or heard from any of them since she and Miranda were put into care anyway. Then all of a sudden the baby was kicking—as if Amy could get rid of it then!

"So I hear you've got a boyfriend, Amy," her caseworker had said one day, eyes back-and-forth-back-and-forth from her files to Amy's stomach. Yasmin was young and nice for a social worker, but Amy couldn't say anything with Mariam sitting right there.

Amy shrugged. She crossed her arms over her belly and stuck her chin into the neck of her hoodie so she could see without really looking.

Yasmin turned to Amy's foster mom and asked if she knew the father, but Mariam just frowned and shook her head. She messed around with her necklace, rubbing the little gold cross between her fingers and thumb like Jesus was a genie, able to turn Amy good and skinny and white. Mariam's real daughter smiled down from a photo on the wall, so pretty and happy with her shiny red hair and a graduation cap on top. Patricia had just found out she was having a baby too, and Mariam was kind of excited about that, even if she did say Patricia's boyfriend was no good. Why couldn't she be happy about Amy's baby too? The little ones could play together. It would be so nice.

"I told you from the start—teens only. It's bad enough having this one's little banshee sister around. I'll not have another toddler after she's outta here, and I'm definitely not having a newborn screamin' through the night."

"We'll find the girls another arrangement just as soon as we can."

"Well, I don't know why you'd bother moving *Amy*." Mariam sighed. "It's a lot of work for me having to take in someone new, you know. It's not like they'll let her keep the baby anyway. A nice family should have it. Raise it right."

Amy's heart thumped like Rodney's basketball. Yasmin reached over and squeezed Amy's arm, pretty red and gold bracelets clinking on her thin brown wrist. Amy looked up.

"I'll do the best I can," Yasmin whispered, her eyes locked to Amy's. Amy didn't think she looked so sure. Between the chimes of Yasmin's bracelets and the beating of Amy's noisy heart loud in her ears, she couldn't hear what Mariam said next.

Instead, Amy pushed her head deeper into her sweatshirt, trying to hide her red-hot cheeks. She knew people wanted babies, knew they got scooped up real quick, but she hadn't thought about not even getting a say. So a couple weeks later, when Rodney's cousin showed up in a lady-driven Dodge Spirit four months too late and gave her five hundred dollars to get rid of it, Amy asked for the car instead and disappeared real quick and quiet.

The pains are coming every eight minutes now, so Amy drives to the Grey Nuns Hospital. The road blurs when her gut seizes and she has to work hard not to swerve. It's like driving with Rodney but the opposite. The hospital's only twenty minutes from the mall, but she forgot she'd need change to park so she stops across the street and just hangs out. The earlier she checks in, the more questions she'll have to answer.

Amy's plan is:

Sleep

Get in just in time

Have baby

Pretend to not speak English

Sneak out

See Rodney

Amy closes her eyes and tries to sleep but can't. Then she remembers the Benadryl in the glove box.

In her dreams, they're all staring down at her: Shannon and Larry and Yasmin, all weird smiles, Mariam's black tooth hanging like a bat ready to bite. Amy's stomach is torn open and they reach into her until their elbows are sticky red. They're pulling her guts out like giant worms and she whimpers, *no please stop owie, owie*, like a little child. Then her guts change into pieces of the baby and they're ripping the baby apart and it's sick and it's terrible. And then Rodney's there, and he's holding her hand and telling her it's okay, it's okay, and she pushes her face to him, but he's tricked her too and, *please stop, please stop, Mommy, Mommy, Mommy!*

Amy wakes up screaming *Nikâwiy!*, what she used to call her mom when she was just a little kid. Suddenly, the pain stops. She hears that same song about courage that was playing before and thinks hearing a thing twice in one day has got to mean *something*. She opens her eyes and, oh no, it's way too dark. She's all wet, too, like she peed again. And then, oh no, she shouts out again and bends into the wheel and, oh, oh, oh—it's like she's turning inside out!

People are standing around in front of her car and she realizes she's parked in front of a restaurant. Stupid, stupid, stupid, why didn't she look? The pain starts again and she sees two girls looking at her like she's crazy while they smoke.

I'm dying, I'm dying, she tries to shout, but it just comes out like "I'm Di, I'm Di!" and the girls throw their smokes and walk away, smug smirks on skinny legs in high heels. She's going to die here all alone and her poor baby too. Poor baby, she thinks, poor, poor baby. Why doesn't somebody love you?

The driver's side window gets dark. Death. Death is coming; this is what it's like. And then there's a face. Not death, a man. Oh no, who's this? Black skin, dreadlocked hair, big eyes staring. Why's he looking at her?

He raps the window with his knuckle.

"Open the door!"

"I'm having a baby!"

"I know, open the door!"

Amy starts to cry. Drive, she thinks. Drive to the hospital. Beep the horn. They'll rescue you. But that pain happens again, and oh no she's going to be sick.

She opens the door and the man steps into the space and she throws up on his shoes. He doesn't care though and gets in even closer and almost kneels right in the puke.

"Can you walk?"

She shakes her head. All Amy can do is cry and cry.

He tries to scoop her out of the car but she screams and clings to the seat.

"I can't, I can't, I can't," She drops and crawls on the asphalt and the lights from cars and the hospital windows across the road all blur and swim around her. "I'm dying!"

"No, Mama, you're having a baby." He pulls her up by her armpits and she clings onto his jacket. "I'm gonna put you on the backseat and drive you to a hospital, okay?"

Amy points to across the street. "There," she gasps. "My sister was born there."

The man shakes his head. "The Nuns is just a clinic now, kiddo. They don't do labours anymore." He opens the door and she falls into the back and feels something cut into her belly.

"Can you take off my pants?"

"What?"

She screams again. "Take off my pants!"

"Grey Nuns it is."

She moans and arches the best she can while he slides his hands under her, and then her bum and belly and legs are bare and cold and it's so good and who cares about being embarrassed and oh no, no, no, it's not good, OW!

The pain runs out just as the man gets into the driver's seat and she remembers the seat is wet.

"I'm sorry." She starts to cry again, big tears running into her ears. "I had an accident."

He *shush, shush, shushes* her, and she feels the car lurch forward.

"I need you to focus on me, okay? Don't push. I'm gonna keep talking and you just keep listening—don't push. We'll be there in a minute."

"You're gonna have that sweet baby in your arms tonight, okay, Mama? You think of that. You gonna meet your sweet little baby tonight! Gotta be strong now. Gotta be a mama bear, gonna fight for that lil' baby bear, now, okay? Don't push."

Amy moans. She pulls her knees as close to her chest as they'll go. She can barely breathe. Her head is on the pile of folded clothes and everything smells like wet dog. She fights the urge to push, focusing on his words and a hole in the floorboard, the street flying by underneath. How's a baby gonna live back here?

"I don't know what to do."

"Only two things anyone's ever got to do, okay? You gotta be brave, you gotta be kind. Those the only two things anyone's gotta do."

Amy closes her eyes and the car stops and he shouts out, his voice real high, like he's scared. Then there are more voices and a woman opens the car door and then Amy feels fingers between her legs and she's on a rolling bed and everyone is yelling and playing with tubes and needles and that man's gone and Amy keeps thinking *don't say anything,* except she wants to because a woman with short fluffy hair is holding her hand and right now all Amy wants is her mom. Sandra, the woman says her name is, and Amy thinks of sand, soft and warm, grains slipping too fast between her palms at the beach.

She's there by the lake building sandcastles with Nikâwiy and little Miranda, and then there's a whitecap wave and Amy is swept away.

It's all blurs

and shouts

and lights

and pain.

And then the pain stops. Something large is pulled from her, but everything's alright. The room is dark, and voices are calm, and the bed . . . the bed is so soft and so warm.

The next thing she knows, Amy's clothes are clean and folded on the bench opposite her bed. Her keys are on top of them and there's a tray of food beside her. That's good because she is so hungry and tired and—

There's her baby.

Courage.

Amy peels the sticky white tape off her arm and slides out the IV. She sits up and holds her breath and leans over the baby's plastic cradle. He's beautiful and small and his hair is all curly like hers when it rains. She wants to pick him up but he's so quiet and his little wrapped-up body is so nice and neat and sweet that she takes her hand away. She's never wanted anything as much as she's wanted this little boy, and a little voice in her head says, *except Rodney,* and she half laughs and half cries because that's all so stupid now.

She knows what she's got to do, but it's hard to think so she reaches for the napkin on her food tray and finds a pen and makes a list. She pulls on her grey sweatpants and ignores the way her nose stings and her body aches, and she grabs her keys and kisses his sweet soft head and wishes him every last little bit of happiness and she puts the napkin in his cradle:

To Do:
Be brave
Be kind
And then she slips real quick and quiet out of the room, out of his life, and, just like Mom, no one's looked for her yet.

ACKNOWLEDGEMENTS

I ONCE READ that your first book by far takes the longest to write and I really hope that's true because, in my case, it took thirty-four years. In that time so many have helped me that I'm sure to miss thanking a few. For that, I apologize but remain so very grateful.

I owe deepest thanks to my husband, Freddy Bickell. Once upon a time, he fell in love with a girl who dreamt about writing a book and then he spent almost twenty years helping make that dream come true. Honey, thank you for the space heaters placed around drafty offices, for camping trips interrupted by editing breaks, for every morning you woke up alone to the sound of my fingertips on the keyboard downstairs. With my whole heart, thank you for the life we built together. I love you.

I'm indebted to the Alberta Foundation of the Arts for providing me with funding support while I wrote *Always Brave, Sometimes Kind*. I'd also like to thank the Writers Guild of Alberta and the Alberta Literary Awards for the extra financial support (and invaluable morale boosts) that happened twice during its creation, and to literary award supporters Vanna and Guy Tessier and Nicole Duley. Also, thank you to the team behind *Alberta*

Views fiction contest, and to 2014 guest judge Marina Endicott for pulling "Northside Delacroix" from the pile. There was a point in this process where *Always Brave, Sometimes Kind* hit a production snag and online readers banded together to provide funding for professional editing services. These donors were: Holly Whitaker, Patty Hartman, Linda Green, Moe Mouallem, Jennifer Hansen, Erin Shaw Street, Kim Mulholland, Kara Risk, Omar Mouallem, Brittany Gambler, Jodi Dealexandra, Alyssa Westcott, Dr. Donna Mcarthur, Blair Cronk, Samantha Weald, Jen Henderson, Norma Bernas, Andrea Gilroy, Beverly Baptiste, Megan Kempel, Tammi Salas, Chelsea Setter, Melissa Burden, B. Mullenberg, Sondra Primeaux, Emily Smith, Dawn Hope, Jackie Simpson, Jessica Kluthe, Esther Zimmer, Chrystal Olsen, and Kristy Mcfarland. My friends, you worked a small miracle and I am so grateful.

I also couldn't be more thankful for the team at TouchWood Editions. Thank you for seeing the potential in *Always Brave, Sometimes Kind* in its early stages, and thank you for your dedication in bringing it into the world. I'm especially grateful to my publisher, Taryn Boyd, my editor, Claire Philipson, and TouchWood's editorial coordinator, Kate Kennedy. Thank you all for your honesty and for your thoughtfulness. Without you, this book wouldn't be what it is. Thank you also to marketing and publicity coordinator Tori Elliott, to Renée Layberry for the careful proofreading, to Tree Abraham for the book's cover, and to George Webber for the cover photography. Profound thanks to Nav Nagra of Breathing Space Creative, who performed the important work of a sensitivity read. I'm grateful, also, to Breathing Space Creative Founder and CEO Chelene Knight—thank you for being kind, and for helping me be brave.

Earlier versions of the chapters that make up this novel were published in the following publications: "Ascension" (published as "To Do:") and "But For the Streetlamps," *Tahoma Literary Review*; "Northside Delacroix," *Alberta Views Magazine*; "A Reason to Bend," *A Cappella Zoo*; "Tell Me What You Want," *Punchnel's*.

There were many people who made this book greater than the first draft. No one spent as much time with the text as Margaret Macpherson, the skilled and fearless midwife of this novel. Margaret, there is no way to adequately thank you for all the ways in which you nurtured me. This book would not exist without you. Janice Zawerbny, thank you for your keen eye and vibrant imagination; your gentle pushes toward the development of more minor characters made this story so much richer. Several chapters were also made immeasurably better by the skills of other professional writers, editors, and artists. Thank you, Joe Ponepinto, Tim Bowling, Carla Ulrich, Stephanie Sinclair, Natasha Deen, Colin Meldrum, Traci Cumbay. I must also give thanks to Chelsea Vowel, author of the Cree language website apihtawikosisan.com, for the incredible resources found there.

To my children, Cailena and Chloe Bickell, thank you for your patience in repeating all those questions every time I answered one with a "Hmmm?" while I was writing or researching. Thank you for the immeasurable ways you motivate and encourage me, and for proving always and again that this world must be a good place because, after all, there are people like you in it. I've written stories since I was younger than you girls are now, but you, my daughters, are the true masterpieces of my life.

There are four fundamental figures I must also thank. To my mom, Angela Mulholland, thanks for helping me turn the old treehouse into a writer's studio, for getting me a typewriter when I'm sure you must have thought it was a strange Christmas present for an eight-year-old, and for all the novels you read to me at bedtime. Thanks, also, for doling out essays as punishment when teenage me crossed all those lines. The extra work killed neither my desire to write nor to misbehave, but it did help me understand why I like to do both. Dad, it turns out you don't have to mail yourself unopened copies of stories to protect your copyright, but thanks for spending my twelfth summer doing that with me anyway. To date, no one has plagiarized any of those stories or poems and I credit Paul Mulholland for the protective measures. Thanks, also, for all the stories around the campfire and the dinner table and the fairy stump. Thank you for always encouraging critical thinking and open debate, no matter how often our views refuse to align. While I wrote most of these chapters on a small desk in the closet of a spare room, a great amount was written at the home of my parents-in-law. Gale and Fred Bickell, thank you for always treating me like I'm one of your own, and thank you for raising such an incredible son (Marcella and Wayne Francis, and Shelena Bickell—thank you for your contributions in that effort, too!).

To my siblings Kim (and Kyle) Henry, and Danny, Jay, and Jarrett Mulholland: thank you for your patience when I monopolized so many conversations with news about this book at family gatherings. I know I'm insufferable and bossy and, most certainly, lucky to have you guys.

Throughout my life I've been so fortunate to have many exceptional teachers—far too many to list. But there are a handful who stand out for never making the dream of authorship seem like an unreachable notion, despite the tiny northern town they taught me in. Thank you Mr. Brett Arlinghaus, Ms. Linda Green, Ms. Deborah Tourangeau, Mr. Terry Mosher, and Ms. HelenJane Shawyer.

I'm deeply grateful to the friends who have loved me. There are too many to name but there are some people I'd like to thank for inspiring me, teaching me, or helping me in specific ways while writing this book: Liz Pomeroy, Courtney Pytyck, Stephany Kruger, Angel Auger, Constable Pam Bolton, Lisa Daley, Erin Regnier, Nicola Ramsey, Shianne McDermott, Jamie Linington, Chelsea Setter, Danielle Larivee, Deanna Rausch, and Erin Giese. There are also three women who vitally inspired elements of this book and/or kept me travelling onward while writing it. Those women are Laura McKowen and Holly Whitaker of Home Podcast, and Scarlet Bjornson, whose selfless work founding "No Woman Without. Period"—a campaign to supply girls and women in need with feminine hygiene products—directly inspired elements in the chapter "Ascension."

And of course, I must mention Tweakers (Tweak) Tweakerson (2006–2019), "Dog of My Life." Thank you for dragging me from my desk for an hour every day at twelve noon, sharp. Rest in peace, my darling. Willow Claudia Bee Bickell, you have tiny but mighty paw prints to fill.

Lastly, I must thank my home for the inspiration it continuously lends. Certain people, organizations, landmarks, and businesses directly influenced or even appeared in *Always Brave, Sometimes Kind,* and I'd like to acknowledge them here: Peter Mansbridge, Ralph Klein, Ed Stelmach, Global News Edmonton, CBC Radio-Canada, Joel Plaskett, Sheryl Crow, Lloyd Robertson, *Canada's Got Talent,* Jann Arden, Joni Mitchell, University of Victoria, Sherwood Park Kings Athletic Club, Tim Hortons, Don Cherry,

Bobby Orr, Nickelback, Grey Nuns Hospital, the Tragically Hip, Gord Downie, Sam Roberts, Edmonton *Sun*, Northern Lakes College, Alberta Teacher's Association, West Edmonton Mall, Bissell Centre, the REDress Project, the City of Edmonton, Strathcona County, the Temper Online Magazine, Ascension Books, Rachel Notley, Justin Trudeau, Hope Mission, Vancouver Island, Coombs Market (Goats on the Roof), Tofino, Long Beach, St. Paul's Hospital, YEG International Airport, University of Alberta, Rundle Park, Royal Alexandra Hospital, Edmonton River Valley, Calgary Stampede, the City of Calgary, Lesser Slave Lake, Slave Lake Friendship Centre, and Strathcona County Millennium Place.

Thank you, Alberta.

Thank you, Canada.

Photo by Chloe Bickell

KATIE BICKELL emigrated from England to northern Alberta in 1990. Her fiction has been published in the *Tahoma Literary Review* and *Alberta Views*, and her essays have appeared in *WestWord Magazine*, *HERizons Magazine*, and on *The Temper*. Chapters from *Always Brave, Sometimes Kind* have received the Alberta Literary Award's Howard O'Hagan for Short Story, the Writers Guild of Alberta's Emerging Writer Award, and won the Alberta Views Fiction Prize. Katie lives in Sherwood Park, Alberta, just outside of Edmonton. Find out more at katiebickell.com.